AN UNEXPECTED ROLE

LESLEA WAHL

eLectio Publishing

Little Elm, TX

An Unexpected Role
By Leslea Wahl

ISBN-13: 978-1-63213-304-5
Published by eLectio Publishing, LLC
Little Elm, Texas
http://www.eLectioPublishing.com

Printed in the United States of America

First Edition.

5 4 3 2 1 eLP 21 20 19 18 17 16

The eLectio Publishing editing team is comprised of: Christine LePorte, Kaitlyn Campbell, Lori Draft, Sheldon James, Court Dudek, and Jim Eccles.

Publisher's Note
The publisher does not have any control over and does not assume any responsibility for author or third-party websites or their content.

The heart of this story is really the deep bonds between mothers, daughters, sisters, and friends. So naturally I want to dedicate this book to the most important women in my life.

To my mother - the first person to support my writing and creativity. Thanks for always encouraging me to be myself.

To my sister - my first and greatest friend. You were a wonderful big sister and deserved a less pesky younger sibling.

To my daughter whose strength, confidence and creativity inspire me daily. I wish I could grow up to be more like you.

Chapter 1

"YOU RUINED MY LIFE!" I scream as I burst through the door, not caring that I probably just permanently scarred my vocal cords.

Okay, possibly a bit overdramatic but the severity of the situation needed to be conveyed.

My mother looks at me for a moment, her cell phone plastered to her ear. She covers the mouthpiece, then says, "Hi, sweetheart. What are you talking about?"

"Your stupid book!" I screech and toss a copy of *Saving Sadie* on the kitchen island. Her newest masterpiece pirouettes across the smooth gray-speckled granite, colliding with the fruit bowl. Two precariously perched oranges roll off the counter and plummet to the floor.

I spin on my heel, march up the stairs and into my bedroom. The slam of my door punctuates my exit. As I flop on the bed, my face buried in the down-filled pillow, I wonder how my life could be destroyed in a matter of mere hours.

This morning when I woke up I was an ordinary teenager, thrilled that it was the last day of school. I was on the verge of becoming an upperclassman. The curtain was at last closing on my lowly sophomoric life. I just had one final day to suffer through then I would no longer be the unworthy bottom of a high school social class system where upperclassmen rule and freshmen and sophomores haven't earned the right to be cool. Jocks, cheerleaders, and poms are the popular crowd, the top of the hierarchy. If you're unlucky enough to not only be an underclassman but also not be involved in an acceptably deemed activity then you are basically nonexistent. And that was exactly where I had found myself for the last two years. But that was about to change. I still wasn't in with the cool kids, and probably never would be, but I was at least about to be an upperclassman, safe from the tyranny.

I only had to survive one final day and then the most amazing summer ever would begin. Teenage Utopia. Relaxing afternoons at the pool, glorious weekends at the lake. Here in Lake Forest, Minnesota, there is an unwritten rite of passage. Juniors and seniors overtake the lake on Sunday afternoons. (Such irony that in the land of 10,000 lakes we only have one nearby to enjoy.) The families frantically pack up their picnics, stuff the floaties in the back of their minivans, and flee the lake before teenagers flood the area, music blaring. To pacify the community the local police make their presence known so all stays innocent. Of course, I've only heard the legendary stories of adolescent joviality since I've been too inconsequential to enjoy it myself. But that was all on the verge of changing. This morning I had envisioned the promising future ahead of me. What a waste.

My mother knocks on my door, then—not waiting for an invitation—enters like she owns the place.

"Josie, what's this all about? Are you rehearsing a scene?" Her tone is somewhere between worry and annoyance.

"No, Mommy Dearest," my voice muffled by the fluffy pillow. I roll on my side, fresh air filling my lungs. "This is not a problem that can be solved with a big musical production. This is my life and you have completely destroyed it!"

"What's wrong?"

"I can't go anywhere without being ridiculed and laughed at, that's what's wrong. How could you humiliate your own daughter like that?"

She takes a deep breath. "I don't know what you're talking about."

How can she be so clueless?

"Your book!"

"My book? I think I need a little bit more to go on here."

"Next time you decide to destroy my life can you at least warn me first?"

She sighs, then sits on the edge of my bed. She's wearing her usual mom clothes, a T-shirt and yoga pants. The woman's array of yoga pants can rival any sporting goods store's collection. I'm not sure if she actually ever does any yoga but she's always well prepared if the mood hits. "Honey, I still don't know what's wrong."

"You mean besides the fact that I can no longer show my face around this town *and* that you have ruined what was supposed to be the most epic summer ever?"

"What does this have to do with my book?"

"How could you write those *things?!*"

"Josie, calm down, nothing in the book is about you."

"But no one knows that! You always include my most embarrassing moments in your books."

As cool as it seems to have a mom who's an author, it's actually a total pain. My mother loves to scatter my unfortunate mishaps throughout her books. It's not that I'm a total klutz, I mean everyone has moments of ineptitude, right? I'm just lucky enough to have mine set in print for all eternity. Actually, I pride myself on being a pretty graceful dancer. But I have this horribly bad habit of diving headfirst into life without contemplating the outcomes. My classmates in elementary and middle school called these incidents "Josie moments." The kids were like mini detectives scouring the pages of Mom's novels in search of them. Her last book included my very dramatic fainting episode during the school choir concert in second grade, and my unfortunate panic attack in the corn maze during the class field trip. Hey, getting lost in miles of towering maize can be extremely traumatizing.

"That's ridiculous. It's a fictional novel," my mom says dismissively. "No one will think it's about you."

"You made the lead character a sophomore in high school who's in the theater club. Of course everyone thinks it's me!"

"I think you're overreacting."

"Then why did I get a hundred texts calling me Jailbait Josie?"

"Oh, honey, it'll blow over," she says in the same patronizing tone she used when I was five and thought my world was over because I didn't get the part of the gumdrop in the *Nutcracker* pageant.

"No, Mom, it won't blow over. And do you know why I know it won't? Because today my locker was covered in tampons thanks to you. Not one little metal inch was left showing."

She cringes a little, then defensively says, "But those things I wrote never happened to you."

"It doesn't matter, the damage is done. No one will listen. They all believe that it was *I* who lost my bikini top while jumping off the diving board trying to impress a guy and that *I* am the one who started my period and stained my white skirt while up on stage giving a speech. Thanks, Mom. I'm never going to be able to face any of these people ever again."

"Come on, honey, let's go make some popcorn and watch an old movie. That always cheers you up."

"Mom, seriously, this isn't some little problem that you can tidy up like in one of your books with some lovely mother-daughter time. You wrote those horrible things and now I have to live with the consequences. My amazing summer has been stolen from me."

I bury my head back in my pillow. She eventually takes the hint that I don't want to talk and leaves.

Even now in the safety of my room a wave of nausea sweeps over me as I think back over the horrific events of the day. I can still feel how the curiosity of seeing the enormous crowd gathered in the hallway turned to pity when I realized they were laughing and pointing at some poor, unsuspecting soul's locker, which quickly turned to panic with the realization that the locker in question was mine and that it was covered in feminine hygiene products.

As I stood there staring in disbelief, the blood throbbing in my head, someone yelled, "Hey, that's her. That's Josie DelRio." I watched as the mob turned toward me like lions about to pounce. The pointing, laughter, and whispers made my knees weaken. How could this be happening? Why was it happening?

Before I could collapse from the sheer force of the mortification, a strong arm yanked me into the bathroom. Thank goodness for best friends.

Liz instructed me to sit on the tile floor, then left to track down some answers. I sat there stunned, wondering what could possibly have sparked the incident. But as the bell rang and the crowd dispersed I heard someone in the hallway say, "If you think that's bad, wait until you get to Chapter Four."

And I suddenly knew who was responsible for the collapse of my world. My own mother.

***

I hole up in my room the rest of the afternoon, trying to calm myself. But a comprehensive check of all forms of communication leaves no doubt—my life is officially over. The repulsive things people are posting sicken me. If this is what social media has come to, I opt for being antisocial.

But seriously, how could people be so cruel? Even if all those things in the book had happened to me why would people be that horrible and exploit my misfortunes? What a stupid question. They don't care who they hurt, they just want to look cool. I learned long ago most people in that school will do whatever it takes to be accepted and avoid the wrath themselves.

Depressed, I fall back on my bed and contemplate my mom's stupid book. What kind of person comes up with this stuff? Who is this woman who gave birth to me? Suddenly it doesn't seem possible that I could have her genes coursing through my body.

Maybe these parents of mine picked up the wrong baby at the hospital sixteen years ago. Maybe they have unknowingly been raising someone else's child. It would explain a lot, like how no one in my family seems to understand me or why I'm the only one in this house who can somewhat carry a tune and remember the order of gifts in "The Twelve Days of Christmas."

I picture my real parents, totally rich and chill, right now probably hanging out on their yacht in the Mediterranean, martinis in hand. They're watching their daughter pondering how she, of nerdy brains and unusually strange sense of humor, could be from their uber-cool loins.

Unfortunately, my switched-at-birth daydream shatters when I remember how I break out in hives whenever I wear wool, just like my dad. And how my kindergarten photo looks eerily like my mother's—same crooked smile, big blue eyes, and curly brown hair sticking up in odd places, all Medusa-like. Alas, I guess I'm stuck with the parental units I have. A mom who writes adolescent fiction, loves old movies, her church, and of course those yoga pants, and a straight-laced lawyer dad whose idea of fun is finishing the Sunday crossword puzzle.

Eventually my mom knocks on my door.

"Sweetie," she says tentatively, "Cameron's here. He's waiting for you on the front porch."

Cameron. My boyfriend—for about the last month anyway. Over the last two years, we've done every Lake Forest High theater production together. Our Broadway-obsessed drama teacher specializes in musicals. I'm primarily a dancer but sometimes get a minor role. Cameron always gets the leads. Even as a freshman he won the coveted roles. He's tall, good-looking, and has been blessed with a knee-weakening tenor voice. He's used his claim to fame to go out with most of the freshman, sophomore, and even a few of the junior theater girls at one time or another. For the longest time I never understood his appeal. Immune to his charms, I recognized him for the conceited and totally full of himself jerk that he is.

That is, until the spring musical, *The Music Man*. As I was Pick-a-Little-ing around the stage, he was singing about seventy-six trombones. He must be a better actor than I realized because somehow I fell under his Professor Harold Hill spell, just like Marian the Librarian. I mean, when he gazed into perky Katie Phillips' eyes and sang "Till There Was You," well, who wouldn't have melted?

So Cameron and I started going out. Sadly, and embarrassingly difficult to admit, I was always way more attracted to his Professor Harold Hill character than to Cameron Richardson. In real life he never once acted romantic or asked me to meet him at the footbridge or sang a love song—except maybe to his own reflection. Cameron's ego is as big as his stage presence. But it has been nice to have a "boyfriend," especially one that can drive.

I know what you're thinking—because I've thought it many times myself. This girl is desperate and pathetic. Shoot me, but frankly since I don't have my own car, I much prefer being driven to school by a cute guy than by my mom. I live too far from school to walk (unless I want to wake up at the crack of dawn—not likely), but not far enough to take the bus. So yes, I will put up with a lot because there is no way I can show my face climbing out of my mom's SUV now that I'm sixteen. Total target for humiliation. But truth be told, I've been contemplating what to do with Cameron. He doesn't really fit into my summer visions and now that I don't need a ride to school, his usefulness is over.

But here he is, at my door, in my hour of need. I may have misjudged my arrogant crooner. He's actually not the worst boyfriend in the world. Maybe it's good I haven't dumped him yet; at least I'll have someone to hang out with this summer, to shield me from all the haters. I mean, if I overlook his grating narcissistic tendencies, he's actually not that bad. He could help me brave this storm and he might actually learn to think about more than himself. I guess you find out who really cares for you when your world crumbles to pieces.

I sweep down the stairs, all Scarlett O'Hara–like, and push open the screen door to the front porch. There he stands. Sporting his fedora. Seriously? Sure, a fedora can be cool at a cast party, maybe totally acceptable for a night on the town, and certainly appropriate attire if you're an original member of the Rat Pack, but not when you're coming to console your grief-stricken girlfriend who doesn't need any more attention drawn to her. But the concerned look on his face warms my heart. It's nice to know he really can think of others. I throw myself in my leading man's arms, ready to be protected in his strong embrace.

"I'm so glad to see you." I bury my face in his shoulder, trying not to suffocate in the overwhelming scent of his cologne. Does he bathe in this stuff? "You have no idea how bad my day has been."

"You think your day was bad?" he says, and takes a giant step away from me. "This whole book thing is really hurting my reputation."

"*Your* reputation?" I gape at him. He didn't really just say that, did he?

"Hey, I have an image to maintain and your embarrassing moments are not helping it."

"They're not *my* embarrassing moments. They're fiction," I spit out.

"Either way, it's too much for me to handle. Maybe when things calm down we can hang out again."

"Wait a minute. Are you breaking up with me?"

"Hey, it was fun while it lasted, kid," he says with a wink, then quickly turns and saunters down the walkway toward his car.

My fist clutches a begonia from the planter on the porch. Not thinking things through, I yank it out of its pot, clumps of dirt clinging to its tiny little roots, then throw it at Cameron's head. My aim, inconsistent as usual, causes the pathetic flying plant to fall short of its intended target; dirt and leaves scatter the sidewalk. Why couldn't my parents have forced me to stay in sports so I could learn to throw a decent fastball?

I stand on the porch with my hand covered in soil and watch the familiar black sedan pull away, Cameron's *Best of Broadway* soundtrack diminishing as he drives past the immaculately manicured lawns of my boring suburban neighborhood. How do you call someone your own age "kid"? What a loser. Worse yet, I can't believe *he* broke up with *me*.

And there you have it—now my mom has even managed to ruin my love life. At the moment the fact that just this morning I was orchestrating how to break up with him is beside the point. I mean is it too much to ask to have a boyfriend who will be there for me?

I plop down on the porch swing. Face it, Josie—life is not a musical, there are no happy endings. My vision blurs from the tears that burn my eyes. This was supposed to be the best summer ever.

***

Despite my pleas to begin my life of solitude, my parents force me to attend my brother's evening baseball game. Do they really believe fresh air will dull my pain? The thought of being out in public terrorizes me, so even though I'm wearing a baseball hat and dark sunglasses, I beg my best friend, Liz, to meet us at the field.

"You've got to get out of the house, Josie," Dad lectures as we pull out of our driveway. "I'm sure this whole situation is just in your imagination."

"You don't know how cruel kids at my school can be," I answer.

"So, they pulled a tasteless prank. It's over now."

"Did you actually attend high school?" I ask, plastering myself next to the door to avoid being overtaken by Riley and all his gear.

"Relax, kiddo, most people probably won't even read your mom's book."

"Hey," she complains.

"Sorry, it's a great book, dear. I'm just trying to make the point that it's not like the whole town will tease her."

"No, just a few hundred of my classmates," I grumble.

It crosses my mind that the folks may be more understanding if I open up and really express to them how horrific the day was for me instead of hiding behind anger and sarcasm, but sharing my feelings with my parents is just not something I'm very comfortable with.

"Honey," my mom says sweetly, "if it's bothering you so much why don't we pray about it."

Of course. That's her answer for everything. But you know, I've tried it her way and I've never really seen any results. For instance, I spent my whole freshman year praying for a good part in one of the shows and to become cool and witty so the "in" crowd would stop picking on me. But when the prayers just kept going unanswered, I kinda stopped bothering to ask. Hey, I get it—the big guy in the sky has way more important things to deal with like famines, plagues, and stuff. I just learned to handle it myself. And I guess that's what I'll have to do now.

I turn my attention back to my mom. "By the way, since when do you write young adult books anyway? You've always written middle grade chapter books. When you said your next book was being released who knew I had to worry about my friends reading it."

She turns to look at me, her face crinkled in confusion. "Josie, seriously? I've talked about this book for months. Where have you been for the last year and a half?"

"Umm, surviving high school?"

"Josie, you never listen to me."

"Sorry, but it's usually not very important. Mom, you've really got to check for the non-comprehending blank look before you tell me these things."

She shakes her head.

"Can't we have some nice family time, where no one argues?" asks my dad.

"Sure, just one last question: how exactly does one 'accidentally' go on a blind date with their cousin?" I ask.

"I love that scene," snorts Riley. "I mean, how funny would it be to show up to Homecoming with your own cousin."

"How about we not talk about the book anymore this evening," suggests Mom, catching the murderous look I shoot my brother.

10

"Great idea," my dad agrees. "Tonight we celebrate the end of the school year. It's going to be a fun evening. Fun, fun, fun."

"So, what should we do this summer?" my mom asks in an annoyingly ultra-perky voice.

"Won't you be busy touring around with your new masterpiece?" I grumble.

"Yeah, I can't wait to add more postcards to my collection," Riley says. His bedroom walls are plastered with the postcards she sends from each of her Midwestern book tour stops. The postcards are never of the beautiful sites or famous landmarks of the cities she visits but are instead of ridiculously obscure and odd attractions, like a three-story mustard bottle, a life-size grizzly bear carved out of chocolate, or the world's largest ball of string.

"I won't be traveling all summer," she says. "We could do something special as a family."

"Road trip!" yells Riley.

"Oh joy," I mumble.

"Josie, you can't sulk all summer. Riley, that's a great idea. Maybe we could drive to Mount Rushmore," Mom suggests.

"Or the Wisconsin Dells," adds Dad. "You guys always love those water parks."

"Can we go to that weird museum there?" asks Riley. "Nathan told me they have a two-headed cow."

Excellent. My summer went from weekends at the lake to freaks of nature.

When we arrive at the field I scan the area to check for anyone I know. Luckily there's no one from my school in sight. My parents settle into their seats on the bleachers near all the other parents. I sit two rows behind them daydreaming of being a turtle, able to hide away in my shell when the world becomes too overwhelming.

"I see you're coping well from the day's events," says Liz when she finally arrives, scrutinizing my attire.

Liz has been my best friend since forever. When she was little her exuberance was contagious. She reminded me of a puppy, a bundle of energy and fun. Hanging out with her always turned into an adventure. Whether we were Amazonian explorers at the park or secret agents in the candy store, there was never a dull moment. But then in middle school, her parents went through a rather messy divorce. That's when we were introduced to musical theater. Her mom was lonely and dragged us to every show she could find. She could relate to the problems of the protagonists. Cole Porter and Andrew Lloyd Webber became her therapists; the wisdom dispensed in the lyrics of their songs spoke to her. I guess it was more fun and probably cheaper than going to a shrink. Anyway, Liz's zest for life kind of soured after that, which brought a new edge to her.

"Seriously, your disguise is totally sweet, like an incognito rock star."

"Here, put these on," I say, handing her a pair of dark sunglasses and a baseball hat.

"Why do I need to hide?" she asks.

"Because it's obvious it's me if my sidekick is sitting beside me."

"I'm your sidekick?"

I know what she's doing, trying to distract me from the horror that unfolded earlier today. She may be a bit quirky but she's a good friend.

"My partner in crime, my BFF, my alter ego, what do you prefer?" I ask.

"I just always assumed you were *my* sidekick, but we can do it your way," she answers as she dons the lame disguise. "Okay, so if we're putting on costumes I need to know what our role is."

"Can't we just be fans sitting at a ballgame?"

"That's pretty boring."

"Then, maybe we're talent scouts checking out the boys' athletic abilities."

"Talent scouts? Maybe for a blooper reel," Liz says as she watches the boys drop most of the balls thrown to them during warm-up. "Do they know they're actually supposed to catch the balls?"

"Believe it or not they've improved a lot. You should've seen them last year."

"I'll take your word for it," she says. "Hey, not to get all gushy and all but seriously, how're you doing?"

I sigh. "Liz, I don't know what to do. You know how vicious the 'in' crowd can be. They have the power to completely destroy people and they'll never let something this good go. There's enough embarrassing situations in that book to fuel them for months. And since no one wants to face their fury, you're basically the only person who will risk being seen with me now. And to make it worse, my parents don't understand what a big deal it is, and think I'm overreacting. They have no idea how hard we've worked to fly under the radar and go unnoticed to avoid those people. I'm not strong enough to face this battle alone. At least I have you," I say, thankful for the dark sunglasses to hide the tears that well up in my eyes.

"Um, about that—I've got something to tell you," she says, her tone warning me to brace for more bad news.

"What?" I ask wearily.

"Well, my dad wants me to come to his place this summer."

"You go to Chicago to visit him every summer."

"Yeah, but for some reason he wants me to come for the whole summer this year instead of the usual week."

"What?" I furiously try to blink away the tears before they roll down my cheeks.

"I know, I'm sorry. I wish I didn't have to go."

That's it. Final nail in my coffin. I'm all alone. First Cameron dumps me, now Liz is abandoning me. I have no one to hang out with this summer. How am I going to make it through three whole months? I can't go to the rec center, the pool, the park, or the mall without seeing someone from school. I honestly don't know what I'm going to do.

Liz looks at me then leans her head on my shoulder. "You could become a crazy cat lady and adopt every stray you find."

I love her for trying to lighten the mood. "Maybe I'll just turn into a hermit and stay locked away in my house."

"You'd make a cute hermit," she teases. "But seriously, promise me you won't stick with Cameron just so he can drive you around."

"You don't have to worry about that, he dumped me this afternoon."

She stares at me. "He broke up with you? But we had just put the finishing touches on your break-up monologue."

"I know, but he beat me to it. Apparently my problems are too embarrassing for him."

"What a creep. You never should have gone out with him in the first place."

"You dated him as well," I remind her.

"Is it my fault he made an incredibly charming Sky Masterson?" Liz fell hard for him last year during *Guys and Dolls*.

"Well, one thing's for sure, I won't miss him suddenly breaking out in show tunes," I say.

"And you no longer have to pay for your dates when he 'forgets' to bring his wallet," adds Liz.

"And I won't have to avoid walking by shiny surfaces anymore for fear of him trying to catch a glimpse of his reflection," I say with a giggle, happy to forget my problems, even for a brief moment.

"Oh, I always hated that dumb smirk and head bob he does when other girls walk by," Liz adds.

"I know," I agree. "And would it be so much to ask for a guy to open the car door for me?"

14

"Don't hold your breath," says Liz. "My mom says the dumb feminists ruined it for the rest of us. Guys are now afraid to open doors for women or give them their seats for fear of being read the riot act. Face it, chivalry is dead." Ever since the divorce, Liz's mom is still a little (extremely) bitter.

"Well, maybe that's why we both fell for Cameron. He plays these characters from back when guys were gentlemen," I say in defense of our poor judgment.

"Nice try, Josie, but he was playing con men when we fell for him."

How typical, falling for the bad boys and not the sweet nice guys.

"*Shut. Up,*" Liz squeals as she clamps onto my arm.

I follow her gaze to the object of her attention. Out on the field is Ryan McNaulty, one of the high school baseball players. Totally cute jock. As he walks toward home plate in tan cargo shorts, a ref's blue polo shirt, and a backwards baseball cap, I picture him in one of those lame TV movies where the wind blows through the hero's hair as he enters the scene in slow motion, muscles tensing, smile gleaming.

"He's one beautiful specimen," Liz says through a sigh.

"I suppose he's okay if you like the tall, dark, and handsome look. I mean who wants chiseled cheekbones, perfectly styled hair, and chocolate brown eyes?" I tease.

"For your information, his eyes are green. But what's he doing here?" she asks.

"A detective you are not. Notice the clothes, Liz, he's the ump. Usually someone from the high school team is the official for these games."

"And why have you never told me this? I'd have come more often if I'd known that was the case. Ryan's extremely hot— although I prefer when he's in his baseball pants."

"That's right, you were one of the official stalkers of the baseball team this year."

"It's called school spirit. Whenever I wasn't at rehearsal I went to their games. What else was I supposed to do since you were always with Cameron? Besides, baseball is our national pastime."

"But did you ever watch the games or just the guys?" I ask.

"Hey, believe me, if you saw them in their uniforms you wouldn't judge. I don't know what special material those baseball pants are made of but it sure makes them look amazing."

"Polyester, maybe?"

Again she ignores me. "Why do you think they are dubbed the Dream Team? Not because of their baseball skills."

"The Dream Team?"

"Sure, there's Heart Attack Jack, Ben the Perfect Ten, and Scotty the Hottie."

"What's Ryan McNaulty's nickname?"

"Mc*Naughty*."

"McNaughty?"

"Have you ever noticed when he thinks something's funny he does this adorable head tilt and crooked grin thing? It makes him look like he's been caught doing something naughty," she explains enthusiastically.

I stare at her.

"No criticizing. If you hadn't spent all your free time with Cameron you could have contributed."

"Maybe you should focus on someone attainable."

"Who says jocks aren't attainable? He was in my chem class and he's pretty nice," she says with a nod toward the field.

"Um, have you been to our school? Ryan McNaulty is definitely tier one material, which means he dates other tier one people like cheerleaders or the female varsity athletes."

"Just because that's usually how things are done doesn't mean it always has to be that way. Maybe we can change the status quo."

"Like any of them even know we're alive."

"What, you don't think they come to see the theater productions?"

"Highly unlikely," I say as we watch Ryan pull a Keanu Reeves and smoothly matrix-dodge a stray pitch.

"Maybe you can try to get to know some of them this summer when you're at the lake and I'm trapped in Chicago with my old man," she says.

"Like Ryan McNaulty would want to chill with me."

"Well, not him, he's leaving town for the summer, too. I overheard some parents talking at the last game of the season. He was asked to play summer baseball on a farm team out east somewhere. College scouts go check them out or something. It's apparently a big deal for someone going into their junior year to be invited."

"Just as well since I'm probably never going to leave the safety of my bedroom this summer."

"Hey, don't give up. Any of the Dream Team members will do."

I roll my eyes. She's clearly delusional.

"Look! He's doing it!" Liz says as she thrusts her sharp elbow into my side.

I wince from the stabbing pain but turn toward the field. The little rugrats from Riley's team surround Ryan. Just as she described, his head cocks to the side and an amused grin graces his perfect face. He is quite alluring, but I prefer to watch Liz's reaction as she practically melts into a puddle of hormones.

"See, isn't baseball the greatest sport?"

"I admit, I've never appreciated these finer points of the game before," I tease.

"Well, it's a good thing I'm here to educate you. You must not focus on the ball but on all the other things going on around the actual game. That's where the true excitement lies."

"I really have been missing out."

We turn our attention back to the game. Riley somehow makes contact with the ball and hits a grounder to second. After his initial shock, he sprints to first base. The shortstop scurries to the ball and throws it toward first in an attempt to get the out, but the first baseman totally misses the ball. Riley keeps running toward second as the ball rolls toward the dugout. Riley glances over his shoulder and continues on to third, where he pauses. The first baseman finally throws the ball toward third but accidently hits the pitcher in the groin, who falls down and squirms around in agony on the mound. Riley scurries toward home plate and dramatically jumps on the base. Ryan calls him safe, then shakes his head in amusement.

During the third inning of the game of seemingly endless walks, my fears come true. Two of the juniors from the pom squad climb up the bleachers, Missy Harper and Brooke Garfield, along with their lax bro boyfriends—of course carrying their lacrosse sticks like security blankets. Missy's brother plays on Riley's team but she's never graced us with her presence before. Why today of all days must she begin being a devoted sister? When Missy and Brooke see us they stop, exchange a glance, then look back at us. So much for our disguises.

I pull my hat down lower and wonder what my chances are of squeezing through the narrow space between the metal sections of the bleachers and dropping to the ground below. Better not try—with my luck I'd get stuck and the fire department would be called out to rescue me. Out of the corner of my eye I see the foursome climb up the bleachers and head our way. They sit down right in front of us. A tidal wave of dread crashes over me.

"Oh, Mrs. DelRio. I love your new book."

I feel like I'm drowning, sinking to the bottom of an ocean, unable to surface for air, the weight of the book pulling me under.

"Why, thank you," answers my mom as she turns around to look at the group.

"Yes, it was very entertaining and quite *revealing*, don't you agree, Josie?" asks Missy. She giggles, then whispers something in her boyfriend's ear. The beefy jock stifles a laugh and looks away.

"And I don't want you to worry at all about swimming in the lake this summer," Brooke says to me. "I have this lifeguard whistle I can bring and we can have random 'Josie bikini-top checks.' It would be like our very own public service announcement."

"See, we got ya covered, girlfriend—pun intended," adds Missy.

"And we can have everyone bring extra sanitary products for that pesky time of the month. We wouldn't want any more embarrassing leakages to happen."

My parents sit there in shock, their mouths frozen open.

"Gee, Brooke," snaps Liz, "there you go again, proving your IQ and bra size are the same number."

Brooke turns her wrath on Liz. "You're just jealous since you're still shopping in the junior department."

"Well, enjoy the rest of the game," says Missy, unable to keep a straight face. "Josie, we *personally* guarantee it will be a summer to remember."

The four of them get up and move farther down the bleachers, not even trying to conceal their laughter. My parents look at each other, horror in their eyes, then turn back toward the game, like it's the most interesting thing in the world.

"You were right, Dad, this is fun. Fun, fun, fun."

Chapter 2

"You're really leaving?" Liz asks, her concern radiating through the phone.

"Yep, it's all set. In fact, I'm at the airport now," I answer. After saying good-bye to Riley and Dad after mass, Mom and I left for the airport. "I've got to get away from here. Besides, with you gone for the summer who would I hang out with?"

"Well, it's a brilliant idea. Hey! It's your window."

"My window?"

"I can't believe I have to remind you of that great line from *Sound of Music*. You know, something about when a door closes somewhere, God opens a window. The door closed on your summer here but now a window opens leading to South Carolina."

"Maybe. I hadn't thought about it like that."

"Does your aunt at least have a computer so you can post all your adventures?"

"She has a computer but I'm abstaining from technology for the summer."

"Huh?"

"Yep, that way no one can bug me about the book that shall not be named."

"No phone calls?"

"No."

"Internet postings?"

"No."

"Email?"

"No."

"Texting?"

"No."

"Blogging?"

21

"No."

"Cell phone pics?"

"No, in fact I'm leaving my cell here. It's useless anyway due to all the prank calls and texts I've been getting. Besides, I won't need it on the beach."

"How will you survive?"

"I know it'll be hard but I must quit cold turkey."

"You're so brave. But how will we keep in touch?"

"You can write to me."

"*Write* you? You mean like letters?"

"Yep."

"I haven't written a letter since fifth grade and that was to my grandmother. Even she texts now."

"I have to get away from everything. I need a clean break for a while. Maybe then by the start of the school year everyone will have totally forgotten about me and will be onto someone else's crisis."

"Wow. Well, I'll give it a try. It's not like I won't have plenty of free time on my hands, sitting by the pool at my dad's condo every day while he's at work. I'm glad you're getting away. You deserve a better summer than you'd have here."

"Thanks. Well, so long, my friend."

"Farewell."

I'm afraid I'll start crying if I finish the rest of our good-bye ritual so I quickly end the call and hand Mom my cell phone.

"I'm truly sorry, honey," she says. We are at the terminal waiting for my plane. Because I'm a minor she was able to come with me through security—yippee. I would have been fine saying our good-byes at the curb when she dropped me off, but no, she had to stay with me the entire way through the airport. "I had no idea my work would affect you like this."

"I know." I sigh. Mom and I haven't exactly had very cordial conversations the last couple of days. Things around the house have remained tense. Doorbell ditchers and brownies left on the porch, most likely laced with laxatives, have taken their toll on our relationship. Thank goodness Aunt Lily came through with an invite to spend the summer with her.

"I'm praying this getaway is what you need."

"Thanks for letting me go."

"Don't you know, I'd do anything for you." She leans in and gives me a hug, her arms awkwardly wrapped around my stiff upper body.

I know she didn't mean to ruin my life but the damage is done. Hopefully some time away will chill things out.

"Promise you'll go to mass while you're away!" she calls as I make my way down the Jetway.

I wave at her in response.

My stuffed-to-the-max duffel bangs into the seats as I make my way down the narrow aisle of the airplane. Afraid the airlines might lose my luggage again, I jammed my bag with several days' worth of essentials. A repeat of our trip to California when I had to wear the same shorts all week would not be cool. I ignore the angry looks thrown my way. I've faced high school bullies; I can handle a few grumpy airline passengers.

As the plane hurtles down the runway and lifts off the ground, I visualize the weight of the world levitating from my soul.

Somewhere between Minnesota and South Carolina the deep reflection of my life begins. There's nothing like solitude at 30,000 feet to induce self-contemplation.

My high school career has basically been spent trying to go unnoticed, fearful of the upperclassmen. I was singularly focused on not being the brunt of their ridicule and played it safe. So much for that plan. Two years of flying under the radar were wiped away in mere hours thanks to my mom. But now I realize that because of my cautiousness, my life has become extremely boring and predictable. Along the way I lost myself.

Hopefully this summer will be different. This is my chance to reinvent myself. To become cool and confident, or funny and witty, but definitely leave the clumsy, quiet theater girl in the past. It's time to figure out who I want to be—to discover myself. Who knows, maybe I'm a painter like Lily. After all, Mrs. Jones, the art teacher, could have been wrong and I might actually have an ounce of artistic talent. No matter what, this is my chance for freedom, independence, adventure, and who knows, possibly romance.

I picture myself on the beach in my adorable bikini, laughing with new friends, my hair blowing in the sea breeze while cute British guys longingly watch me. Who cares that my daydream strangely resembles my favorite music video. Anything's possible.

This summer I'm going to put myself out there, meet new people, try new things. What do I have to lose? My mom won't be there to record my failings. No one in South Carolina knows me. No one knows my past. I can pretend to be exactly the person I want to be.

The flight continues and my excitement for the new chapter in my life grows.

***

Aunt Lily is easily found. As if she wouldn't already stand out in the crowd with her blond bob, tie-dye sundress, and silver Roman gladiator sandals, she starts squealing the moment I walk toward the baggage claim carousel. With her arms waving frantically she rushes through the crowd, oblivious to the glares from the extras in our personal reunion scene.

It's hard to believe Lily and Mom are sisters. Truly one of the great cruelties of life that Lily got all the laid-back cool genes and my mom got stuck with the uptight serious ones. Lily's whimsically carefree, an artist who paints seascapes for a living and sells them at local gift shops up and down the Atlantic coast. She was never burdened with a husband or kids and lives an enviable life. I've always been drawn to her easygoing attitude. Maybe some of it will wear off on me this summer.

"I'm thrilled you're here, Kitten," Aunt Lily says, using the nickname she gave me years ago, a reference to some comic she read as a kid. Something about pussycats and someone named Josie—who knows.

With her convertible loaded up, I carefully maneuver into the front seat, nudging the piles of espadrilles and sandals at my feet.

"Oh, sorry, no one else usually travels with me."

"No problem. I'm used to Riley leaving his shoes all over the car. Except his are smelly and disgusting, not adorable cute ones that I may have to try to borrow."

"Anytime, Kitten," she says. "I can't wait for you to see Coral Island."

"I was trying to remember how long you've lived there."

"About six months," she answers.

"I was surprised you moved, I thought you liked Charleston."

"I did, but when I began selling my paintings at the store on Coral Island I just fell in love with the place. It was exactly the town I'm always trying to create on canvas. I felt like it had been waiting for me my whole life."

"Wow, that's cool. Tell me about it."

"Well, if I were a tour guide I'd tell you it's one of the smallest of the Sea Islands off the South Carolina coast, and one of those sweet communities where everyone seems to know each other. There are no bridges to the island. The only way to get there is by boat or ferry. Which means it's never been overtaken by the tourists that flock to nearby Hilton Head. The population does increase during the summer due to all the vacation homes on the island. But there are no hotels, only a couple bed and breakfasts, which means it stays relatively quiet."

I close my eyes to picture my summer home away from home.

"But," Lily continues, "since I'm an artist I must describe it like this: When you board the ferry you know you're on a grand adventure. The sparkling ocean surrounds a paradise of soft, silky sand. It really feels like a journey back in time minutes from modern civilization. The people are warm and caring. It has that unique community feel that small towns tend to have."

"Sounds perfect."

"Mostly. Actually we have something odd going on right now. There's been a rash of thefts."

"Oh no. Are there any suspects?"

"No. The locals feel it must be someone here for the summer season."

"Makes sense since the community sounds pretty tight."

"Probably, but there are some islanders that have fallen on hard times in recent years. We're still trying to recover after the downturn in the economy."

"Oh, are you doing okay?" If people aren't spending as much money, her seascapes might not be selling as well anymore.

"I've begun a side business restoring paintings for our wealthy summer residents," she answers.

"That's too bad."

"Actually, I enjoy it. It's a new challenge, plus I get to meet some fascinating people and see their amazing second homes. I've also found, as they get to know me, they are more likely to purchase my paintings," she says with a wink.

When we reach the ferry dock my excitement builds at the sight of the island surrounded by the enticing ocean. As we begin our crossing to the island, I stare at a brightly colored Ferris wheel, a giant spinning pinwheel anchoring the southern end of the island.

"Is that an amusement park?" I ask in disbelief.

"It's a small carnival to attract some tourists from the mainland. Their funnel cakes are phenomenal."

We dock on the west side of the island amid tall sea grasses and sand dunes dotted with driftwood. I fight the urge to abandon my tennis shoes and run through the blanket of sand, letting it sift through my toes. We slowly drive by pastel-colored cottages with white trim that remind me of a box of saltwater taffy, welcoming us to the island. An elderly couple on their front porch swing wave as we go by. Neighbors chat over white picket fences. Children on their bikes try to keep up with us.

We turn on to a beautiful street full of little shops. Striped awnings and lamp posts adorned with overflowing baskets of vibrant flowers line the street. Couples relax at cafe tables and happy families window-shop with ice cream cones in hand. Lily's description of traveling back in time was spot on.

"This is Seaview Boulevard, and that is the Atlantic Ocean." She points to the vast sea that sweeps into view as we pass the last stores. The sun glitters off the ocean as white boats bob along the docks. A large rocky outcropping juts out into the Atlantic to form a natural barrier cutting the marina off from whatever discovery is around the porous rocks.

"It's spectacular."

With the ocean to our right Lily continues up a hill, the dark cliffs anchoring the incline. At the top of the hill sits a park and a soaring white lighthouse. Squealing children chase one another around the playground while their moms chat on a park bench. The road continues past the lighthouse, down the hill, and winds north to the homes situated on the shore. Aunt Lily turns into the third drive from the lighthouse. Flowering bushes line the long driveway and lead toward a sky blue cottage with wraparound porch, the Atlantic Ocean the backdrop of this postcard-worthy setting.

"Come, I have a friend I want you to meet."

My suitcase and duffel bang into my legs as I schlep them up the porch steps. Why did I pack so much stuff? Lily flings the front door open, and a blur of fur flies out. A medium-sized chocolate brown dog with white patches nearly knocks me back down the stairs. The tip of her perfectly looped tail is white like it was dipped in paint.

"Oh, she's adorable!"

"Meet Kahlua, your new best friend for the summer."

The curly furball bounces around me all Tigger-esque, increasing the difficulty of entering with my giant luggage. I try to follow Aunt Lily down the hall toward the bedrooms. But Kahlua grabs the strap of my bag in her mouth and tugs on my luggage, trying to pull me in the opposite direction, toward a living room with overstuffed white marshmallowy furniture. I continue to trail Aunt Lily, pulling Kahlua along. We pass a room with easels stationed on either side of a mammoth window. Paintings in various stages of completion are propped against the walls; drop cloths blanket the hardwood floors. A rainbow of paints and colored pencils bursts from the side wall while a table piled with books sits in the middle of the room. Ah, Lily's studio.

She leads me to the next room, my room for the whole summer. An enticing breeze blows the white gauzy curtains from the open window, billowing out like sails on a boat. The seashell-themed room is filled with the unmistakable scents of ocean and honeysuckle.

We quickly unpack, then curl up in her Adirondack chairs on her back porch. The surf gently tumbles onto the shore. A slight breeze causes the tall grasses off her porch to form a chorus line, swaying and sashaying in unison. She hands me a glass of freshly squeezed lemonade, a lemon slice adorning the rim. Could life get any better?

Maybe I'll be the girl who sits on this back porch all summer and writes poetry. This view is certainly inspiring. "How do you get anything done around here? I'm pretty sure I'd just veg here and stare at the ocean all day."

"That's basically what I do. It's a good thing I found a way to make money doing it." Then Lily breaks the euphoric moment with a parental unit talk. "So, Kitten, tell me about what's going on with you and your mom."

"You mean besides the fact that she's ruined my life?"

"I know you're a fabulous actress but are you possibly being a bit overdramatic?"

"No. Have you read the book?"

"Yes, I found it to be a touching and funny portrayal of the situations young women face and the grace that comes from the experiences."

"You sound like her publisher. Do you remember the part where her lead character has her first stage kiss and gets her braces hooked on the braces of her onstage partner?"

"Of course. You have to admit it was funny."

"Sure, it's hilarious, except for the fact that I had an onstage kiss last year with the nastiest boy in school. I mean you can seriously smell him from ten feet away. He has greasy hair, pimples, bad breath, and who knows what kind of bacteria resides in this boy's mouth. I was extremely worried about catching something from him. When we had our pretend kiss I clamped my mouth shut so tight nothing could possibly penetrate the barrier. When the scene was done I'd run off stage and decontaminate myself. It was awful and until this past week, the most humiliating moment of my life. Well, since the book came out the creep has posted our stupid scene online and updated his status that he's now famous—immortalized in print."

I gaze out toward the ocean hoping she will change the subject, now that she can see my side.

"But your friends must know the truth."

"My boyfriend broke up with me because I was bad for his reputation," I answer without looking her way.

"You're better off without him, then."

"True, but still I needed to get away."

"All right, if you ever want to talk, though, I'm here for you."

"See, you get it. Why can't my mom? Really, the worst part is she doesn't understand. She thinks it will blow over and I'm overreacting, but these kids never forget. The more people they can intimidate the more powerful they feel."

"I think she realizes what her book has done to you. That's why she suggested this visit."

"It was her idea?" I ask, astonished.

"Yep, and I thought it was brilliant. You must know she never would have written any of that if she thought things would turn out the way they did."

"But why did she always have to write about my most horrifying moments in the first place? No one would have thought these incidents were about me if she hadn't written about my mistakes in the past. I mean, does she enjoy exploiting me that way?"

"Maybe you need to ask her."

"Maybe." I'm done talking about this, it threatens to destroy my good mood. "Can I take Kahlua on a walk along the beach?"

"Sure, I need to get a few things done anyway. But don't be too long, I'd like to take you into town for dinner this evening. I want to celebrate you being here."

"Sounds good," I say as I head down the porch toward the beach, Kahlua far ahead of me already.

We start down the well-worn path that leads through the tall sea grasses to the narrow strip of beach. Kahlua scurries around the bushes, then in a blur of fur runs out to the ocean, splashing in the water as she chases something. I kick my sandals to the side and join her in the cool surf. The wet sand oozes up between my toes, my feet quickly buried. The beach is deserted except for an army of seagulls marching along the sand on pencil thin legs. Kahlua, dripping with ocean water, spies tiny crabs that skitter sideways across the sand. She pounces along as she tries to catch them.

I move down the coast, mystically drawn toward the towering lighthouse, the gleaming white pinnacle having the opposite effect of its intended purpose. I've seen lighthouses before, on Lake Superior, but nothing as elegant and majestic as this one.

A sign kindly informs me I'm in Shipwreck Cove. The beach's semicircle shape is surrounded by tall black cliffs; a wooden staircase leads up to the lighthouse. My eyes follow the large outcropping of unique rocks that juts out into the ocean at the southern end of the cove. I assume the town and marina must be on the other side of the natural barrier.

On the beach is a small raft. I had totally missed seeing it, mesmerized by the lighthouse. A figure comes into sight, carrying things to load onto the little boat. I expect an old fisherman, wrinkled by years in the sun, but my heart pleasantly skips a beat as I focus on the totally hot, buff guy with dark wavy hair. He looks slightly older than me, probably a college guy. And lucky for me, his shirt is nowhere in sight, showing off a tanned and muscular chest.

I sink into the warm sand a respectable distance away. Kahlua charges into the water after a seagull while I enjoy this new unexpected view. I have all summer to watch the waves but who knows how long the hunk will be around.

Maybe my new image will be the carefree beach chick with the killer tan. Although I'll have to overcome my boredom of lying out. But if this is what the guys on Coral Island are like, I may have to reassess my priorities. This place is amazing; it's impossible not to feel alive and free and that it really is possible to get away from the damage of that blasted book.

***

We pull up to the marina where Poseidon's, which, according to the front sign, is the premier seafood restaurant on the island, is located. I pluck a flower from one of the bushes outside and after a thorough inspection to make sure no bee lurks inside this time, avoiding a repeat performance of a scene from my mom's third

31

book, tuck it behind my ear. A hostess greets us, a pink streak of hair amidst her blond bob, which totally works for her, not at all beauty-school-dropout-ish. I follow her and her little sailor dress through the nautical-themed restaurant. We follow her past a rusty anchor, the worn wooden steering wheel from a boat, and other artifacts artfully displayed throughout the dining room. The tables fan out from an enormous circular aquarium in the center of the room, filled with vibrant tropical fish and coral. Along the walls are several paintings that I'm pretty sure are Aunt Lily's.

We are led out to a table on the deck where the steel drums of live Caribbean music intertwine with the laughter of happy guests. The tropical feel continues when the waiter brings us a basket of bread and drinks with pineapple and little umbrellas on the edge of the glass.

"Lily darling," says a well-dressed gentleman as he leans in and kisses her cheek. The resemblance to a certain British spy is uncanny. He looks just like the actor who plays the newer rugged version.

"Josie, this is my friend Tom Mullins. He's the owner of this superb restaurant."

"Oh, hi," I say as I shake the man's very tanned hand. I guess Mr. Mullins to be about my parents' age. But I'm pretty sure if my dad ever tried to wear a white linen suit and salmon-colored button-down shirt he'd look like he was going to a lame '70s costume party.

"Tom, this is my niece, Josie. She'll be staying with me this summer."

"Wonderful, we can always use more lovely ladies around here. What do you plan to do while here on Coral Island?"

"Mostly just relax, but who knows. Maybe a summer of adventure awaits me. I could try to solve the town's ongoing mystery."

"I told her about the thefts," explains Lily.

"Oh, you shouldn't bother yourself with our problems, just enjoy yourself," Mr. Mullins says with a smile.

"At least it would give her something to do besides sit on the beach and stare at cute boys," Lily counters.

"I see nothing wrong with staring at cute guys all summer. But I must admit I do love a good mystery," I answer.

"Well, if you get tired of investigating you could come out on one of my new tours. I'm taking advantage of our rich local history and have begun snorkeling and scuba excursions to the shipwreck."

"Shipwreck?" I ask.

"Yes, the pirate ship."

"*Pirate* ship?"

"Lily, how could you not have told your niece about our fascinating history?"

I reach for a breadstick to nibble on while Mr. Mullins continues his story.

"Out by the outcropping of rocks in the cove is a sunken pirate ship, thus the name Shipwreck Cove. It was actually a little cockboat, probably a scout team sent from the larger ship to check out the area. The cove is so secluded we presume they thought it was a safe landing spot. But the ocean's current can be rough along here and most likely caused the little dinghy to crash into the rocks and sink."

"However," Lily interjects, "legend has it that the little boat wasn't just a scout vessel but was in fact loaded with treasure to bury on the island."

"No treasure has ever been found, but when people hear the story they naturally want to explore. I'm happy to provide them the opportunity. We take tourists out to visit the wreck and make a whole day of it: provide lunch, items to dive for, and food to entice the fish. We even have a few helmets for underwater walking. The crew takes pictures with our digital underwater cameras that the guests can purchase back in town. Who wouldn't want a record of their pirate adventure? My nephew Byron oversees that side of the business while I stay focused here at the restaurant."

"Wow, that sounds like fun," I answer and take another bite of my breadstick.

"Hey, I've got someone I'd like you both to meet," says Mr. Mullins. He gestures to someone to come over.

Time stands still as I watch the hunky stranger from the beach approach. There is no way to mistake him even if he does have his shirt on now. Darn. His flawlessly perfect dark Spanish features are breathtaking. I no longer know how to chew and have somehow lost the ability to swallow. All I can do is watch dumbfounded with a chunk of bread still in my mouth as he walks up to our table. At least if I choke I will die happy.

"Niko Consuelos, I'd like you to meet Lily and her lovely niece, Josie."

Niko smiles, deep dimples forming on his cheeks. He takes Lily's hand but instead of shaking it he leans over and kisses it. Oh my. He looks at me with velvety brown eyes, then takes my hand and says, "My pleasure to meet you, Josie." Although in his sexy Spanish accent it comes out "Jozay."

Ay, caramba!

Mesmerized by the beauty that is Niko, I can't take my eyes off him. Boys in Lake Forest, Minnesota, do not look like this.

"Niko is helping me with the pirate ship tours this summer," Mr. Mullins says. At least I think that's what he says—I suddenly have a hard time concentrating on the words coming from Mr. Mullins' mouth.

I force myself to swallow so I don't spit food all over this Latin hottie. "I saw you out at the cove this afternoon."

Niko nods. "I usually am with the small raft in the afternoon. I restock and clean from the tourists of the morning."

"Why don't you just have the tourists help with that? Then you wouldn't have to go out twice," suggests Aunt Lily.

"Oh, Lily darling," says Tom, "you may be a talented artist but you're far too practical for the business world. We don't want our guests to have to do any work. The more luxurious the experience the more they will share the news of our services."

"Tom, you are the quintessential entrepreneur." Lily laughs.

"Always thinking," Mr. Mullins agrees. "So, Niko, what brings you here this evening?" he asks my Latin prince.

"My *familia*," Niko answers in that sultry accent.

Mr. Mullins nods, then turns to us to explain. "Niko's cousins are my Latin band that you are enjoying this evening. They're another find of mine. I had the privilege of hearing them during my last vacation and knew I needed them here for the summer. They spend nine months of the year on a cruise ship entertaining the passengers, then have three months off, when the cruise books other bands. I convinced them to come work here for the summer," he says very proudly. "When they heard of my snorkeling and scuba idea they suggested their cousin Niko to me. Things couldn't be more perfect."

"I agree." I sigh as I stare at the exotic man in front of me.

"Niko, you should take young Josie out on the boat one day."

"I would love that," I blurt out, not caring how desperate I may sound.

"I would enjoy to spend a day with you," answers totally hot Niko. His stunning smile flashes at me.

My cheeks burn as I smile back. Sadly he says his good-byes, then turns and saunters away. My heart flip-flops in my chest. Maybe I could be the girl with the sizzling summer romance. And playing the part of my leading man would be Niko.

"Now that could keep me out of trouble."

Lily and Mr. Mullins laugh.

"Oh, did I just say that out loud?"

Mr. Mullins winks at me, then excuses himself to greet other patrons.

"Well, that was nice of Niko to agree to take you out on the boat," says Aunt Lily as our food arrives.

Her amused look reveals she sees right through my thin veil of nonchalance. I mumble an agreement then dive into my crab legs and enjoy the Latin stylings of Niko's relatives.

A few minutes later the pink-haired hostess walks through the doors from the restaurant to the porch leading a family across the large deck. People around us stop their conversations and turn to watch the most adorable family in the world walk past the tables. They are straight out of a preppy clothing catalogue. The three little kids, all with bobbing blond curls, follow their parents in a perfectly straight line. The two little girls are dressed in matching gingham sundresses and the young boy in a button-down shirt, made of the same material, tucked into navy blue shorts, like a mini Von Trapp family.

But as precious as they are, they're not what catches my eye. A tall guy joins the group. Although I can only see his backside, he's got that lean muscular frame of an athlete. And the way he helps one of the little girls climb into her seat as they settle in at their table is sweet.

I sip on my virgin piña colada, thrilled to have hit the hot guy lottery in this town. This is going to be an epic summer after all. Bolstered by the sultry music and the warm breeze, I try to catch the cute guy's eye as he settles into his seat. I'm struck, though, by how much he looks like Ryan McNaulty, or *McNaughty* as Liz dubbed him, with the same light brown hair gelled up in the front and classic good looks. He must feel my gaze bore into him because he looks up from the menu and our eyes meet. He smiles and I do a double take. He not only looks like Ryan, he looks *exactly* like Ryan. I can't help but stare.

Then he does it. He cocks his head to the side and his mouth forms that McNaulty signature lopsided grin. My stomach drops.

No. It can't be. I quickly look away. Oh no, there's no denying it, it *is* Ryan McNaulty.

I quickly hide behind the dessert menu. How is this possible? Of all the gin joints in all the towns in all the states, in this whole big country, he has to end up here on Coral Island? No freakin' way. What's he doing here?

This was supposed to be my summer away from all things Lake Forest. How can I possibly get away when some jock from home is here? The jerks back home will never forget about me if Ryan supplies them with summer updates and leverage that they can use against me.

"Are you okay?" Lily asks.

"Just end my suffering and shoot me now." I put down the menu and slouch in defeat, my optimism and posture dissolving at the same time.

"Josie, again with the drama?"

"That guy over there goes to my school." I feel like crying but tell myself not to panic because under normal circumstances he really shouldn't know who I am since he's a jock and I'm a theater geek.

"Which one?" she asks as she turns in her seat to search for him.

"The tall one with the light brown hair sitting with the picture perfect family."

"Why don't you go over and say hi?"

"Are you kidding? I came here to get away from home. Besides, I'm hoping he doesn't know who I am."

But when he excuses himself to the cute family I know that stupid book continues to ruin my life. Unbelievable. As a hunter stalks his prey, he starts to walk toward us. I can't comprehend the horror that is unfolding. By the time he reaches our table I'm seething. With nowhere to hide I brace myself for what he might say.

"Hi, Josie. What're you doing here?"

To hear him actually say my name is a shock to my system.

"Um, hi, Ryan. This is my aunt, Lily Baker. I'm staying with her this summer."

"Hi, Ms. Baker," he says as he shakes her hand.

"Aunt Lily, this is Ryan McNaughty."

They both look at me with raised eyebrows.

Oh no, did I just say that?

"I mean McNaulty. Sorry. What're you doing here?" I ask, quickly changing the subject.

"Playing baseball for the Pirates."

"Oh, that's great. Good for you," says Aunt Lily.

"There's a baseball team on this island?" I ask.

"No, the Pirates are over on the mainland," explains Aunt Lily. "The local colleges have a summer scouting program. People around here love baseball. We'll have to come see some of your games."

The glare I shoot her would have made Riley whimper, but she doesn't seem to notice.

"What a small world, for the both of you to be here this summer," Aunt Lily gushes.

"Yeah, it must be fate," Ryan answers with a grin.

More likely bad karma coming back to bite me for my past mistakes.

The two of them chat about the family he is staying with, the Martins, and Lily suggests some things he simply must do while he's in town. I turn my attention to my piña colada in an attempt to appear unfazed by his presence, but I suck too hard through the straw and suffer a brain freeze.

Ryan's eyebrows furrow watching me attempt to not distort my face or bang my head on the table while I wait for the stabbing pain to subside. While he plays nice with Aunt Lily I anticipate the inevitable comment about the book, some slam on me that he will think is incredibly original and amusing. Sorry to break it to ya, McNaughty, I've already heard it all.

"Well, I hope to see you later," he politely says to us when he and Aunt Lily finish talking.

"Nice to meet you, Ryan," Lily answers as he walks back to his table.

That's it? No belittling comment to ridicule me in front of Aunt Lily? What's the matter, big man on campus? Not quick enough to come up with some dis on the fly?

I finish my dinner in silence, so angry that not even the cool Latin music or the thought of Niko the Amazing can lift my spirits. I can't believe I have to worry about the diabolical book's fallout even here. And now my big summer of reinvention will be known by everyone back home thanks to Ryan McNaulty. Why can't anything ever go my way?

Liz,

What's up, buttercup? I thought I'd write sooner but I have been quite busy here in Paradise. Busy relaxing. In fact, I'm writing this letter while on the beach—with Niko, this super hot Latin guy I met. Too bad I've given up technology or I could send you a pic of him. Believe me, him shirtless is a sight to behold.

I have to confess, I haven't actually spoken with him much. He works a lot, bringing tour groups to the beach to snorkel and scuba dive. But since I'm on the beach every day, we see each other often and have this totally flirty relationship going on. And when we smile at each other, I feel this deep connection. When we first met he promised to take me out for a boat ride, hopefully that will happen soon. I'll keep you posted!

Don't worry (I can already hear your lecture), I'm not being all stalker-chickish. There are plenty of reasons to be on the beach every day: to work on my tan, to walk Lily's dog, to collect sea shells, to write letters, to contemplate the meaning of life, etc.

There is one glitch in my whole getting-away-from-it-all plan though. Ryan McNaulty is here. Yes, you read that correctly. Can you believe it? South Carolina is where he's playing baseball for the summer. I seriously have the worst luck. But I've only seen him once so far. And I don't expect to be bothered by him because when I ran into him I totally put him in his place and made it clear he was not going to ruin my summer. Besides he'll probably be busy catching pop flies or whatever baseball guys do. Hope you're having fun at your dad's.

Love,

Josie

Chapter 3

"Kitten," Lily says as she breezes into my room, the aroma of coffee tagging along with her. "How would you like to go with me to check out a painting one of the seasonal residents wants restored?"

"Today?" I ask, lazily stretching in my too-comfy-to-get-out-of pillow-topped bed.

"Yes, that is if you can pull yourself from your busy schedule of Niko watching."

Ah, nothing gets past Aunt Lily. "I suppose I could pencil you in for a few hours this morning."

"Good. It'll be fun. The client is none other than Clive Hollis, the Hollywood movie producer. He built a huge estate on the island last year. I haven't met him yet but everyone's excited to have him here. We're all hoping he'll bring some of his famous acquaintances to visit. I've secretly been hoping for Johnny Depp. By the way, this came in the mail for you," she says, handing me a postcard.

I stare at the picture of the building-sized metal fish with people standing in its open mouth. I guess I'm not exempt from my mom's bizarre roadside attractions tradition after all. I turn it over expecting a note from my mom describing her book event or an anecdote of her travels, but instead is written a bible verse.

> Psalm 55:22 *Cast your burden on the Lord, and he will sustain you; he will never permit the righteous to be moved.*

Typical of her—since she has no idea what to say to me she's going to let God do the talking. Although I don't really see how some bible verses are going to fix anything. And what is that verse even supposed to mean? I actually did have to move away from my burdens—here to South Carolina.

***

41

As we pass each estate on our drive to the northern end of the island I can see the dollar signs mounting. The properties and homes increase in size the farther away from town we go. Apparently the north end is the place to live—that is, if you're a multimillionaire. Eventually we turn and head down a long winding road lined by a living wall of shrubs. We circle around a fountain of jumping dolphins. I gape at the three-story plantation-like home that towers above us. A shiny silver helicopter sits atop the white mansion, adorning it like a crown on a princess.

"Wow," is all I can say.

"I told you coming to these summer homes was fun."

We park behind a sleek black sports car. Before we reach the stairs, the massive front door swings open. A slightly overweight man in an orange tracksuit and really bad toupee hurries down the wide porch steps to meet us. Where's the stuffy English butler or at least a fussy housekeeper?

"Ms. Baker, I presume. I'm delighted to meet you," the man says as he pumps Lily's hand. "I'm Clive Hollis."

You have got to be kidding. This is what a Hollywood producer looks like? Guess I was expecting something a little more sophisticated. At least something less tacky.

"It's a pleasure to meet you, Mr. Hollis," Aunt Lily says, seemingly unfazed by his appearance. "This is my niece, Josie. She's helping me this summer."

He grabs my hand with a firm grip and starts to shake it as well.

"Come in, come in," he says as he scurries past the pillars and into his home.

We walk into what looks like a hotel lobby—an extremely lavish hotel lobby, one that would impress Daddy Warbucks himself. The space is so large I'm pretty sure my entire theater department could put on a whole production right here in the entryway. Two sweeping staircases frame the foyer, the curved wood of the banisters and ornamental swirls of the iron railings reminiscent of the waves of the ocean. The chandelier dangling in the center of the room is like nothing I've ever seen before. I'm awed by the dazzling hand-blown glass masterpiece, which looks like a mammoth tangle of blue streamers and balloons tumbling out from the soaring ceiling. Centered under the stunning light sits a massive, ornately carved wooden table with a giant model of a pirate ship.

Drawn to the intricate details of the miniature mast and Jolly Roger, I wander closer to the model. The click of my sandals on the white marble floor reverberates through the space. I fight the sudden urge to tap dance across the tiles. Our "Forget about the Boy" routine from *Thoroughly Modern Millie* would sound phenomenal in here.

"Oh, you have already discovered my passion," Mr. Hollis says to me. "Ever since I was a little boy I've been fascinated with pirates. You must see my collection."

We follow him through the impressive entryway and down a long hallway. I glance into the rooms we pass: a library with white bookshelves soaring two stories to the ceiling, a dining room with a seemingly endlessly long glass table and wall of French doors that lead out to a patio surrounded by flowers. Off the patio, a well-worn pathway leads down to their private beach. But the seashell-shaped pool is where I'd like to spend some time.

When we reach the end of the house, Mr. Hollis dramatically pauses at a set of double doors, so large they must be on steroids. Then, with the flourish of a magician, he pushes them open. The two-story room is lined from eye level to ceiling with ornately framed paintings. I've been to museums with less artwork. The majority of the paintings are of pirate ships tossing in the ocean.

"You have an amazing collection, Mr. Hollis," Lily says in awe. "Oh my, is that a Howard Pyle?" She rushes over to a painting of a snarling pirate on a beach, the bold red of his sash in sharp contrast to the muted colors of the rest of the piece.

"It's wonderful to have visitors who appreciate art. Most people don't understand my obsession. And they don't realize the caliber of renowned artists that are represented here."

"I would expect to find some of these only in museums," Lily agrees, much to Mr. Hollis's delight.

"It's good to be wealthy."

That's the understatement of the century.

He shows us around the room but the names and dates he keeps emphasizing mean nothing to me so I just follow along silently, nodding in fake appreciation. Mr. Hollis grins like a mischievous child as we near his imposing desk.

"You have a Wyeth?" Lily grabs onto the edge of his desk to steady herself.

Even I'm mesmerized by the painting in question. A pirate ship crashes through the rough waves, a glow from the golden sunset in the distance. I'm sure the boat will burst through the canvas and into the room at any moment.

"Josie," Lily says breathlessly. "N. C. Wyeth illustrated *Treasure Island*. My father loved that book. I remember staring at the beautiful pictures wondering how he could capture so much emotion on paper."

"A master storyteller through his art," Mr. Hollis agrees.

Eventually he leads us to a painting leaning against a wall. The faded picture is of a mermaid sitting on a beach, her tail curled behind her. She gazes across the ocean toward a ship with billowing sails. Massive dark clouds give the scene an ominous feel. "This is the painting that I would like your help with."

"It's beautiful."

"Well, it could be. Do you think you might be able to bring it back to its original splendor?"

"I'm confident I can help you," says Lily, and they begin to discuss what the project would entail.

I wander around the room and try to decide what I would collect if I had Mr. Hollis's wealth. Old movie posters? Signed playbills? Dorothy's ruby slippers? My deep thoughts are interrupted by a ten- or eleven-year-old girl as she pirouettes into the room. A cyclone of purple, from her eyeglasses to her matching tennis skirt and socks, she spins around me.

"Cyd, you know there's no dancing in the gallery!" calls Mr. Hollis.

"Sorry, I wondered where you were. Can we go to the beach now?" asks the girl as she twirls a strand of long blond hair around her finger.

"Cyd, I'd like you to meet some people. This is Lily Baker. She's going to be restoring a painting for us. Lily, this is my daughter, Cyd."

"Ah!" Cyd gasps as she stares at Aunt Lily, her huge eyes magnified by her glasses. "You're Lily Baker? *The* Lily Baker!" she squeals.

I lean toward Aunt Lily. "I didn't know seascapes were so popular with the kids these days."

"I didn't either." The three of us stare as Cyd spins around again.

"Dad, don't you know who this is?" she asks her father in disbelief.

"My art restorer?"

"No! This is Tabitha Baker's sister!" she yelps.

My heart plummets.

"Who?" he questions.

"Only my favorite author, that's who! The bookstore owner in town told me you lived here on the island. I can't believe this!"

Neither can I. My mom's number one fan is on this island? Unfreakin' believable.

"Cyd loves your sister's writing," explains Mr. Hollis. "She has read the books so many times, they're all falling apart."

"They are good books," Lily agrees.

"Good? They're the best!" Cyd screeches. "I just love all the clumsy characters."

Of course she does.

"I'm bummed, though. The bookstore here doesn't have her newest novel yet. And Dad wouldn't let me order it online," she whines.

"That's because as soon as you get the book I will not be able to get you outside again. And a young lady needs plenty of fresh air and sunshine."

"Besides, you won't like the new book," I blurt out. They all turn to look at me.

"This is Ms. Baker's niece, Josie," Mr. Hollis informs his daughter.

"Niece? OH MY GOSH!"

I've never encountered anyone with such an ear-splitting voice before. It's a miracle the crystal chandelier above us doesn't shatter.

"That means you're . . . you're *her* daughter! The one who inspires her writing, which means the books are about you!" She fans herself like she might faint.

"No!" I state. Lily turns to look at me, her eyebrows raised. "My mother is Mrs. DelRio, Lily's other sister," I say, proud of my quick thinking. It's not a complete lie, my mom *is* Mrs. DelRio at home. I don't have to acknowledge the fact that she writes under her maiden name.

"But that doesn't make any sense," Cyd says. "According to the biography on her website, Tabitha Baker only has one sister."

Why does this pint-size fan know so much?

"It's a long story," I say, not sure where this tall tale will take me. "You see, there are three Baker girls, one of the daughters, my mother, was tragically separated at birth. A crazy nurse at the rural hospital where she was born fell in love with the sweet tiny baby and took her home. She raised her as her own and was a wonderful mother. Oh, and grandmother," I quickly add, remembering this is my pretend family I'm talking about.

"It wasn't until my mother was browsing in a bookstore one day, looking for a book for me, that she came across the first clue. She picked up one of Tabitha's books and was stunned when she saw the author's photo. The resemblance to her own face was uncanny. A few days later she asked her mother if they had any relatives with the last name of Baker, and told her about the photo she had seen. The old woman, my grandmother, who was dying of cancer, confessed to her daughter of the terrible thing she had done so many years ago. DNA testing confirmed it, and the sisters were recently reunited." I wince as I finish my monologue, feeling a twinge of guilt for lying.

Young Cyd stares at me, her mouth hanging open.

"That would make a great movie, it's absolutely unbelievable," says Mr. Hollis.

"It truly is," adds Aunt Lily.

"The books aren't about you?" Cyd asks. Her shoulders sag with disappointment.

"No. Sorry."

"Well, she's still your relative so you can tell me all about her. Which book do you like the best?" She starts to reel off the titles, beginning with her favorite.

"I guess you now know my daughter's passion," chuckles Mr. Hollis.

"She's darling," Lily says with a warm smile.

"Cyd, we don't have time for the beach now. The tennis pro will be here any moment for your lesson," says Mr. Hollis.

"We should be going," Lily says. "I'll be back tomorrow to wrap the painting and transfer it to my studio."

Mr. Hollis walks us out. Cyd follows along reciting her favorite misadventures from the books, many my own mishaps. I can't believe this is happening.

As we pull away from the Hollis estate, Lily turns to me. "Okay, what was that about?"

"That book ruined my life back home, I'm not about to let it mess everything up here. In case you didn't notice, the kid is not exactly a quiet little wallflower. If she knows who I really am she will tell everyone in town. And the moment the book arrives on this island everyone will assume it's about me since my mom states on her website I'm her inspiration. And then once again I will be humiliated."

"I see your dilemma, but people around here are not like the kids back at your high school. It doesn't seem right to lie about who you are."

"I just want to be a different person this summer and not be compared to the characters in those books. The whole point of coming here was to get away from all the drama."

"Could you have made your story any more unrealistic?" she teases.

"Hey, improv is not as easy as it seems."

***

In the evening Lily's neighbors come over to play poker. Mr. and Mrs. Thompson are quite a bit older than my grandparents, but still full of life. Mrs. Thompson is a tiny little lady with curly gray hair and wire-rim glasses. Mr. Thompson towers over his wife, his tight white curls in sharp contrast to his dark skin. After repeatedly trying to tell him my name I deduce he's hard of hearing.

Lily mixes up some cocktails for the adults while I bring out bowls of snacks to the back porch. Mrs. Thompson pulls out some cards and starts to shuffle them.

"Josie, what're you going to do this summer while you're visiting?" asks Mrs. Thompson as she deals the cards.

"For now, just relax on the beach."

"What? Teach?" hollers Mr. Thompson.

"No, dear, she said relax on the beach," Mrs. Thom

"Oh. That's a waste of time," Mr. Thompson grumbles.

"Well, I'm also going to help Lily with her restorations and I may try to figure out who's robbing everyone in town," I say defensively as I arrange the cards in my hand. I don't want them to think I'm a total slacker, but geez, I am on vacation—what's wrong with a little beach time?

"Now, that's a good idea," says Mr. Thompson. "No one else around here seems to be doing anything about those burglaries."

"Yes, we really need to figure out who's behind it all," Mrs. Thompson adds as she fans out her cards, her arms extended from her body. I turn slightly to avoid seeing what she's holding.

"Could be someone new in town. We get quite a bit of summer help," says Lily.

"Could be a local for all we know," adds Mr. Thompson.

"I don't think it's a local. Why would anyone want to steal from their neighbors?" asks Mrs. Thompson.

"That would be pretty bold," I agree.

"Fold? You fold already? Me, too. That was a short hand," says Mr. Thompson, laying down his cards for us all to see.

Mrs. Thompson punches him in the shoulder. I stifle a giggle.

"What?" he asks his wife.

"Nothing, dear," she answers and starts to reshuffle the cards.

"Nancy, I'm glad you're not like all those other teenagers wasting all their time. You have spunk, I think we're going to be great friends."

"Dear, her name is Josie."

"I know that but she could be our Nancy Drew and solve this mystery."

"She probably doesn't know who Nancy Drew is," says Mrs. Thompson.

"How could she not know who Nancy Drew is?"

"She's from a different generation, dear. I hate to burst your bubble but usually great friends have something in common."

"Nonsense," he grumbles, "we are like two peas in a pod."

"That's right," I agree, enthused by Mr. Thompson. "What books do you like?" I ask, searching for some common ground.

"Books about war."

"Movies?"

"Historic fiction."

"Music?"

"Blues."

"Hmm, TV?"

"Documentaries."

"Talk show hosts?" I ask, grasping at straws.

"There hasn't been anyone interesting since Ed Sullivan."

Mrs. Thompson sighs.

"Oh, I know him," I say excitedly. "In *Bye Bye Birdie*, Conrad has his 'One Last Kiss' on *The Ed Sullivan Show*."

The three of them look at me; Mr. Thompson's white eyebrows burrow.

"See!" he exclaims to his wife. "I told you—two peas in a pod."

"Besties," I agree.

***

So go my days on Coral Island, mornings spent perfecting my tan and riding my wakeboard, which of course gives me a great excuse for Niko watching as he dives with the tour groups. I keep hoping he'll have time to come over and talk to me but sadly I only get a smile and a wave.

During the afternoons I lounge on the deck reading or help Lily as she works. At least I like to think I'm helping her. I really just talk and hand her the supplies she needs. The evenings are my favorite. Aunt Lily makes cooking dinner fun. At home my mom just prepares the meals for us. But here it's an event. Aunt Lily turns on the music and pours herself some wine. We dance around the kitchen and sing along to songs like "Brown Eyed Girl," "Margaritaville," and other songs I didn't even know I liked, while cutting up vegetables and sautéing the meat.

After dinner we relax on the porch or stroll along the beach with Kahlua. Some nights we play cards with the Thompsons. Mr. Thompson usually loses but keeps us entertained with his military tales, like the time he snuck a donkey into the general's stateroom. I love it here. My problems seem so far away. Ah, if only I could stay here forever.

Chapter 4

The restoration of Mr. Hollis's painting has consumed most of Lily's time the last few days. But this morning she tells me she needs to go into town to talk with a shopkeeper about an order of paintings. I decide to break up my usual routine of lounging on the beach hoping for a chance to talk to Niko, and join her.

In true beachy style we ride to town on bikes that you would never be caught dead riding back home, the kind with high handlebars that make you sit up straight, wicker baskets, and bells. Somehow here they are perfect. We ride down her long driveway to Seaview Boulevard, follow the bike path up the hill toward the lighthouse then down the other side toward town.

Even though it's Friday, the town has its usual Sunday afternoon laziness about it, families window-shopping with that slow pace that vacations bring. We park our bikes outside a little retro burger and malt shop.

"Here, Kitten," Lily says as she hands me some money, "can you order me a cheeseburger and chocolate malt? I'm going to run across the street to let Polly know when those paintings will be finished."

"Sure."

She turns and crosses over to the shop with the light blue curtains framing the window.

I enter the vintage burger joint. Black-and-white floor tiles and red vinyl booths and chairs fill the space. An Elvis tune plays from the jukebox in the corner. Records along with black-and-white photos decorate the walls, completing the 1950s set dressing. If only I had brought my poodle skirt and saddle shoes from *Bye Bye Birdie*. Not only would they fit in perfectly but I would fulfill my promise to my mom that I would indeed wear the outfit I begged her for, again. I place my order at the counter with the sweetest little old man, who has probably been making malts since the '50s.

Footsteps rhythmically descending stairs at the side of the shop divert my attention. Like a daydream coming to life, my leading man Niko appears. Our eyes meet across the not so crowded room. His dark chiseled face makes my knees weaken.

Muy caliente!

"Hi," I gasp, when he smiles at me, sure my cheeks are as red as the vinyl chairs.

"One of those you bought for me?" he asks in his completely endearing choppy English style as the malts are placed on the counter in front of me.

"Of course," I say. Hey, Aunt Lily can fend for herself.

"No, no," he laughs, "but I hope not for a boyfriend."

Is he flirting? "No, just Aunt Lily."

"Excellent," he says as he follows me to a small round table in the back corner.

"How are you, Jozay?" he asks as he pulls out a chair for me at the cozy table for two. Impressive.

"I'm great. What are you doing here?" I ask, staring into those chocolaty brown eyes.

"I am living here. My cousins and I have an apartment to rent upstairs, from Mr. Spencer," he says, glancing over at the little man behind the counter who's hard at work on my food order.

"Oh." I may have to enjoy these malts more often.

"I believe you must like the beach. Often you are there."

I hope he doesn't think I'm stalking him even though I kinda am. "Being from Minnesota, I have to take advantage of the beach whenever I can."

"I do not know Minnesota. It is cold?"

"Yes, that's why I need to work on my tan."

He smiles and I try to think of something else to ask him.

"Where are you from?" I finally come up with.

"In the Dominican Republic is where I was born."

"Oh, wow," I lamely mutter because I have no idea where that is and don't want to make a fool of myself. That's what I get for passing notes to Liz during geography instead of paying attention. Who knew school was so useful?

His cell phone buzzes and he reaches for it. The distraction gets me off the hook for being completely ignorant.

"Excuse me, Jozay," he says. He reads his text message and frowns.

"Is something wrong?"

"No, Mr. Mullins asks me to take care of something."

"You seem to work a lot. Do you get many days off?" I ask.

"There are some. Are you going this weekend to the dance?"

"What dance?"

"A kick-off of summer dance," he answers.

"Will your cousins be playing at it?"

"Yes, it is at the park of the lighthouse Saturday night. Tomorrow."

"That sounds fun." And romantic.

"I hope that you may be there," he says.

"I wouldn't miss it," I answer, my eyelids batting under their own volition. "Maybe you'll save a dance for me."

"Of course," he says with a smile, dimples a-dimpling. "*Nos vemos mañana, hermosa*," he says with a slight bow.

I have no idea what he just said but it was beautiful. Spanish—a class that probably would have been more helpful than the French I've been taking.

He smoothly saunters toward the door. Outside he climbs into a large black pickup parked out front. With a sigh, I shift my gaze back to the counter to see if my order is ready yet. Startled, I see someone watching me. Ryan. Are you kidding?

He grins, then struts over to my table, his backwards baseball cap annoying me for some reason. Without waiting to be invited to sit, as a gentleman would, he grabs the chair Niko had been sitting in and flips it around in one fluid motion so it's facing backwards.

Then he straddles the poor innocent chair, his arms resting on the back.

"Hey."

Seriously? "Hey" is the best he can come up with?

I take a deep breath then brace myself for his best one-liner. Bring it on. I'm in too good of a mood about the upcoming dance; nothing he throws my way is going to ruin my day.

I lean back in my chair, cross my arms, and answer, "Hey."

"Enjoying your malt?"

"As a matter of fact, I am."

"What've you been doing since you got here? Swimming?"

Let the games begin.

"Yes, and I haven't even had any problems with my swimsuit, thank you," I answer, ruining his punch line.

"What?" he asks, looking confused. "I just thought you looked tan. You know, losing the Minnesota pallor. Have you been spending a lot of time at the beach?"

"Yep, and if I get stung by a jellyfish I don't need you to pee on my foot." Rim shot, please. Oh, this boy should not have tried to mess with me today.

"Um, okay. Are you planning on staying here all summer?" he asks.

"Why? You trying to figure out how much longer you have to torment me?"

"What? Why would I torment you?"

"Just go ahead and get it over with."

He rubs his temples with his left hand like I'm giving him a headache. "What're you talking about?"

This clueless routine is getting old. There is no way I'm going to fall for his innocent act.

"Your big joke . . . the funny cut-down. Come on, I've heard it all. Just go ahead and get it out of your system so I can continue on with my summer."

He stares at me blankly. "I have no idea what you're talking about."

Boy, he's good.

"You expect me to believe you haven't heard about my mom's book?"

The light bulb comes on and he nods. "Oh, that. Yeah, I heard something about a book."

"Oh yeah, that. Don't play stupid. I'm here to get away from all you morons back home who have nothing better to do than give me grief. I will not have you ruining my summer."

I'm proud of my speech and wish I had someone to high-five. But his grin only gets bigger. He's like sand rubbing my skin raw.

"You think I'm here to give you grief?" His eyes crinkle in amusement. I'm glad he finds this funny.

"Go ahead and tell your dumb jock friends back home all about my summer. I don't care. I'll deal with that next year but right now I refuse to worry about Lake Forest High School and all the petty people that go there."

He continues to smirk. How can Liz think that totally obnoxious grin is cute?

"Do you feel better now?" he asks.

"What?"

"Now that you got that off your chest, do you feel better?"

I'll just have to ignore him; there's no reasoning with this guy.

"Whatever. Say what you want to say then get out of my face," I snap.

"I was just going to ask if you wanted to come to one of our games this weekend."

"What?" That was not what I was expecting. "I don't know, I may be busy."

"With Rico Suave?" he asks with a head tilt toward the door Niko exited.

"His name is Niko, and who I choose to do things with is none of your business."

"Duly noted. So are you meeting someone?" he asks as he looks down at the two malts on the table.

"My aunt, if you must know. She's across the street at the souvenir shop."

"She might be a while. I heard that store was robbed last night."

"Oh. She told me there's been a lot of robberies on the island in the past few weeks, right as the summer tourist season started. Lily thinks I should investigate and try to figure out who's behind it all."

"That's a great idea. In fact, I'll help you," he says enthusiastically.

"Why would I want to do that?" I ask.

"What? Help solve the mystery?"

"No. Work with you."

"It'll give us something to do while we're on this island," he says.

"I don't need anything more to do, I'm quite busy already."

"Doing what?"

"Going to the beach, helping my aunt with her business, and meeting interesting new people like Niko and his cousins who are here from the Dominican Republic for the summer."

"Oh, well, according to my sources the robberies started about the time your Romeo and his cousins moved to town," he says with a shrug.

"You're accusing Niko?"

"Just telling you what I heard," he answers.

"That's ridiculous, he would never do that."

"How do you know? Do you even know anything about him?"

"I'm a good judge of character," I say.

"I bet you I'm right about him," he counters.

"You're insane."

"Maybe, but I still think I'm right."

"You're completely off base here. Unlike you, Niko is a nice guy and would never annoy anyone, let alone rob them."

"Then prove it," he challenges.

"Why should I waste my time disproving your delusions?"

"Afraid of what you might find?"

"No, because there is nothing to find," I snap.

"Then work with me."

"You're not going to let this drop, are you?" I sigh.

"Nope."

"Why?"

"I'm also a good judge of character," he says, throwing my own statement back in my face.

"Fine, if it will get you to shut up, I'll work with you."

"Good. You find out from your aunt which residents have been burglarized and I'll get a list of the businesses. Then we can figure out who the likely suspects are."

"You apparently have too much time on your hands."

He smiles, then stands up. "By the way, there's a game tonight if you're interested." He turns and walks away. His long legs stride toward the counter. Mr. Spencer hands him a bag of takeout then thankfully he leaves.

I sit there sorting out our strange conversation. He never did make fun of me. Probably wasn't prepared for me to head him off. Maybe he's luring me in, getting me to spend time with him, then he'll turn on me when I'm not expecting it. He could be more dangerous than I thought.

Out front he leans against a motorcycle and chats with Aunt Lily after she crosses the street. Why does he have to be all polite to her? Hopefully if I just keep anticipating his comments and he realizes he can't get to me he'll get tired of this stupid game and leave me alone. I watch him climb on his motorcycle and buckle his helmet. The resemblance to '50s heartthrob James Dean, from those old movies my mother loves, is uncanny. I just wish this rebel's cause was not to torture me.

Lily sweeps in and chats with the elderly gentleman at the counter. He follows her over to my table, carrying a tray with our burgers and fries.

"Josie, I'd like you to meet my dear friend, Larry Spencer."

"Hi, Mr. Spencer," I say as he hands us our food. "It's nice to meet you. I love the fifties vibe of your restaurant."

"That's sweet of you to say. I guess I'm a little nostalgic for the old days."

"The fifties never go out of style," Aunt Lily says.

"Are you a friend of Niko's?" he asks me.

"Sort of. We keep running into each other," I answer. Out of the corner of my eye I see Lily smile.

"Him and his cousins are the best tenants I've ever had. They're such polite young men. They even help me out around here when they have free time."

I smile, glad to know there's more to Niko than just a pretty face.

"I hate to think how lonely it will be around here when they leave," Mr. Spencer adds with a touch of sadness.

"Maybe you could go back to the dating scene," Aunt Lily teases.

Mr. Spencer laughs heartily; his frail frame shakes with glee. I can't help but laugh, too, his joyous demeanor contagious. He then shuffles back to the counter.

"Sorry it took me so long. I also ran into Ben, the mailman, and he gave me my mail." Lily hands me another postcard, then focuses on squeezing ketchup all over her fries.

I tuck it into my back pocket to look at later. "Thanks. Ryan told me your friend's store was broken into."

"Yes, poor Polly. They jimmied open the cash register and took the money, then smashed the display case and grabbed the more expensive jewelry. The place is a mess, glass everywhere."

"Can the jewelry be tracked if it's resold?" Seems like something they could do based on TV shows I've seen.

"The police are pretty sure the gold will be melted down then resold. With the high price of gold these days it's a hot commodity. The thief seems to be getting braver."

"Well, that could be good. Maybe he'll get sloppy and get caught then."

"Ryan told me that the two of you are going to investigate," she says with a smile.

"I'm just trying to get Ryan off my back."

She nods. "I told Polly I'd go back over after lunch and help clean up the mess. Do you mind riding home by yourself?"

"No problem, I think I can find the way. Even if I turn the wrong way, it's an island and I'll circle back around eventually."

"By the way, do you have any big plans the next few days?"

"You know me, my social calendar is awfully full," I tease. "Why?"

"I need to take some paintings to a few shops and galleries along the coast. I thought we could make a road trip out of it."

"What about the dance tomorrow night?" I ask.

She smiles. "Oh, you heard about that, did you? Did Ryan ask you to go?"

"Ryan? No, no way."

"Why? He seems nice and you've got to admit he's cute."

"I'm pretty sure he only wants to make my life miserable. No, Niko told me about it. He's going to save a dance for me." I try to say that last part with an easygoing attitude but feel a blush roll over my face.

"Niko, huh?" she slyly says. "He seems a bit old for you."

"Aunt Lily, don't be such a mom."

"I thought we could leave town after mass on Sunday. I want you to see the beautiful little parish in town. Does that work for you?"

"Sounds good."

After we eat I ride back toward her cottage. My burning quads emphasize how steep the hill between town and Lily's house is when heading this direction. At the top I take a detour and ride through the park, hoping to get a glimpse of the perfection that is Niko down at the cove. Unable to see the beach from the bike path, I park and walk closer to the cliffs. Below, the ocean gently laps onto the shore. Unfortunately, no Niko in sight but I walk along the edge toward the lighthouse soaking up the feeling of peacefulness. Maybe if I store up enough, I can take it home with me and use it when things get tough there.

I sit on one of the rocks near the wooden staircase that leads down to the beach and finally look at the postcard from my mom. The picture is a replica of the famous English landmark Stonehenge but it's made out of old junky boats. How do people think of these things? On the back is another Bible verse written in her beautiful script.

Psalm 23:2–3 *He leads me beside still waters, He restores my soul.*

I gaze out at the peaceful blue ocean. I'm a bit annoyed my mom keeps sending these motivational postcards but I can't help but be drawn to the verse. I really am ready for my soul to be restored and here by this awe-inspiring water seems like the perfect place for it to happen. But my reflective moment is ruined by a loud rumble coming from behind me. I turn to see a motorcycle pull into the park. Panic sets in when I realize it's Ryan. I look toward my bike but there is no way I can reach it without Ryan seeing me. To avoid another confrontation with him I quickly rush into the lighthouse.

"Nancy, what brings you here?" The gruff voice startles me as I burst through the door.

"Oh. Hi, Mr. Thompson."

"Tracking down a lead in your robbery investigation?"

"No, just hiding from my problems." I use my best theater voice and project to make sure he can hear. My words echo off the metal walls.

"Hmm, in my experience that never works. Problems have a tendency to follow you."

"You can say that again. Wow, what is this place?" I wander around the small lobby of the building set up as a museum of lighthouse memorabilia.

"Oh, it's the town's way of preserving our history. These pictures and articles are all about shipwrecks and hurricanes that have impacted the island. I'm the volunteer caretaker. It keeps me out of Mrs. Thompson's hair," he says.

"This is great. I had no idea this was here."

"Come here, I've got something to show you," he says and leads me to a spiral staircase. I'm thankful for information and photos displayed along the walls heading up to the viewing area, a convenient excuse to stop and rest on the long climb up the tower. I'm impressed with how fit Mr. Thompson is. While I'm gasping for breath, he looks like he's on a leisurely stroll. I grasp the railing as I follow him, not wanting to slip on the steep metal steps. A summer at the beach sporting a cast would not be cool. Although it would give my mom new ammo for her next book. Finally we emerge at the top.

Breathtaking.

The vast ocean in front of us sparkles like a field of diamonds. The Atlantic stretches out as far as I can see. Far off on the horizon the deep blue of the water intersects with the clear blue of the sky.

Behind me in the center of the space is an enormous light, which he tells me no longer works. He points out the landmarks as we walk around and admire the 360-degree views. The black ribbon below us is Seaview Boulevard; it stretches north where I spot Aunt Lily's house sheltered among the trees. To the south is the park below us, the cliffs, and part of the town beyond the rocks. I spot

Ryan in the parking lot, leaning against his motorcycle eating his lunch.

"A friend of yours?" Mr. Thompson asks.

"No, just another one of my problems," I say.

"Are problems what brought you to Coral Island?" he asks, staring out at the endless ocean.

"Yes, I had to get away from home," I admit. "There were lots of rumors going around about me. I needed to remove myself from the lies."

"People can make life very difficult."

"No kidding. That guy is one of the popular kids at my school who happens to be here this summer. I really thought this was my chance to get away from the whole ordeal but now he's here and I'm worried he's going to keep following me and tell the kids back home lies about my summer that will just fuel the whole situation even more."

Mr. Thompson nods thoughtfully. "But the ones who matter will know the truth and not believe the lies. You should just be yourself and not worry what others say."

"Can I be honest with you?" I ask him.

"Of course, we're besties now, right?"

"Right. The thing is, I don't really know who I am anymore. My high school is very cliquey and if you're not one of the cool kids you get harassed. I've spent so long trying to avoid being noticed by any of them that I haven't been myself and now I'm not sure who that is. I'm hoping this summer I can somehow figure it out." It feels good to confide in someone.

He nods. "Do you know what's in an army ration?"

"Um, no," I reply, realizing he mustn't have understood what I just said. So much for baring my soul to a hearing-impaired military vet.

"Once when my ship was off the coast of Korea, a group of us had shore leave. We went into a village that was supposed to be friendly. Some buddies and I went to a bar, a known hangout for the troops. We met a group of Army privates and were having a great time shootin' the breeze. That evening the place was ambushed. Most of the guys in that bar were taken hostage, but a few of us near the side door escaped. We ran through the jungle until we came across an abandoned shack and holed up there.

"There we were in enemy territory, no means of communication, and no way to know what was happening in the village. In the distance we could hear gunfire and saw the glow of burning buildings. We were terrified that we would be found. The Army guys had their duffels so we did have some weapons and their rations. We were in dire circumstances but all I could think about was how much I hated the biscuits in those Army rations and that I was glad I had enlisted in the Navy."

I stare at him, not sure what to say. Maybe that strenuous climb depleted the oxygen to his brain. "Oh."

"We were eventually rescued. When we were heading back to the ship, I learned the captured men had been tortured and were being held as POWs. I couldn't get over the guilt I felt that I had obsessed over food for days and not worried about those men." He keeps his eyes on the ocean as he speaks.

"Wow," I say, still not sure how this story is relevant to anything.

"Don't you see, you must put the POWs before the rations," he states emphatically.

"Okay." Clear as mud.

"I didn't want to be someone who always thought of themselves first and didn't care about others. See, the key to finding out who you really are and what your beliefs are is to focus on those less fortunate than you. When you help someone else with their problems yours dwindle in comparison. It seems like you have plenty of rations in your life—you may not like them but you have them and you're surviving. But some people are like the POWs and are struggling and really need prayers and assistance. If you focus on them you'll see how lucky you are. Suddenly your priorities and beliefs will come into focus."

"Hmm. It sounds like wise advice."

"It's something I still adhere to. Once a week I head to the mainland and volunteer at the veterans' hospital. You should join me sometime."

"I'll think about it. Thanks, Mr. Thompson."

"Mr. Thompson sounds too formal coming from my new bestie." He grins.

"We'll have to think of something," I say, going in for a hug. "Maybe Captain Von Awesome," I whisper into the folds of his cotton golf shirt that smells of cologne and peppermint.

"No. That would be Rear Admiral Von Awesome."

I pull away, embarrassed. "I'm so sorry, I didn't mean any disrespect. I was just . . . Wait. You heard that. You're not really hard of hearing, are you?"

He winks at me. "Shh, don't tell anyone. Sometimes it's nice not to have to talk to people I don't want to deal with."

"Your secret's safe with me. I totally understand but I don't think it would work for me. Although sometimes I do wear my earbuds just so people will think I'm listening to music and they'll leave me alone."

"See, great minds think alike," he says with the knowing smile of a cohort.

Josie,

What's the scene, jellybean? You are not going to believe this! My dad is having a full-blown midlife crisis. So, he picks me up at the airport in his new convertible sports car. He thinks he's lookin' all fly in his preppy shirt and designer jeans. Really? Where are the khaki pants, tucked-in polo, and brown belt that I've known my whole life? And you should see his hair. It's all gelled and kind of spiky. What's with that? Then he drives me to lunch. He stops at some ultra trendy tapas place. I'm thinking who is this man and what has he done with my dad? As we walk in he tells me—all nonchalant like, "I'd like you to meet a friend of mine." Then we head over to this table where this bleach blond chick—way closer to my age than his—is sitting. She jumps up and squeals then kisses him! Yuck! Who wants to see their dad play tonsil hockey with someone named Chrissy? Yup—Dad's got himself a girlfriend. Should be an interesting summer.

Love ya,

Liz

P.S. McNaughty, huh? Go watch one of his games for me. And when you see him ask him about the baseball trick he does. Trust me, it's cool.

P.P.S. You suck—my hand's totally cramping. My dad thought it was such a great idea to handwrite our letters so he's making me be all 19th century, too. Thanks a lot.

Chapter 5

Lily invited Tom Mullins over for dinner and cocktails before the big dance. Their relationship has me stumped. They've met for lunch and coffee a few times since I've been here but seem mostly like friends. If I could pay attention to their conversation I might be able to piece together what's going on between them but my mind is elsewhere so they morph into the adults on the Charlie Brown shows. Wah, wah, wah, wah, wah.

I can't get Liz's letter out of my head. What is wrong with the adults of this world? Can't they act normal? My mom has to pretend she's cool and write young adult stories—like she knows anything that goes on with teenagers these days. And Liz's dad can't face the fact that he's getting old and is acting like a fool. I hope I turn out like Aunt Lily, who figured out how she wanted to live her life and is doing it with no regrets, no living off someone else's experience, no reliving her glory days.

After a dinner that I barely touched, Mr. Mullins walks with us up the beach toward the lighthouse. It's a perfect evening for an outdoor dance. The stars are shining and a slight breeze refreshes the air. The quiet roar of the tumbling waves adds a tropical background soundtrack.

"Tom, it was sweet of you to close the restaurant early tonight so the whole town could enjoy your new band," Lily says, her arm wrapped around his and the tailored sports jacket he wears.

"Of course," he says. "Besides, the more everyone wants to hear the guys the better for business. Hopefully people will come in for dinner to see them again."

"Your diving tours also seem to be a big hit," I add.

"Yes, they've been popular. Have you heard the buzz around town?" he asks.

"No, but I see the packed tours when I'm on the beach," I explain.

"Josie has been spending a lot of time at the cove since she got here. Although, I'm not sure if it's the amazing ocean view she's been enjoying or your young tour guide," teases Lily.

"Oh, I can see the appeal of both for a young lady," answers Mr. Mullins with a wink to me.

How embarrassing.

"How's your new restoration project coming along?" asks Mr. Mullins. "You told me it was a painting of a mermaid and pirate ship."

"So far so good. It's always a slow process but I enjoy it," Lily answers.

"Rumor has it that Clive Hollis has quite the art collection."

"You could say that again," I chime in. "But it's pretty limited to pirates. I don't think he ever outgrew his childhood fantasies."

"He is a bit eccentric," agrees Lily.

"I gathered that," says Mr. Mullins. "One night he and his daughter came to the restaurant. He asked me about my small collection of shipwreck items then told me about some of his own treasures. I'd love to see them. Maybe I could help you deliver the painting when you finish."

"I'm sure he would enjoy showing them to someone who shares his interest. Although you better plan on taking the whole day off for it, he's very animated when it comes to his collection," Lily says.

The wooden staircase that leads us to the park and lighthouse vibrates to the band's warm-up notes. The entire town seems to have shown up. There are no empty spots in the parking lot and the overflow of cars lines Seaview Boulevard. The thousands of twinkling lights strung along all the trees and the tiki torches blazing around the park blanket the scene in a magical glow. I don't see Niko anywhere but do spot Mr. and Mrs. Thompson.

"Nancy, you look as lovely as a South Pacific island this evening," says Mr. Thompson when he ambles over to us.

"Nancy?" asks Mr. Mullins.

"Coral Island's own Nancy Drew," says Mr. Thompson.

"Josie and her friend Ryan are investigating the robberies," explains Lily.

Begrudgingly. But it does give me a chance to try out Mr. Thompson's theory about helping others in order to find myself.

"Ah, well hopefully someone will solve it soon," Mr. Mullins answers.

One of Niko's handsome cousins takes the mic and in impressively smooth English welcomes everyone. They start off the evening with one of their Latin songs. The crowd flows to the makeshift dance floor.

"Could I please have this dance, Lily?" Mr. Mullins asks.

Aunt Lily accepts and I watch as they take to the dance floor, the dashing secret agent and his beautiful girl. Her skirt flares; the sequins shimmer in the light to create a couture disco ball. Mr. and Mrs. Thompson desert me as well.

"Do you salsa?" asks that smooth Spanish voice I can't stop thinking about. Ah, my leading man, here to sweep me off my feet.

I turn to see Niko. His eyes sparkle in the moonlight. The cream color of his button-down shirt sets off his bronze skin. A gold chain with a cross hangs around his neck.

"No. That is definitely not how we dance in Minnesota. Could you show me?"

"Of course," he answers and holds out his hand to me.

I'm not exactly sure me and salsa dancing will make a great pair. I mean, give me some choreography to rehearse and I'm golden. But when I wing it, that's when the trouble happens. The memory of the tap dance recital when I wanted to jazz up the routine and double flapped instead of doing the planned buffalo, causing the whole line of dancers to trip and topple over, flashes into my mind. But I'm not going to miss an opportunity to dance with the hottest guy on the island. Besides, my mom's not here to take notes on this attempt.

The warmth of his hand causes my stomach to tighten. Niko leads the way to the pavilion and maneuvers his way through the swishing skirts and fast-moving feet. He suddenly stops, turns, and pulls me toward him. I gulp as his free hand goes to the small of my back, our faces inches apart.

Do not hyperventilate.

He begins smoothly swaying his hips, then steps forward and back to the beat. I smile at him and try to keep up. I've never danced like this before or with anyone who could move like this. The boys at Lake Forest have no idea what to do unless a dub step is involved.

He leans in, his mouth next to my ear. "Let your heart feel the music." His whisper stirs through my hair.

But the only thing my heart is feeling is my chest wall as it pounds as loud as the band's conga drum. I concentrate on relaxing and letting him lead, which is extremely difficult with him so extremely close to me. We don't look precisely choreographed, but amazingly, it works. He effortlessly moves me with him. When he twirls me out then pulls me close again, I can't help but giggle.

The song finishes and the crowd erupts in applause for the band. Niko's hands float off my body, leaving me chilled despite the warm summer evening.

"Would you like to sit out for this one?" he asks.

"Sure."

He leads me back out through the crowd.

"Niko!"

We turn to see a tall thin man with dark hair and a serious expression approach us.

"Niko, I need to talk to you," the man says, not even giving me a glance.

"Jozay, this is Byron Mullins. The nephew of Tom Mullins."

This is Mr. Mullins' nephew? He sure got the raw deal in the family genes department. Where Tom Mullins is suave and sophisticated his nephew has redneck written all over him.

"Oh, nice to meet you," I say and reach out to shake his hand.

He barely glances at me. "I need to talk to you now."

"Can it not wait until tomorrow?" asks Niko.

"No," Byron states.

Geez, what a grump.

"Yes. Jozay, will you excuse me, *por favor*? I should not take too long."

"Of course. I'll wait at the playground."

Byron and Niko move toward the parking lot while I retreat to the swings. I sit and gently sway, reliving the dance. That was amazing. Dancing in Niko's strong arms was the most incredible thing ever. I hope I remember this feeling forever.

The clear night and twinkling stars lull me into doing something I used to do back home in Minnesota. I quietly sing "Goodnight, My Someone" from the spring show. Only this time when I close my eyes, my someone has a face—Niko's. Just as I'm starting the second verse and about to wish him sweet dreams, I lean back in a pretend dip, my right leg kicking up.

"Ooff!" I hear as my foot hits something.

My eyes fly open to see a guy doubled over in front of me. Relief washes over me when I realize it wasn't Niko I just incapacitated with a kick to the unmentionables.

Just Ryan.

"That's what you get for sneaking up on people," I say defensively.

"Technically I don't think it's sneaking up if you approach someone from the front," he says, grimacing in pain. "Do you always practice karate kicks while swinging?"

"If you must know, it was more of a can-can kick."

"Ah, from what show?" he asks as he slowly straightens up.

"*Guys and Dolls*. I was a Hot Box Girl."

"I'll pretend I know what that is."

Glancing over to Niko, I use my imaginary psychic powers and will him to hurry back to me. But Niko and Byron Mullins are still deep in conversation. I turn back to Ryan. It appears he'll make a full recovery. His jeans, white T-shirt, and short hair gelled up in the front reek of high school boy, not Latin summer romance.

"What do you want?" I snap.

"Nothing." He holds his hands up in surrender. "Just came over to say hi."

"Hi," I say suspiciously. What's he up to?

Again I turn away from him hoping to see Niko coming over to rescue, me but no such luck—he's still talking with grumpy Byron. Hello? Now would be a good time to save your damsel in distress. Maybe he can swoop in and challenge Ryan to a duel or something.

"Won't your Music Man be jealous of your summer fling?" Ryan quietly asks.

Confused, I spin my head to look at him. My Music Man? Cameron? Could he really be referencing the spring musical? No. There's no way *he* saw that thing.

"What?"

"Your boyfriend, from home, you do remember him, don't you?"

"As a matter of fact we broke up," I answer, still surprised he knows about Cameron. Of course, Cameron is hard to miss. Ryan probably caught him serenading himself in the boys' bathroom or something.

"It hasn't taken you long to get over him."

"Why is this any of your business?"

"Because I don't trust that guy." He nods toward Niko. "He could be the one who's robbing everyone. Which is why I came over here, to see when we could begin our investigation."

"Drop it. He's not the thief."

"How do you know?"

"Because he's a nice guy."

"Josie." He sighs. "You make a horrible Watson."

"I'm Watson?" I ask, offended. "Why aren't I Holmes?"

"To be Holmes you would need to take this case seriously."

"Unless I'm a Robert Downey, Jr. type of Sherlock. Then my brilliant mind would still work on the mystery despite distractions."

"Well, we can't rule out your *distraction* as a suspect unless we can verify his alibi for when the gift shop was broken into."

"You've never told me why you're suspicious of Niko anyway."

"There's just something not right about him."

"Fine. If you stop annoying me, I'll look into some things." Relax—just keep focusing on putting the POWs in front of the rations.

"Great, I don't have practice tomorrow morning since it's Sunday. I can pick you up around eleven, then we can go into town to talk to all the business owners that have been burglarized."

"There is no way I'm getting on that motorcycle with you."

He grins. "Fine, I'll meet you at the gift shop."

"When we prove that Niko had nothing to do with this will you finally leave me alone?" I ask.

"Probably not," he says.

"What's your problem?"

"Hey, just looking out for you."

"No, you're not," I say, fed up with him and his cocky attitude. "You're looking for some kind of information you can get on me and report back to the idiots back at home who are having a heyday torturing me." I can see him being all Danny Zuko-ish from *Grease* and insinuating to everyone back home that my sweet summer romance is something not so innocent. The ridicule would begin again.

"Why would I do that?" he questions.

"To get on the good side of the popular crowd and boost your social standing in the fall."

He just stares at me.

"I see right through you," I add.

"Are you still obsessing about that? Why do you care what any of those people back at home think?" he asks.

"I don't, but it's a little hard to ignore them when they attack with a full frontal assault. I came here to get away from all the pranks and cattiness. And no spoiled, insensitive, self-absorbed rich boy whose good looks, cute butt, and athleticism have secured him a spot in the 'in' crowd is going to ruin the only true fun that I've enjoyed in two years."

He watches me as I gather my composure. Maybe God helped me after all by letting me confront him. I must admit, blasting him felt rather liberating.

"Am I supposed to be the spoiled, insensitive, self-absorbed rich boy?" he asks.

"Gee, you catch on quick."

"Just making sure," he says, then tilts his head and does his signature McNaughty grin. "You really think I have a cute butt?"

"You are so annoying," I snap.

His focus shifts over my shoulder and his easygoing McNaughty expression darkens. I turn to see Niko approach.

Finally.

"Hi, I am Niko," my Spanish savior says as he holds out his hand.

Ryan shakes it but looks like he'd rather strangle him. What's his problem?

Not wanting Niko to think I've been flirting with another guy, I decide introductions are probably necessary.

"This is Ryan, he's from my hometown. He's here to play on the Pirates baseball team."

"Oh, that is great. The team I hear is good. I also played baseball in the Dominican, mostly the catcher. What is it you play?" he asks.

"Shortstop," Ryan answers.

"Maybe Jozay and I will soon to come watch a game." He says it so smoothly like we have been a couple forever and do everything together. I can't help but shoot Ryan a satisfied smirk.

Ryan holds my gaze. "That would be great. I invited Josie but she apparently hasn't had a chance to come yet."

I squirm under Ryan's intense look, guilty for ignoring his invitation. But why would I subject myself to him any more than I have to?

"It was good to meet you," Niko smoothly says.

"See you tomorrow, Josie," Ryan says, then walks away.

Am I a glutton for punishment? Why did I agree to meet him?

Niko places his hand on my elbow and leads me back to the makeshift dance floor as beautiful guitar notes fill the summer evening. I know this song. *"Bailamos."* I've always had a weakness for this romantic slow song by Enrique Iglesias. I shyly look up into Niko's deep brown eyes and smile.

He smiles back, dimples appearing; his firm hand pulls me even closer, scandalously close. We begin moving to the music. The heat of the night increases with each sway of the hips. His face brushes my cheek and he begins to softly sing in my ear, smoothly alternating between English and Spanish. His sultry tone makes me melt. I've always been a sucker for a guy who can sing—as evidenced in my complete lack of judgment with Cameron.

Wrapped in his arms, I close my eyes and breathe in his scent, totally lost in the moment and unaware of anyone else around. The music sweeps over us like a fairy tale while we spin around the floor.

The rest of the night continues to be magical. Niko and I spend the whole evening together, dancing, talking, and laughing. Finally, taking a break from the dance floor, we find an empty park bench.

"This has been the perfect evening. Where did you learn to dance like that? Back on Hispaniola?" I ask, happy to show off my newfound knowledge of the Dominican Republic. Who knew it shared an island with Haiti? This information would have been simple to uncover via the Internet if I hadn't sworn off technology for the summer, but the library turned out to be quite helpful.

He laughs. "You have done some research, I believe."

Shoot, so much for acting worldly.

"Well, I wanted to find out more about where you're from," I answer with a shrug.

"Jozay, you are sweet. Dancing and creating music is what my family loves to do. I have many memories at holiday of us singing and playing instruments. My *abuela* would keep asking for us to play more." He smiles at a memory. "It has been very long since we all gathered together. My cousins found work to play for the tourists on the cruise ship. And my parents and I have immigrated to Miami a few years ago."

"Oh. Well, I'm sure it's fun to be reunited with your cousins again. They're very talented."

"I must introduce you with them."

"That would be nice. You know, you're a great singer. Why don't you join them?"

He laughs. "Val is much better than I. And to be on a cruise ship for nine months I would not like."

"Yeah, I suppose that would get old. Are you heading back to Miami after the summer's over?"

"Mr. Mullins may have me to stay here. I can make more money that I send home."

"I'm sure you miss your family, though."

"Yes, but the people here I like," he says and grins at me.

I smile and am thankful he can't see me blush in the moonlight.

"Well, I'm glad you're here," I answer. "Who else would have taught me to salsa?"

"You were wonderful, Jozay. I wonder would you be free tomorrow?" he asks.

"Yes." OMG, he just asked me out!

"You can snorkel?" he asks.

"Snorkel? Sure," I answer, surprised.

Of course, he doesn't need to know the first time I tried, instead of breathing in clean air through my tube, I sucked in a bug, which caused me to spit out my mouthpiece in total disgust and gulp in a mouthful of saltwater, causing me to choke. Luckily he hasn't read any of my mom's books to know of this little incident. I could get used to this anonymity.

"I can pick you up at noon?"

"I'll be in town in the morning. I can meet you at the marina."

"I will bring a picnic for us."

A picnic? Sweet and sensitive. He really is a genuinely nice guy.

We share a few more dances before the evening ends. I hope he will offer to walk me home but he says he must help his cousins with their equipment.

"Thanks for the amazing night," I say.

"I soon will see you, *bella dama*," he says and squeezes my hand as Aunt Lily approaches.

"Goodnight."

Lily smiles at me. "Have a good time tonight?"

"The best. How about you? Where's Mr. Mullins?"

"He's going to help the Consuelos boys take everything back to the restaurant. He'll pick up his truck later."

Feeling very Eliza Doolittle-ish I twirl around in the moonlit sand on our walk home, humming "I Could've Danced All Night."

"Listen, Kitten," Aunt Lily says as I dance around her. "I'm all for summer romances but I don't think your mother would be happy that you're spending so much time with an older guy."

"Aunt Lily, don't worry. Niko's sweet."

"Well, it better stay innocent or I'll ship you home," she says seriously.

I stop dancing and look her in the eyes. "You don't have to worry."

"Good, because I don't want to be policing teenage hormones."

"Aunt Lily!" I say in mock indignation, amazed how easy it is to talk with her. If my mom said such a thing I'd be mortified.

"Well, don't be surprised if I keep my eye on you. I may trust you but him I don't know," she says. "He does seem very sweet, though," she adds with a smile.

"He is. And what a great dancer. He even made me look good. This is turning out to be the best summer ever!" I tousle her hair then skip down the beach.

Chapter 6

Aunt Lily graciously agreed to put off our road trip for one more day so I can go snorkeling with Niko. I tell her she's my favorite aunt. She reminds me that she's my only aunt. Except if you include my new made-up family tree where my mom is now my aunt, which reminds me of that weird "I'm My Own Grandpa" song. Dad and I once spent a whole afternoon trying to analyze it.

Lily took me to the most adorable little church for mass. The gorgeous stained glass windows depicted biblical scenes having to do with water like Jonah and the whale, Noah with his ark, and Jesus walking on water. The windows sparkled with the most brilliant blue and turquoise bits of glass that I'd ever seen. The light reflected in such a way that the scenes seemed to come alive with movement.

Something about this church made me feel more spiritual than I'd ever felt at home. Maybe it was those dazzling windows or the fact that I hadn't felt forced to come. Whatever it was, something really connected within me. The elderly priest, a small, energetic gentleman, told jokes and made everyone happy to be there. But as endearing as he was, it was his homily that really made an impression. I couldn't tell you about many homilies back at home, I never seemed to be able to follow along or stay focused. But this one was different.

He spoke about praying. He pointed out that if Jesus is our friend, and hopefully our best friend, our prayers should reflect that. He asked what kind of relationship we like to have with our earthly friends. Do we like hanging out with people that only talk about themselves and are selfish? Do we like being around people that don't care about our accomplishments or what is important to us? Do we want to be friends with someone who never thanks us for things we do for them or takes us for granted? No, usually not.

So why, he asked, are we that kind of selfish friend to Jesus? This little priest with the engaging smile went on to say we should instead tell God how much we love Him. We should thank Him for all He's done. Thank Him for sending Jesus to save us, thank Him for creating such a beautiful world and for bringing all the good things we have into our lives. We should think of others and pray for them, which of course made me think about Mr. Thompson's words of advice. We can tell Him our problems but don't demand the outcome; instead, ask Him to guide us through it.

And most importantly we should be a good friend who listens. Because only by having quiet time and listening do we hear God guiding us.

What?! Mind blowing!

Why had I never heard any of this before? It made so much sense and suddenly I felt terrible. I've only ever prayed for myself and had one-way conversations with God. This new concept seemed very logical and I vowed to give it a try.

So as I ride my bike into town to meet Ryan, I try out a new prayer.

> *Hey, thanks, God and Jesus, for all that you have done for me. Thanks for bringing me here to this island and letting me meet Mr. Thompson and the cute little priest. They both have such powerful words that I'm really going to try to follow. Um, I'm still pretty upset about what happened at home so could you please just give me some strength to deal with it all? Thanks. Amen.*

Granted, it's not perfect yet, but it's a start. As I continue on my ride, my reluctance to meet Ryan fades a little as I decide he's not going anywhere so I may as well work with him. Not only can I keep an eye on him but I can hopefully help the residents of the town by discovering who's robbing everyone. Maybe I'm the beach chick who in her free time helps the local residents.

But as I ride down Main Street and see Ryan smugly sitting on the back of a bench with his feet on the seat, a twinge of annoyance passes through me. I park my bike next to his motorcycle in one of the angled parking spots in front of the stores.

"Nice ride. I especially like the basket," he says in greeting.

"Well, a beach bike happens to be the ideal transportation when you live on an island."

"True, but you can't get anywhere very fast."

"The beauty of summer on an island is that there is no need to be in a hurry."

I brush past him and make my way to the gift shop. Ryan trails behind.

The outside of the shop is a soothing classic beach cottage, pastel shutters, and white wooden flower boxes. But when we open the door, the bell joyously jingling, we are bombarded with an explosion of beach paraphernalia. We make our way through the quiet store, squeezing past racks of T-shirts and floral dresses. Shelves bursting with beach towels and trinkets line the walls. The only thing that doesn't scream typical tourist junk are Lily's paintings—an oasis of calm amid the chaos of tacky. At the back of the store sits a display case, or what's left of one. My keen detective eye notices the plywood that covers the areas smashed during the robbery.

A huge man in a Harley T-shirt emerges from the storage room, his long hair pulled back in a ponytail. Coils of rope loop around his massive tattooed arm. Worried that we just walked in on another burglary, I shift closer to Ryan.

"Can I help you?" the man asks very politely.

"Umm, is the owner in?" I ask cautiously. I peer around his massive body toward the back room, wondering if Polly is tied up or something. Maybe she's gagged and desperately trying to scoot toward the door to signal us. Possibly we're her only chance of getting through her ordeal unscathed. I wonder if we could somehow overtake him. But one look at the giant inked bicep tells me no.

The towering hoodlum follows my gaze over his shoulder. "I'm the owner," he states.

"You expect me to believe your name is Polly?" I say, trying to sound tough.

83

"My dad was Paul so to avoid confusion I became *Paulie*," he explains.

"*Really?*" It's hard to hide my disbelief. While the store screams for a tasteful makeover it does not have a Hell's Angel vibe.

"Really," he chuckles. "It was my mom's shop. I took over after she died."

"Oh," I answer, still not sure if I should believe him. "Well, I'm Lily Baker's niece."

"Of course. How are you? Josie, right?" he asks and gently shakes my hand.

"This is my friend Ryan," I say, satisfied there would be no way he could know my name unless he knew Aunt Lily.

"We were wondering if we could ask you a few questions about the robbery," Ryan tells him as they shake hands.

"Sure, but there's not much to tell."

I pull out a pad and pen then stick an extra pencil behind my ear.

Ryan watches me, then whispers, "What're you doing?"

"It's called method acting. I'm taking on the persona of a good investigator." Duh.

He smirks, then shakes his head.

"Can you tell us what happened? Please don't leave out any details," I say to the big burly man.

"I came in that morning and realized immediately something was wrong."

"Why?"

"There was glass everywhere and items were gone."

"Did you have an alarm set?" I ask.

"No. I have one but don't usually set it. I've never had a break-in, just an occasional shoplifter, so I haven't thought much about security. Believe me, I'll be more diligent from now on."

"Did you notice anyone strange that looked like they might have been casing the joint?"

"No," he says with a grin, seemingly amused by my inquisition.

"Do you have any idea who could have done it?" Ryan questions.

"No. If I did they would be in a world of hurt right now." He cracks his knuckles in emphasis. "One thing, though. They knew what to take."

"What do you mean?" I ask, ready to scribble down his answer.

"It was no 'snatch and grab.' They selected the pieces they wanted. Took the expensive stuff and left the junk, even though it was all in the same case."

I look at all the worthless souvenirs; it would take some skill to find the valuable items amid all the costume jewelry, especially in the dark.

"So, they must have been in here before and knew what they wanted. Maybe someone who lives or works nearby," Ryan says. I know what he's doing, subtly implying Niko and his cousins who live across the street.

"Maybe. The cops thought it was a pro. Beyond that, they don't have any leads. I doubt you'll be able to find out much more than them, but good luck anyway."

I ask a few more questions, then we say our good-byes and leave the store.

"Niko would have the perfect vantage point to watch the store since he lives right across the street," Ryan says.

"Anyone could be watching these shops," I counter.

"True. I wish we could find out where Niko and his cousins were that night. We could look into their alibi and see if it holds up."

"You are totally off base here but I'll be happy to prove you wrong and ask him when I see him this afternoon."

"You're seeing him today?"

"Yes, he's taking me out on the boat." I can't help smiling in anticipation.

Ryan's eyebrows furrow before his face quickly brightens. "Oh. Well, good for you. Your plan actually worked."

"What do you mean?" I ask.

"Well, throwing yourself at a guy is one way to get his attention."

"I didn't throw myself at Niko."

"Hey, if that's the only way you can get him to ask you out, then go for it."

"It's not like that."

"Whatever you say," he says smugly and starts walking down the sidewalk.

"You are such a jerk," I say, as I follow him. "In fact, I didn't want to go with him. I thought we should do it another day. But he talked me into it. He said, 'Josie, if you collect too many tomorrows all you'll have gathered are a bunch of meaningless yesterdays and I for one don't want to waste one more moment.'"

He stops walking, then turns and stares at me.

"What?" I ask.

"He said that?"

"Yes."

"Really?"

"What?" I demand.

"Nothing. I just didn't peg your Latin Romeo to be a fan of musical theater. Because if I'm not mistaken that sounds a lot like the line the music professor used on his librarian love interest in your spring musical."

"I may have been paraphrasing," I snap.

He laughs.

Dang. How did he know that?

86

"Isn't he a little old for you anyway?" he asks.

"He's only eighteen," I answer defensively. "And I'm sixteen, going to soon be seventeen," I add, then literally have to bite down on my tongue to keep from singing the *Sound of Music* classic. But it's too late.

"OK, Liesl," he says, shaking his head. "Feel free to sing the song, I know you want to."

"No. I'm good," I snarl at him, then turn and start walking again. But a familiar sight interrupts my annoyance.

"No!" I yelp.

"Problem?" Ryan asks, coming up alongside of me.

"Look." I point to the window of the bookstore next door, piles of *Saving Sadie* on display.

"That *is* strange, a bookstore with books."

"That's my mom's book."

"Great."

"No, not great. Horrible. I don't want people here reading that thing." Then I see the unmistakable exuberance of Cyd in the store. Her sundress flairs as she spins around the store in excitement. Her father, dressed again in a polyester tracksuit and ridiculous toupee, expertly diverts her from knocking into the counter. The bookstore owner rings up two copies of my mom's book for them.

With a death grip on Ryan's arm I yank him past the bookstore before Cyd can see me. We burst into the neighboring building; bright colors and the competing musical sounds of a toy store engulf us. I ignore the curious looks from the customers and duck behind a bin of rainbow-colored Hacky Sacks to spy. Cyd skips out of the bookstore swinging the bag with Mom's books. Her father trots behind her and almost bowls her over when Cyd stops abruptly at the toy store window. I drop to the floor to hide.

My mom's latest postcard comes to mind. The picture on it was of a palace made of walnuts. On the back she had written another verse—Psalm 32:7 *You are a hiding place for me; you preserve me from trouble; you surround me with glad cries of deliverance.* The verse seemed to fit my present circumstance well, although this wasn't exactly what I had pictured my hiding place would be when I first read it. Funny how those verses of hers keep circling around in my brain.

"Do you always act like this?" Ryan leans against a shelf, his arms crossed, and grins down at me.

"Like what?" I ask casually from the tiled floor.

"A paranoid schizophrenic."

"There's someone I don't want to see."

"Who? That innocent-looking little girl?"

"She may look innocent but she's not. She's trouble with a great big bold capital T."

"Clearly she's a menace to society."

I ignore him.

"Okay, I think I'm going to go introduce myself to her," he says as he edges toward the door.

"Stop!"

"Then explain."

"Fine. She's my mom's number one fan. And I don't want her to know who I am. It's bad enough that you're here and know about the book. I just want to be anonymous this summer. Please keep my secret." I look at him with the biggest puppy dog eyes I can manage.

"What does my being here have to do with this?" he asks.

"Those creeps back home made my life miserable. I couldn't go anywhere without being mocked and made fun of. I've even given up my cell phone for the summer because the messages were so horrible. Coming here was my chance to get away from all that and I hoped with me away they would forget about it all. Then, here you are. Someone who could easily tell everyone back home what I'm doing and give them more ammunition. Then to make matters worse my mom's biggest fan lives here and she knows my mom writes about me. I don't want her to know who I am; otherwise, the whole island will read the dumb book and think all those horrifying scenes are about me. And the torment will start again." I pause for a breath and to readjust my position since the cold hard floor is killing my back.

"You really think I'm like those idiots back home?" he asks.

"I don't know you. How do I know what you'd do?"

"Making your life miserable is not my intention," he says.

"So, you just do it unintentionally then?"

"Precisely." He laughs.

"Will you please keep my real identity a secret from Cyd?"

He studies my face. "Your secret's safe with me. Under one condition," he finally answers.

"What?" I ask warily.

"I'll keep quiet if you come to one of my baseball games."

I sigh. "Deal."

"Good," he says, then begins to wander around the store.

I edge up to peek out the window again. Thankfully, Cyd has decided not to come into the store. She and her dad walk across the street to Spencer's Ice Cream Parlor.

But we're trapped. If we leave now, she'll see us and probably run over to tell me she got the new book. I dust myself off and watch Ryan as he examines a baseball.

"What're you doing?"

"Well, if I'm stuck here I may as well browse."

"You don't have enough baseballs?"

"I'm thinking of getting something for the Martin kids."

"Oh. Hey, that reminds me. Liz told me I need to ask you about some trick you do with a ball."

He looks at me with raised eyebrows. "Oh, so you've been discussing me with your friend Liz."

Oh, geez. "What? No," I mutter, knowing my cheeks are burning. The last thing I need is him thinking I've been talking about him. His ego does not need stroking.

He grins like the Cheshire Cat.

I try to come up with an explanation. "I just mentioned to her what bad luck it was that I was stuck on this island with McNaughty."

"*McNaughty?*" he asks, amusement twinkling in his eyes.

"It's her dumb nickname for you. Something to do with . . . Oh, never mind. I'm just going to slither back to the floor now," I say, totally mortified.

He laughs. "Here, throw me one of those." He nods to the bin of Hacky Sacks.

I take aim and zing it at his head. His reflexes are fast and he easily grasps the ball.

"Nice try. Another, please." I toss him another one. "One more."

I toss him a third ball and he begins to juggle. He starts with a low arch, then the balls start to fly higher.

"Okay, one more."

I toss one and he somehow snags it, not dropping any of the flying orbs.

"One more," he says, and I gently toss another.

The fifth ball disappears into the rotation. The five Hacky Sacks move so fast I can hardly keep track. He throws them high, nearly touching the ceiling, then low, barely rising to his chin. He lets two of them drop and begins to throw the remaining ones a different way. Two moving arches form. The store keeper and the families that were shopping have gathered around us, mesmerized by his performance. One at a time he tosses the three remaining balls to some of the kids intently watching him.

I can't help but be impressed and clap with the rest of the crowd. He takes a bow. "Wow. Where'd you learn that?"

"Oh, it's just something I picked up," he says.

"Can you teach me?"

"Well, I'll try, but from what I hear, coordination is not your strong suit," he teases.

"Hey, you can't believe everything you read."

"You didn't knock out a teammate with a volleyball?"

"I knocked her off her feet, but she never lost consciousness," I answer defensively, then start to giggle. "Actually, you may want to take cover."

"I'll take the risk," he says, then patiently explains the process of juggling.

He has me start with one ball, tossing it in an arch from one hand to the other. We then add another ball. After numerous tries I finally get the hang of how high to throw the Hacky Sacks so their air time is consistent. Confident in my newfound skills, I add a third ball. But it totally messes up my consistency and somehow flies into a nearby tower. Small plastic bricks fly everywhere.

"Oops."

Ryan can't stop laughing as we crawl around the store in search of the bricks, ignoring the frowning store owner.

"I warned you," I say.

"You were doing great. For now just keep practicing with two, but not around priceless heirlooms. When you get comfortable then you can add the third. You'll be an expert in no time."

"Time. Shoot, I forgot about the time. I need to go meet Niko."

"Of course you do," he grumbles. "Let me at least walk you over."

"You don't need to do that. I can ride my bike to the marina. Thanks for the lesson," I say and shove a handful of the bricks at him, then hurry out of the store.

Chapter 7

In reality the distance between Paulie's gift shop and the marina is maybe a block, but my excitement to spend the afternoon with Niko makes it feel like an eternity. The opening night jitters that fill my insides make it difficult to pedal the short distance. When I ride into the parking lot, Niko waves at me. He and Mr. Mullins are deep in conversation near Mr. Mullins' fleet of vehicles. I may just be the luckiest girl alive with this chance to be alone with Niko on a boat for the whole afternoon. It's going to be a fabulous day—we'll laugh and flirt and he'll whisper sweet nothings in my ear. Hopefully it won't tickle or I'll laugh inappropriately when he's trying to be all romantic.

I park my bike next to the three big black trucks with correlating vanity plates, MLLNS 1, MLLNS 2, and MLLNS 3, then grab my bag out of the basket.

Mr. Mullins, a nautical British spy today, wears a navy blue sports coat over a crisp white button-down shirt. "Josie! I'm glad Niko finally got his act together and is taking you out for the day."

"Thanks, Mr. Mullins, for letting us use the boat."

"Anytime. Let me know if he doesn't show you a good time. I may have to dock his pay," he jokes. "Niko, I left some supplies on the deck. Can you take care of them for me?"

"Of course, Mr. Mullins."

"How is your lovely aunt today?" asks Mr. Mullins, turning his attention back to me. "You two ladies were the loveliest of them all last night."

"Thank you."

"I hear the two of you are leaving for a tour of the beach towns tomorrow?"

"Yes, we're delivering some of her paintings."

"She told me. I insisted she take my SUV in order to take more pieces along."

"That's very nice of you."

"That's what friends are for," he replies.

Again I wonder just how close they are.

"I have a few minutes to spare, please indulge me while I give you a tour of the *Jewel of the Sea*," he says proudly as he leads us down the dock to the boat.

It's a beautiful vessel, larger than most of the other boats on the dock. *Jewel of the Sea* is swirled on the side in navy blue paint. He tells me all about "her," then shows me the deck and the cabin with fatherly pride.

I glance at Niko as Mr. Mullins continues his brag-a-thon about the boat. Niko winks and smiles.

"It's quite impressive, Mr. Mullins," I say.

"This is just the beginning," he replies. "I have already made plans to purchase a much larger boat that can be used for dinner cruises. Hopefully next summer that will be up and running."

"I love that idea."

"Well, I suppose I better get back to the restaurant and let you two get on your way."

Finally. "Thanks for the tour, Mr. Mullins. I don't know much about boats so it was really interesting."

"You two have a good time," he says, climbing down the ladder to the dock.

He reminds me of my dad when I borrow his car as he stands protectively watching Niko untie the lines and maneuver us out of the marina.

Niko masterfully takes the boat straight out into the ocean. My hair blows in the wind as we speed along the water, most likely causing me to resemble a dog enjoying a car ride. I really should have taken the hair tie off my wrist and pulled my hair back before we started this journey.

"Can I ask why you and your family left the Dominican Republic and came to Miami?" I ask when he slows the boat down.

I make a feeble attempt at tamping down my crazy wind-blown tresses.

"My parents dream for me to attend American university so we came to finish my high school."

"You're in college now?" I ask.

"Not yet. I graduated my high school early, in December. Now I work to earn money for college."

"Oh." I feel guilty knowing my parents will probably just whip out the checkbook to pay for my higher education. Of course, it is kind of thanks to me that my parents are successful. I mean it is my life that Mom writes about. So in a way I guess I've earned my college tuition. "Miami sounds like a cool place to live," I say, changing the subject.

"I do not know it much. We live in a Hispanic community, my parents feel more like at home there. I did not 'hang out,' as you might say. When classes were out I would work at the restaurant of my parents. Last year, I also began work at a scuba shop. And I do work at the refugee center to help teach English." He says it so nonchalantly while he veers the boat toward the cliffs.

Once again, I'm stumped. It's obvious that my sheltered life in Minnesota is nothing like his background. I wrack my brain trying to remember what the difference between an immigrant and a refugee is. Really, how did I get such good grades? I seem to know nothing important.

He glances my way, then continues to explain. My face probably gave away my ignorance. Blank looks tend to do that.

"We were lucky, Dominican is a good country. There are poor. My cousins, they make more money on the cruise ship than any job they would work back at home. They support many of our family back in the Dominican. To be away so long, it is hard. But we were never persecuted. At the refugee center there are people from all over the world I meet. Most are forced to leave their country for their religion or ethnicity and must live at refugee camps. If they are sent to the US or other countries they have found luck. Many do not know anyone and cannot speak English or Spanish. And they are parted from their families."

"How awful." Sadly, my knowledge of different ethnic groups is pretty limited to *West Side Story* and the rivalry between the Polish-American Jets and the Puerto Rican Sharks.

"Yes, but they are such a happy people. They are so grateful to be alive and have safety here."

Worrying about my reputation and some stupid high school pranks feels rather shallow at the moment. Mr. Thompson was right. Focusing on others' problems totally changes your perspective.

"Do you hope to go back and work with the refugees after college?" I ask, noticing the way his face lit up when he talked about them.

"Yes. I think to go to law school first would work best. The refugees do not know the ways of America and can be taken advantage of. I would like to help with their rights."

My Prince Charming: handsome, sweet, and noble.

He steers the boat into Shipwreck Cove then lowers the anchor. As usual, few people are on the beach. I watch as he pulls off his shirt, curious if his abs are as rock hard as they look. Following his lead, I pull off my shorts and T-shirt. I shoot up a slightly selfish prayer that my bikini top stays put and that my mom's book is not a premonition of what will happen when I jump off this boat. Niko flings two large waterproof bags over his shoulder, grasps my hand, and together we leap into the water.

After confirming all is in order with my swimsuit—*thank you, Lord*—I suggest we race to shore. He easily beats me even with his cumbersome load. A few minutes later a beautiful picnic lunch is spread out on the beach: sandwiches, potato salad, lemonade, and grapes. Is there anything this guy can't pull off? I try to emulate his casual demeanor as we eat but am suddenly extremely self-conscious sitting on the blanket in my bikini.

"Do your cousins help you sometimes with the snorkeling tours? I think I've seen some of them here with you."

"Yes, Val and Marco, they help the restock of chests," he says, leaning back on his elbow, his bronzed skin glistening with sea water.

"Chest?"

"Pirate chests." He grins, running his fingers through his dark, wavy hair. "Mr. Mullins has the tours to be a pirate theme. Snacks and supplies we keep in pirate chests."

"Oh, I've wondered what you were loading on and off the raft. Where are these pirate chests?"

"I will show you after our lunch."

"If the experience is so authentic why don't you wear an eye patch?" I tease.

"I may have you to walk the plank," he threatens, although it's hard to take him seriously with those deep dimples.

We easily chat during lunch. He puts me at ease as he describes his parents and the restaurant they run in Miami. I tell him about my life back home, which seems pretty meaningless compared to his. I purposely leave out the part about my mom's book and what really brought me to South Carolina—no need for him to know about all that. I'm amazed how easy he is to talk to, like I've known him forever.

While he packs up the lunch I contemplate how much depth he has. I mean he's not that much older than I am—he just graduated high school six months ago. But unlike the annoying kids back in Lake Forest where football games and pep rallies are the only things of importance, he seems worldly. He is seriously the nicest guy I've ever met, thoughtful, interesting, and caring. My eyes are definitely opening and I hope I don't fall back into the usual routine of high school self-centeredness when I get back home.

"Please come, I have something to show to you." He grabs the bags, then we walk toward the black cliffs.

I have no idea where we're going and am nervous he may want to climb up the sheer rocks because I'm pretty positive rock climbing is not my thing. When we get closer I see a sliver of a passageway in the rocks. On second thought maybe scaling the cliff would be better than this. A flying bat entangled in my hair is one experience I prefer not to relive. He leads me through the narrow tunnel, and, fighting the panicky feeling of claustrophobia, I cling to him, a possessive vine wrapped around his arm. With me plastered to Niko's side we round a natural curve in the rocks, and the light from the beach diminishes.

He gently peels my hands from his arm. "Do not worry. Stay right here."

With actual blind trust in him, since I can't see anything, I wait. One by one, Niko flicks on battery-operated lanterns anchored into the rock, revealing a cave.

"This is incredible," I say as I look around in awe of the bedroom-size cave. Pirate chests line the perimeter on the soft sand. "How did anyone find this place?" I ask, exploring the space.

"Mr. Mullins said people who search for the pirate treasure found it."

"Maybe the pirates really did bring the treasure here. You've got to admit, it's the perfect hiding spot."

"Mr. Spencer told me people still cannot agree if the little pirate boat was crashed while it was out to scout a location or while it brought a treasure to land."

"No treasure was ever found?"

"Not that is known. But it could have long ago been found."

"So this is where you and the tourists disappear to."

He opens one of the chests and places the supply bag inside between some snorkel gear and first aid items.

"Some treasure for the tour," he says, indicating the bag. "You would be amazed how coins of plastic thrill children who have everything."

"I still think you should dress as a pirate," I say.

"Oh, Jozay, please do not give Mr. Mullins a new idea." He laughs.

I lean against the rocks and smile at him. My insides flutter as he slowly leans in close.

He looks in my eyes, then smiles. "Shall we go to snorkel?" he asks instead of making any kind of move.

"Um, sure."

Back on the beach, Niko pulls two sets of snorkel gear from his waterproof bag, then secures the lunch bag over his shoulder while I pull my tangled hair in a ponytail. We slip into the ocean and slip on the flippers, goggles, and mouthpieces. He motions for me to follow him and we swim close to the rocky outcropping. *Okay, God, you helped with the bikini situation—can we continue the streak and eliminate any snorkeling mishaps today? Thanks.*

Then I remember not to be a selfish friend. *Oh, by the way— you're awesome! I love you!* Okay, this new prayer life needs a bit of help.

Little striped fish swim around us as we near the rocks. From the surface the rocks are dark and plain but underwater they are covered with swaying plants and bright coral, transformed into a Technicolor dream world. We swim around the first ridge of rocks and I'm stunned to see a small boat below me, wedged into the rocks. The pirate ship. Barnacles and algae have overtaken the rowboat shape. Colorful fish play a game of hide and seek amid the wreckage.

Expertly holding his breath, Niko dives down, scaring a crab who skitters away. I stay floating on the surface, sure I'll swallow seawater if I attempt the dive. When he surfaces, we continue on to explore the cliffs and the sea life at their base. The constant motion of the schools of fish and coral create a living kaleidoscope.

Eventually we make our way back to the *Jewel of the Sea.* In one fluid motion Niko climbs on board then easily pulls me up with one muscular arm. I collapse on the bench, exhausted.

Instead of pulling up anchor and heading back to the dock, Niko grabs us some sodas from the galley and sits down next to me.

"Did you like the day?"

"It was wonderful. The ocean is spectacular. I wish I could see more of it."

"Would you like if I teach you to dive?"

"Scuba dive?"

"Yes."

"I would love that." Me at thirty feet below the surface sounds a bit sketchy but it would mean we could spend more time together and get to know each other better.

"Good. I am a certified instructor so with me you are safe."

Ahh.

"Jozay, may I ask you a question?" he asks.

"Sure." Is he going to ask me out on another date or maybe if he can kiss me?

"What is the relationship with Ryan?" he asks, totally out of the blue.

I start choking on my soda, thankful it didn't spurt out my nose. "What? Why do you ask?"

"Last night after you left the dance, he asks to talk to me," he says. His deep brown eyes search mine, for what I'm not sure.

"What did he want?" I ask cautiously.

"To warn me."

"*Warn* you? About *me*?" I ask, furious that Ryan would try to turn Niko against me.

Niko chuckles. "No, no. He did not warn me about you. I believe he wanted to be sure if I was honorable. His team is to leave for away games and I think he wants to know you will be safe while he's away."

"What?" I ask, stunned.

"He worries for you."

"No, he definitely just wants to annoy me. Believe me, the only person Ryan McNaulty worries about is himself. But I hope he didn't scare you away."

He grins. "I do not scare so easily."

Liz,

What's the plot, Camelot? Sorry it has taken me forever to write. There's a lot to tell you. Niko is just as wonderful as I thought he would be. He's sweet and romantic and makes me feel beautiful and graceful. He even taught me to salsa dance! I haven't kissed him yet, he's too much of a gentleman to rush things. Yes, there actually are chivalrous gentlemen out there.

Speaking of non-chivalrous guys, I can't get rid of Ryan. He's completely annoying, I don't know what you see in him. But we're kind of investigating some local crimes together. I'd rather just do it on my own but I'm hoping if he thinks we're working together he will be less likely to tell the idiots back home about my summer.

Right now Aunt Lily and I are on a road trip traveling up and down the coast to other beach towns to deliver her paintings. In fact, I'm writing this from Virginia Beach. At each town we explore and shop, sometimes staying the night. It's been so much fun sampling the seafood and saltwater taffy. And at every stop we've made I've bought a t-shirt so I can make one of those t-shirt quilts when I get back home. Maybe when I curl up with it during the long Minnesota winter it will remind me of my amazing summer.

Tell me how it's going with the girlfriend—so unbelievable!

Miss you!

Josie

Chapter 8

"Do we really have to go to this thing?" I whine to Aunt Lily as I join her on the back porch. We just got back from our East Coast road trip and the last thing I feel like doing is going to Ryan's baseball game.

She looks adorable as usual in capri jeans, a red tank under a men's white dress shirt with sleeves rolled up and tied in front, and red sandals. I purposely dressed down, making a protest statement, in jean shorts and a blue T-shirt, and I have my hair pulled back in a long ponytail.

"I still don't understand why you don't want to go to the ball game."

"I told you, I don't want to see Ryan. I'm here to get away from home—not keep running into it every couple of days," I say. It was nice to be away for a few days and not be reminded of the past. Besides attendance through blackmail does not make for enthusiasm. I just can't help being a little wary of Ryan and his intentions. He seems nice but I can't shake the feeling he's up to something.

"It was very sweet of the Martins to invite us to sit with them. And besides, the Pirates put on the best fireworks display in the county. Last year—"

Before Lily can finish her thought a brown blur tears up the back steps and hurtles onto her lap.

"Kahlua!"

"Something tells me she missed you," I say as Lily tries unsuccessfully to avoid slobbery doggy kisses.

Mr. and Mrs. Thompson slowly amble up the porch steps to join us.

"Thanks for watching her while we were gone. I hope she wasn't this hyper the whole time," Aunt Lily says to the Thompsons.

The four of us stare at the energetic dog as she hops off of Lily then bounces around the patio like she has springs in her legs.

"Watching her makes me tired. Maybe I need a nap," says Mr. Thompson, lowering his large frame into one of the lounge chairs.

"She was a good girl," says Mrs. Thompson, who hands Lily a stack of mail they collected for us then joins Lily and me at the table. "How was your trip?"

"Great. We had the best time," I say. "We stopped at all these picturesque coastal towns."

Kahlua stops bouncing only to begin running circles around the table.

"We brought you back some fudge for watching Kahlua," I say. "I couldn't decide between that or saltwater taffy."

"Good choice, Nancy. Taffy will pull out my dentures," says Mr. Thompson, his eyes shut.

"The seafood was incredible," I tell them.

"Except Josie was a bit freaked out by the soft-shell crab sandwich. You should have seen her face when the waiter brought it to her," laughs Aunt Lily.

"Who decided eating a crab, shell and all, in a sandwich was a good idea? Gross."

"If you think that's bad you should have seen some of the foods we ate when I was stationed in Asia, like fried spider or ants on toast," says Mr. Thompson.

"Dear, we better change the subject. Poor Josie's turning green. Anyway, we're glad you're back. You missed some excitement though."

"Did Mr. Thompson learn to play poker?" I tease.

"Hey, I heard that," he grumbles, his eyes still shut.

"No. Mullins' restaurant was the latest place to be burglarized."

"Oh no," gasps Aunt Lily. "I texted Tom that we were back with his vehicle but he didn't mention it."

"Did they take much?" I ask.

"I haven't heard all the details yet," replies Mrs. Thompson.

As they continue to talk I pull a postcard from the stack of mail. It's of a tall tree with a giant boulder stuck high in the branches. Psalm 27:1 *The Lord is my light and my salvation. Whom shall I fear? The Lord is the strength of my life. Of whom shall I be afraid?*

I reread the verse, feeling strangely connected to it. During our trip I had lots of time to think about things. I tried following the priest's advice and used the quiet time to listen and let God speak to me. I hadn't had any big revelations but was feeling more peaceful. During those meditative moments I kept thinking about the ocean and for some reason the lighthouse at Shipwreck Cove. This verse somehow brings it all together. God could be my own personal lighthouse keeping me safe during the storms of life. Cool.

The low hum of a motorboat cuts through the air, gradually getting louder, disrupting the relaxing quiet of the morning. After a few moments it comes into view. Niko and one of his cousins are steering the small fishing raft in our direction. My heart skips a beat as it stops moving and idles offshore from us. Niko hops out, splashing through the water.

Lily, Mrs. Thompson, and I watch as he jogs up the path toward Lily's cottage. His hand runs through his thick dark hair, seawater dripping from his bare chest. I imagine him rushing up the porch, gathering me in his arms, telling me how much he missed me—that my absence made his heart grow fonder.

When Kahlua sees him she stops her laps and runs down to meet him. He pats her head, then she calmly trots up the steps beside him.

"Good afternoon, Mr. Mullins told me you are now back," he says.

"Yes, we got back a little while ago," I answer.

"Jozay, I am happy to have you here," he says.

My heart leaps to my throat.

"We're going to the Pirates game this afternoon, would you like to join us, Niko?" asks Aunt Lily.

Yes, please.

"Thank you, but I am to work at the malt shop for Mr. Spencer. His grandchildren will take him to some fireworks. Carlos and I just finished the refill of supplies at the cave. I wanted to stop by to say hello. I cannot stay or he may leave without me," he jokes. "Jozay, I have a question to ask of you. Tomorrow after the restaurant closes the employees are to have a clambake at the cove. Would you join us?"

I glance over at Lily for approval even though clams don't sound particularly appetizing. She nods in agreement even though her eyes are glued to Niko's chest.

"Sure, I'd love to," I say.

"Wonderful. I will find you at the beach at ten?"

"Great, thanks for inviting me."

"Have a lovely evening. You will enjoy the game. It was nice to see you all again," he says.

Mrs. Thompson, Lily, Kahlua, and I all watch as he jogs back down the beach and splashes in the ocean, then easily leaps into the raft. The motor whines and they pull away, off toward town.

"He is very handsome," Mrs. Thompson says, fanning herself.

"You can say that again," agrees Aunt Lily.

"Ladies," I say, "don't be so superficial. There is much more to him than his looks. He happens to be the nicest guy I've ever met."

"You're very wise," Mrs. Thompson says. "Looks can fade. Personality is so much more important."

"That's right," adds Mr. Thompson, his eyes still closed. "Not everyone can be as lucky as Mrs. Thompson and have married someone who has kept their charming personality and devastatingly good looks all these years."

I smile while Mrs. Thompson just rolls her eyes.

***

The ocean breezes keep the July afternoon from becoming too hot. After a quick ferry ride and drive to the college, we arrive at the ball field.

We easily spot the Martins when we enter the stadium. The five of them are perfectly patriotic today. I wonder if they always coordinate their clothes. The little girls wear white sundresses with blue trim and sparkly fireworks on them, their blond curls gathered up in red scrunchies. The little boy is his dad's mini-me in a matching T-shirt with a waving flag across the front.

"Thanks for joining us today," says Mr. Martin.

"We've been wanting to have you over for dinner while Ryan is here," adds Mrs. Martin.

"Yes, but instead you get stadium hot dogs," jokes her husband.

"Yum, you can never go wrong with ballpark food," I say.

"It's amazing that someone from Ryan's hometown is here," says Mrs. Martin.

"Yeah, amazing," I reply.

"We love having Ryan stay with us," Mrs. Martin gushes as we settle in beside them on the bleachers. "He's such a wonderful young man. The kids absolutely adore him, and he's so polite and helpful."

And he obviously knows how to turn on the charm.

"Hi," says the oldest of their children, as she snuggles in next to me. I guess she's maybe six. "I'm Brianna."

"Hi, Brianna, I'm Josie."

"Are you Ryan's girlfriend?"

"No." Definitely not.

"I wish he was my boyfriend," she says, her blue eyes shining up at me.

"Me, too," says her little sister, who can't be more than three, her little cherubic face beaming.

Mrs. Martin laughs. "I told you they are crazy about him. The team was traveling most of the week and the kids missed him terribly while he was away."

"It was nice of you to open up your home to him," says Aunt Lily.

"When our dear friend Matt told us that one of his friends needed a place to stay, we couldn't say no. I totally understand why Ryan's parents didn't want him to live in the dorms with the older boys. Even though it's probably a pain for him to have to take the ferry over every day, it has worked out well. If Brady grows up to be half the young man Ryan is, we'll be proud." She tousles her son's blond curls.

"Are Ryan's parents coming out this summer to see him play?" asks Aunt Lily.

"No, they can't get away. But I promised them we'd take extra special care of him and treat him like one of our own."

I wonder if it strikes anyone else odd that the McNaultys would send their son halfway across the country to stay with strangers for the summer and never come to visit him.

The crowd rises as the players run out onto the field to warm up. Ryan glances up at us and grins. The kids wave furiously while I stand there feeling completely awkward.

Brianna shares her popcorn with me as we settle in for the game. Since Ryan is younger than the rest of the players I assumed he'd sit in the dugout most of the game. So I'm surprised when he jogs out to be the starting shortstop.

Watching him on the field, I almost forget how irritating he can be. When the batter hits a ball his way he effortlessly catches it off a bounce, rotates around, and fires it to first base, getting the out. The crowd cheers. The Pirates get two more quick outs then take their turn at bat.

Ryan's third in the lineup. The first batter walks and the second hits a single. With two runners on base Ryan strides up to home plate, confidence pouring out of him. He raises the bat over his shoulder and doesn't even flinch as the first ball goes by. *Strike.* A nervous knot forms in my stomach. He lets the next one go by. *Ball.* Come on, do something.

The pitch comes, and the muscles in his arms tighten. He whips the bat around. The loud crack makes me jump as he sends the ball flying far into the outfield. Without thinking I jump up and yell with the rest of the crowd as he sprints to second base. Both runners in front of him score.

Lily leans over. "See, I told you these games were fun."

I roll my eyes at her. She sounds just like Liz.

Ryan leads off the bag, ready to run to third. The pitcher throws a ball. Then as he prepares to throw his next pitch, Ryan takes off. I grab onto Lily's arm. He slides feet first toward third then effortlessly pops up on the base. Wow.

Lily shakes her arm free. Geez, this is nerve-wracking.

The excitement is palpable. The metal stands vibrate from the cheers, whistles, and foot stomping. I watch in frustration as the next guy up to bat strikes out. Come on. The following batter hits a line drive to first. Ryan takes off. I jump to my feet. The first baseman grabs the ball, steps on the base getting the runner out, then pulls back his arm and hurtles the ball toward the waiting catcher at home plate for the double play. I hold my breath as I watch Ryan slide toward home. A cloud of dust rises as he rockets through the dirt, obscuring my view. Did he make it?

The crowd falls silent in anticipation of the call.

"Safe!" bellows the ump.

Brianna and I hug each other while the fans scream. For the rest of the game I'm mesmerized by his athleticism. There's no denying he's amazing to watch as he dives, jumps, and catches every ball that comes his way. No wonder Liz liked going to the games. I find myself cheering as much as the rest of the Martin clan.

The Pirates win the game. Ryan's white uniform is a complete mess, dirt and grass stains evidence of his hard work. As we wait for the team to change and the sky to darken we climb down from the bleachers to spread blankets on the grass in anticipation of the fireworks. Brianna and Brittany Martin hold my hands as we make our way to the outfield.

"Can you come to more of Ryan's games?" asks sweet little Brianna, her big blue eyes pleading.

"They are fun. Do you guys come a lot?" I ask, purposely not answering the question.

"Yep. But Brittany sometimes falls asleep."

"Do not!" Brittany whines.

As we settle onto the blankets Aunt Lily tells the girls that I'm a dancer in my school shows. This thrills them and they beg me to start dancing with them, which basically consists of twirling around in circles until we're dizzy, something I haven't done in years. Luckily for my equilibrium, Brianna and Brittany are soon distracted. They squeal and run across the field, their little legs a blur. I turn to see Ryan approach, fresh out of the shower, his hair still damp, wearing jeans and a white T-shirt. Liz would probably have a stroke if she saw him now.

As the girls plow into him he bends down and scoops them up, one in each arm. He lifts them over his shoulders like two sacks of potatoes. They squirm, their small legs flailing. When he reaches the blanket he kneels down, unloading the girls while Brady climbs on his back.

He looks at me and grins. Despite myself I smile back.

"Hey, you finally made it to one of my games," he says as Brady tumbles over his shoulder practically onto my lap. Brady scrambles up and starts to chase his sisters around the grass.

"I was holding up my end of the bargain," I answer.

"Well, I'm glad you came." He smiles at me.

Uncomfortable, I glance away.

"We just got back from a series of road games but I hear Poseidon's was broken into. Do you have any new theories?" he asks.

"No, I just heard about it this morning. Lily and I were out of town as well."

"I was thinking we should check with the homeowners that have been hit. When are you free?"

"You know, we're both really busy. If we split up we can cover more ground. I can finish talking with the shop owners and you can visit the residents." It seems like a great idea; that way I can still investigate but don't have to work as closely with him in case he is up to something.

"Did you ever ask Niko where he was during the gift shop burglary?"

"No, I didn't have a chance to ask him." I wasn't about to ruin my time with Niko by bring up Ryan's ridiculous theories.

"Josie." He sighs. "I'm not asking you to put on ruby slippers and chase after a wicked green witch to steal her broom. I'm just suggesting you ask a few questions."

"Hey, nice musical theater reference," I say, slightly impressed.

"I've been working on my Josie-speak."

"You seem to know quite a few musicals. Maybe you missed your calling and should join the theater department," I tease.

He laughs. "I only know a few shows. Thanks for the offer but I think I'll stick with baseball."

"Well, I'll admit, the game was fun. You were quite impressive out there." I probably shouldn't stroke his ego but what else can I say?

"More exciting than your brother's baseball games?"

"I don't know, his are awfully entertaining," I say with a laugh, then stop when I realize the meaning of what he just said.

I, of course, noticed him at Riley's games but why would he have noticed me?

"Wait. How do you know I have a brother?"

"I've been the ump at three of his games." He states the obvious, his eyebrows raised.

"I know, but it's still surprising that you'd know who I am."

"Why wouldn't I know who you are? We've gone to school together for two years," he answers, looking at me like I'm a moron.

"Yeah, but you're a jock and all."

"So?"

"Everyone knows the jocks. We all see you at the assemblies and games and stuff."

"Well, we go to your plays and stuff."

"Yeah, right." He's such a liar. I've never seen any jocks at our productions.

"What, you don't think we support our fellow students?" he says to my skeptical look.

"No. I'm sure you were forced to see the spring show for extra credit or something."

"No, actually I went to that one because I wanted to. In fact, I've seen all your shows this year," he says with that grating-on-my-nerves confident grin of his.

"I don't believe you."

"Test me," he challenges.

"Fine, tell me something about the winter show."

"*The Curious Savage*, in which you played an insane asylum patient. Quite well, I might add." His smug look is exasperating.

"Well, what about the fall show, Mr. School Spirit?"

"*Thoroughly Modern Millie.* You were an adorably dorkish tap-dancing secretary," he says, leaning back on his elbows. His eyes crinkle in amusement at my shocked expression. "In fact," he continues, "I bet I've been to more of your activities than you've been to mine."

"Highly doubtful."

"I don't remember seeing you at any of our baseball games this year."

"I had rehearsal," I say, defensively.

"Didn't stop your friend Liz from coming to cheer us on."

I have completely underestimated Mr. Baseball. He is very perceptive.

"Liz is quite the fan," I concede.

"Maybe you will be now, too," he answers with his McNaughty grin.

Before I can think of something clever to say Mr. Martin calls the kids over to us for a photo. Brittany sits on my lap, and Brianna and Brady plop down on either side of us—cute curly blond bookends. Ryan puts his arm around my shoulder and we all lean in for a picture. The kids then start telling us ridiculous knock-knock jokes until the stadium lights go out and the crowd cheers in anticipation. Ryan lies back on the blanket with his hands behind his head and his ankles crossed while the National Anthem plays through the loudspeakers. Brady lies down on the other side of Ryan, duplicating his pose. Brittany plops down between Ryan and me, clapping her chubby little hands. Spectacular fireworks light up the dark sky. Somewhere during the lineup of patriotic songs, Brianna comes and snuggles up beside me. I give her a hug and realize, with surprise, that tonight was actually fun.

Thanks, God.

Chapter 9

"Lily, are you positive Cyd won't be there?" I question as we drive to the Hollis estate to deliver his newly restored painting.

"There are only so many ways I can say that Cyd is out of town."

"But are you sure this isn't some plot you and Mr. Hollis orchestrated to get me to talk to Cyd about the book?"

"Paranoia doesn't suit you," she answers. "For the third time, she's in New York with her mother, shopping and attending some fashion shows."

Gee, that kid has a rough life.

"I thought Mr. Mullins wanted to help you return the painting so he could see Mr. Hollis's collection up close and personal."

"He did but is still busy dealing with the fallout from the theft."

We pull into the long drive; the immaculately groomed shrubs lead us to the house. I half expect Cyd to jump out from behind the bushes or drop down from a tree like the Von Trapp kids in *The Sound of Music*, but all remains quiet as we near the home. My anxiety eases slightly when I see the helicopter is not perched atop the mansion.

Mr. Hollis scurries past the maid who answers the enormous door. Every time I see him I'm confused. Today this powerful movie mogul is wearing another jogging suit with a crooked Angels baseball cap covering his bald head. He's a living, breathing oxymoron.

"Ms. Baker, I've been anxiously awaiting your arrival. You have no idea how I've missed my beloved painting."

He helps Lily carry the carefully wrapped painting into the house and down the hall to his gallery. Lily gingerly removes the packing materials like she's opening a present and hopes to preserve the wrapping paper. She reveals the newly restored work. The faded, cloudy painting now vividly clear.

117

Mr. Hollis says nothing as he slowly circles the gilded frame, examining every inch. He stops and stares at the painting. His forehead crinkles, scrutinizing the restoration. Aunt Lily looks confident, but I start to squirm as he sighs and frowns. He leans in closer, then crosses his arms. Finally, he backs away and turns to her.

"*Bravissima*, mademoiselle." He beams. "She is lovely."

Lily smiles, unfazed by his foreign language mismatch. "I'm glad you're pleased. Would you like me to help you hang it?"

"No need. I have a security company coming this afternoon. They'll be installing sensors on all the paintings. They can hang it then."

"Sensors?" I ask.

"Well, we had a scare last night. Someone tried to break in through the French doors by the pool. But I have the latest technology and the most secure home on the island. I'm just thankful Cyd wasn't here."

Lily gasps. "Oh my goodness."

"I almost told you to keep the painting a while longer but I thought she'd be safer here with me."

"Have you contacted the police? Has a CSI team been called?" I ask, jumping into investigative mode. Too bad I didn't bring my notebook with me—or maybe a magnifying glass.

"Oh yes, they were here for hours. They assume the perpetrator thought I was away since the helicopter is gone. That usually does mean I'm off the island but I had the pilot take Cyd to New York and told him to enjoy a few days off. I thought some time here by myself would be nice."

"Wow, I'm glad you're all right and none of your priceless items were taken," Lily says.

As he escorts us to the door I can't help but ask, "Mr. Hollis, I've been wondering. Do you have any movie stars coming to visit soon?"

"No, I prefer to keep Hollywood away from here. This place is my haven for relaxing and figuring out my next film. I'm always searching for that one special project and it helps to have a little quiet time to do that. Which can be hard to come by with my daughter's exuberance. But lately she's been nose deep in your other aunt's new book. It must be a good one, because I haven't seen Cyd much, although I keep hearing her gasp every once in a while. It was hard to convince her to go to New York until I agreed she could take the book with her. I think she's already on her third read-through. Her newest idea is to take a photo with you and email it with a letter to Ms. Baker. She's sure that if your aunt sees proof that Cyd knows you, she will send a signed copy of her book."

"Wow, that's an idea all right." An incredibly horrible idea—then my cover will be blown because my mom will of course tell her the truth. I've got to continue to avoid that kid.

"She also told me that this new book is a bit shocking. She couldn't believe your cousin went through so many ordeals," he adds.

Lily glances at me. "Yes, my poor niece has had to deal with quite a lot."

We wave good-bye and pull away from the grandeur of the Hollis estate. "Kitten, we haven't talked about it lately but he's right. You've been through a traumatizing time. You're incredibly strong and will get through it."

Her words of encouragement remind me of my mom's postcards. This morning's latest installment was a picture of the curviest street in the world with a very similar verse to what Lily just said.

> Colossians 1:11 *May you be made strong with all the strength that comes from his glorious power, and may you be prepared to endure everything with patience.*

It's weird how my mom seems to anticipate my thoughts.

"Are you ever going to talk with your mom, Kitten?" Lily asks.

"I don't know. I despise confrontations. I guess I'm hoping it will all just blow over."

"Avoidance could work but you and your mom have always been close. I hate to see this come between you. Maybe you should tell her how it makes you feel when she writes about you."

"I think she knows."

"I'm not sure. I remember you used to like those sections. You had me guess which things had happened to you. It's kind of cool to have your life written in a book. Not many people can say that."

"Except this time they weren't about me but I got ridiculed anyway. And they weren't silly juvenile problems but the worst teenage humiliations you could ever think of. Although I must admit that the longer I'm here the less I care what everyone back at home thinks."

"It's good to get away sometimes to see the big picture," she agrees.

"Exactly. Back at home life seems to only be about high school and the cliquey teenagers. Here, there's so much more—new people, new experiences—I don't know, it's just different. That life and this life don't seem to mesh together."

"I completely understand. Why do you think I left Minnesota and never returned?"

"I never thought about it."

"I didn't like who I was there. I would fall back into a routine that didn't feel like me. Here on the coast, I'm free and totally myself."

"I know what you mean." She's the coolest. I could never talk to my mom like this.

***

"Well, I'm off to the clambake. I hope they're better than those horrid soft-shell crabs we tried."

"I think you'll like the clams. Have fun and don't be out too late, okay?"

"Okay," I say, and give her a quick hug, then head down toward the beach.

I walk along the lapping water, the hem of my skirt dampening as it brushes the waves. It felt great to talk with Lily this afternoon. She encapsulated my feelings perfectly. My new life here just doesn't fit with my old one. And when I think about going back home this overwhelming sadness settles in. I don't really like the person I was there, always worried about what everyone thought. Too bad I can't stay here forever. Or figure out a way to feel different back there.

I stop for a moment and stare out in the distance. The beauty around me is truly overwhelming. *God, you're amazing. This ocean is unbelievably incredible and awe-inspiring. It really is the perfect way to soothe my soul. Thank you for creating it.*

The enticing smoky aromas and the pulsing tempos from a radio lure me toward the wider beach at the cove. Tonight is going to be amazing. I can just picture Niko and me, wandering along the water holding hands. With the stars and moon as our backdrop he will probably look into my eyes and serenade me with some beautiful Spanish love song.

As I get closer to the group, Niko sees me and strides over, the warm glow of the fire behind him. My pulse quickens when I see him. Of course he looks amazing in his cargo shorts and gray V-neck T-shirt, but it's more than that. He's genuinely such a nice guy and so incredibly interesting that I really enjoy spending time with him no matter what we do.

"Jozay, I am glad you came," he says as he comes up to me, his eyes twinkling in the firelight. He smells of campfire and awesomeness. "Tonight you look beautiful."

Oy vey.

We join the others lounging on blankets and beach chairs around the bonfire. I recognize some of the workers from

121

Poseidon's, including the hostess with the pink hair. His cousins start a barrage of Spanish. It's not hard to figure out from their tone and laughter that they're giving Niko a hard time.

"Jozay, these are my cousins, Val, Marco, Carlos, and Juan."

I shake their hands and smile as they continue to tease him.

"He must always keep the pretty ones to himself," says Val.

"That's because he's the baby of the family and doesn't know how to share," adds Juan.

"Don't listen to them, Jozay," says Niko. "This is Tina," he says, introducing the pink-haired hostess. "She somehow puts up with Marco."

"Nice to meet you," I say and shake her hand.

Behind the fire, tables and coolers of drinks wait in anticipation of the meal. A few feet away several people stand guard as smoke rises from a mound of seaweed in the sand. The aromas are mouthwatering.

"I've never been to a clambake," I admit to Niko as we settle onto a blanket near the fire.

"Oh, you'll love it," says Tina. "A couple of the chefs grew up in Maine so they're our clambake experts."

The laughter from the group bubbles up around us. Jokes and stories bounce around in a verbal ping-pong match. I know they're just together for the summer but I love being part of such a fun group and wish it could last forever.

The chefs declare the food to be ready and uncover the cooking pit, removing layers of seaweed. My stomach growls in anticipation. As they scoop out the food I'm glad to see that it's not all clams; crab legs, lobster claws, potatoes, and corn on the cob are also pulled from the pit. Huge platters of food fill the tables and everyone serves themselves. Niko patiently shows me how to eat the clams after my first attempt lands in the sand. Turns out, I'm not a huge fan of the smoky slimy clams, but the crab legs are phenomenal.

As we eat, Niko's cousins share stories from the cruise ship, like the lady who couldn't understand that the food was part of the price of the cruise and kept stashing items in her purse at every meal. They tell about the magician and his assistant who got in a huge fight on board and in revenge the assistant began to throw the props overboard in front of all the passengers. As the stories flow and the food disappears, several couples snuggle up to one another. When I wrap my arms around my legs and shiver, Niko—unlike the other guys who use the cooler temps as a reason to put an arm around their girls and pull them closer—drapes an extra blanket around my shoulders.

The large group eventually dissipates into smaller conversations and couples that walk hand in hand down to the water. I suddenly remember what Mrs. Thompson said about the restaurant and ask Tina about the burglary.

"I heard the restaurant was broken into."

"Not exactly," she answers. "It was Wednesday right before we opened for dinner. We were all there setting tables and preparing for the evening when the fire alarm went off. We smelled smoke and everyone immediately headed outside to wait for the fire department to arrive. After a thorough search of the area they informed us someone had set a fire in a sink in the ladies' bathroom to create a diversion."

"Oh . . . did they take much?"

"All our purses and personal items were taken since we had all exited right away and we hadn't had time to go back to our lockers."

"Oh no."

"And Mr. Mullins' gold trophy from last year when he won a sailing regatta," adds Niko with a laugh.

"Yes, his prized possession," Tina agrees. "Actually quite a bit of his memorabilia was taken. He had a fairly large collection of pirate artifacts that could have been valuable. Luckily the next day the sheriff found our purses in a dumpster over by the carnival. All the money, jewelry, and electronics were gone, but at least our credit cards and driver's licenses were there."

Marco kisses Tina's neck then pulls her up. With their arms around each other's waists, they head off toward the water. Niko asks if I'd like to walk with him. Heck yeah.

We take off our shoes and stroll along the ocean in a scene straight out of a movie: the full moon shining off the water, the lingering notes of the music, the cool water rolling over our feet as we walk along the surf.

We pass a couple huddled together on the beach. I'm envious of their connection, how they gaze into each other's eyes like they're the only two people on earth. I let my hand brush Niko's.

"I am glad you could come tonight," he says, not reacting to my not so subtle hint. "I enjoy to spend time with you."

"This has been an amazing night. I love your cousins, they're so much fun. I could listen to their adventures all night. You all are incredibly interesting."

"I am sure your life is interesting also. You do not talk much about it."

"Oh, my life is far from interesting or important." The last thing I want is for him to know about the book or for that matter my theater career. I don't think he'd get it; besides, those elements don't really fit into my new beach chick persona.

"Oh, I almost forgot. I got you a present while I was gone," I say, changing the subject.

"Is it an eye patch?" he asks warily.

"No, Dread Pirate Niko." I pull a shark tooth necklace with a cool leather chain out of my pocket.

"Thanks, Jozay, you are very sweet," he says, then puts it on.

He smiles at me then *finally* reaches out and takes my hand. The heat from his touch radiates through my body. I feel like I could swoon, despite the fact that I don't know what that would actually entail.

We continue walking, the moon's reflection dancing on the ocean. I describe the towns Lily and I visited. He recounts his week and the guy on his tour group that had his rental car keys in his swim trunks and lost them when he jumped in the ocean to snorkel. He tells me how he spent half an hour diving down to the shipwreck to find them. Again, I marvel at how easy it is to be around him and how he has this ability to make me feel like what I have to say is fascinating.

"Your cousins have great stories from the cruise ship. It must be fun to work on one for a while."

He pauses before he answers. "Yes, they have good times but it is hard. Most of the workers on the cruise ship are coming from really poor countries. Juan dates a woman from Haiti. Back in Port au Prince, she has two children she only can visit on her three-month break. Her entire family lives on what money she makes, while the children are raised by her sister. But she sacrifices because she is making enough that someday her kids can go to university and will not be in the poverty. Always the crew works extremely long hours, month after month, and worry about their struggling relatives back at home while they must tend to passengers who will complain when their bed is not turned down to their liking or their daiquiri is not tasting right."

"Wow, I will never think of cruise ships in the same way again." I can't believe I never thought about things like that before.

"I hope you do not misunderstand my words. It is a hard life but it does provide people an opportunity to care for their families that they otherwise would not have. They can be grateful for that. And yes, they do as well have some fun."

When we get to the pathway that leads up to Aunt Lily's we stop walking and turn toward each other. The moon shines down on us like a spotlight. Gazing into his deep brown eyes causes my heart to do a jeté leap to my throat. This is it. He's going to kiss me here on the beach. The setting is absolutely perfect as the warm sea breeze blows through our hair and the moonlight caresses our skin.

There could be no better moment. In my mind the music crescendos and my leading man draws me toward him for a kiss.

But in Realsville he doesn't.

"Jozay, I would like to spend more time with you," he says instead. "I can start you to scuba tomorrow."

Como say what?

He must notice my confusion.

"You said you may like to dive?"

"Oh. Sure. I would love that."

He squeezes my hand then leans down and kisses my forehead. My forehead. Really? I could sure use the help of a little red crab with a Jamaican accent singing subliminal romantic suggestions right about now.

"*Buenas noches y dulces suenos*, Jozay."

"Bye," I answer and try not to sound disappointed about our goodnight scene, then make my way through the grasses to Lily's house.

Of course I should have known he would take his time, he's too much of a gentleman to rush things. But I think I've had enough chivalry.

Chapter 10

"We miss you, kiddo." This has become Dad's usual mantra during the weekly family phone call. The ringing phone greeted Lily and me as we walked into the cottage after mass and another inspiring homily.

"Miss you guys, too." A little.

"I can't believe you're learning to scuba dive."

"Yeah, learning all about buoyancy and decompression has kept me really busy the last few days. But I think remembering all the hand signals is the hardest part. I kept giving a thumbs-up sign to signal I was okay but that actually means I need to surface, so we wasted a bit of time that first day. But once I got that straightened out it's been good."

"Please be careful."

"Don't worry, it's with a certified instructor." One who's also my new beau but dear ole dad doesn't need to know that part.

"Well, there isn't much new around here," he says. "Your mom's been traveling to promote the book. Grandma is coming for a few days to help with Riley. Right now he's planted in front of the TV watching an endless supply of shark shows. In a week he'll be an expert. Let's see, what else, it's been humid as usual and we've had a lot of mosquitoes."

I shiver realizing that depressing description had almost been my summer. I barely escaped in time. "Gee, sounds like I've been missing all the fun. Well, tell Riley congrats on passing his knot-tying test during scout camp."

"Let me put Mom on."

"Oh. Okay."

"Hi, sweetheart," she says, the tentative tone still in her voice. Our relationship has not become any less awkward over the weeks. We tiptoe like ballerinas on pointe around the whole reason I'm here. "Lily sent lots of texts and pictures from your trip. Sounds like you two are having a great time. But you know you can always come home early if you want."

I almost start laughing at the absurdity of her statement. "Thanks, but I'm really having the best summer ever. It's great having no one around who knows about the book." Well, almost no one except for the pesky superfan and of course McNaughty.

She sighs—quite heavily, I might add. "Josie, every week you remind me how your life has been ruined and every week I apologize profusely. I get it. I screwed up and shouldn't have written about you. I'm sorry your school is full of a bunch of spoiled rich kids who have nothing better to do than tease you. But there's nothing more I can do. I can't keep apologizing forever and quite honestly, life doesn't revolve around you. You need to get over it and move on."

I actually have no words—completely stunned into silence.

She continues. "I love you very much and will keep praying that this situation will soon be resolved. We'll talk to you next week." And then she hangs up.

Aunt Lily watches me closely as I put the phone down. "What's the matter? Everything okay at home?"

"She was annoyed with me. Can you believe it? After all she's done, she cops an attitude and is frustrated with me for not forgetting about the whole book thing."

Lily smiles. "Well, it's about time."

"What?"

"Josie, what happened to you was horrible but if that's the worst thing you face in life then you're extremely blessed. Hanging onto the hurt seems a little self-centered. Your mom is a great mom and it's probably time to forgive her."

She gracefully makes her exit to her studio. Kahlua dutifully prances after her.

I know she's right and actually the longer I'm away the less the book bothers me, but for some reason I can't quite let go of my anger. I start to feel better, then something happens when I talk to my mom that draws me back down to the despair I felt. Not wanting to focus on the hurt and—in Mr. Thompson's words—my rations, I decide instead to focus on those I can help.

I pop my head into Lily's studio. She looks up at me with a pencil behind her ear, one paintbrush in her hand and a smaller one in her mouth.

"I'm heading out and riding the bike into town."

She removes the smaller brush from between her teeth. "I thought you weren't meeting Niko until this afternoon for your scuba lesson."

"I'm going to go talk to Mr. Mullins about the break-in. I haven't had a chance to ask him about it yet."

"Oh, good idea."

***

I pedal up the hill toward town, my eyes on the lighthouse. *Dear God, thanks for this summer. Please continue to be my lighthouse and guide me through this storm in my life.*

When I ride into the parking lot of Poseidon's, for some reason Ryan, wearing cargo shorts, white T-shirt, dark sunglasses, and backwards baseball cap, is leaning against his motorcycle, his arms and feet crossed.

"What're you doing here?" I ask as I climb off my bike.

"Waiting for you," he answers with a grin.

"How could you possibly know I'd be here? I just decided I was coming like five minutes ago. You're a mind reader and a juggler? Let me guess, you come from a circus family, The Magnificent McNaultys."

"You should see me walk a tightrope," he jokes.

"Seriously, how'd you know I'd be here?"

"I know you well," he answers. Then in response to my skeptical look adds, "Or, maybe your aunt told me where to find you."

"Why were you looking for me?" I ask, confused and honestly a bit suspicious.

"I finally had a free morning and thought maybe we could hang out."

"Hang out? Just the two of us?"

"Yeah, I don't have anyone my age to just chill with."

I watch him, trying to ascertain his sincerity.

"I don't really have the time to just chill," I answer. "I'm actually here to do some investigating."

"Great. I'll help you."

"Fine." I sigh and we climb the big white porch steps to enter Poseidon's. "Did you hear that the Hollises were targeted by our local crime lord as well? But lucky for them their high-tech security system scared him off."

"No, I hadn't heard about that one. Good thing you are privy to all this insider information."

Lily must have warned Tom Mullins as well of my visit since he's waiting for us in the lobby. He's very charming and dashing as usual as he shows us around the restaurant, pointing out what was broken and what was taken. I jot down as much information as I can in my investigative notebook. Finally he leads us to the comfortable chairs in the lounge.

"Josie, I'm of course thankful for any help with this investigation, especially now that I've been personally affected, but I must say I'm surprised you have time. I was under the impression you and Niko were spending a lot of time together."

Ryan sighs heavily and leans back in his chair.

"Oh, we are. But I have a little time while he's out on his morning dive tour," I answer.

"I hope he's being a gentleman."

"Nothing but," I say.

"So, getting back to the robbery," Ryan says impatiently. "It sounds like you had a few large items stolen. I'm surprised they could be taken in the middle of the day with a restaurant full of employees."

"Yes, it was rather brazen," agrees Mr. Mullins. "But the police think a van or truck must have been parked in the back alley. The businesses around here get a lot of deliveries so no one would have been suspicious. And since everyone evacuated to the front parking lot to wait for the fire department, they had free access to the place."

"Any idea who would be interested in your collection?" I ask.

"My collection was rather rare and extensive, especially for local pirate and shipwreck items. Their intrinsic value is high."

"Oh, I didn't realize the pieces were valuable. I just thought they were decorations," I admit, feeling rather dumb.

"I've been collecting eastern seaboard artifacts for a number of years. But my fascination really lies with the pirate boat and treasure that sank off our island. I like to believe somewhere once upon a time the treasure was here. In fact, my new dinner cruise will have a pirate-themed evening for families."

"Kids will love it," I say.

"And I can tie everything together. If we tell stories during dinner of the sunken ship, we can promote the scuba and snorkeling tours. The tourists will also want to come here to the restaurant to view my collection. Once I build it up again."

"If the items were rare can they be traced if someone tries to resell them?" I ask.

"Not easily. I have photos on record for insurance reasons but many old maritime items look the same. Rusty anchors, worn flags, and pieces of ships are hard to tell apart and authenticate."

"You seem calm about losing so much of your prized collection," says Ryan.

Mr. Mullins shakes his head in response. "You should have seen me a few days ago, I was furious. But I realized at least everyone is safe and what was taken from me were just items, albeit rare items but still just items. Besides, part of the fun of collecting is the search, so now I get to hunt for more treasure."

"Do you have a security system?" I ask.

"Yes, a rather sophisticated one. That's probably why they decided to hit during the day."

"No video monitors?" quizzes Ryan.

"Just out in the front parking lot."

"Well, thanks for your time, Mr. Mullins," I say, since I can't think of anything else to ask. This detective stuff is harder than it looks.

"Thank you," says Mr. Mullins. "I don't have much confidence in our local authorities so maybe you will be able to uncover something. But don't spend all your time on this; remember to have fun, too. That's what being a teenager is all about. Before you know it life will be filled with mortgages and responsibilities. Enjoy your freedom now."

Ryan and Mr. Mullins shake hands, then we make our exit.

We sit on the porch steps outside the restaurant to plan our next move in this big investigation that at the moment seems impossible to solve.

"Now what?" I ask. "Is there anyone else in town that has been hit?"

"You mean besides Paulie at the gift shop, who you practically accused of being one of America's most wanted?"

"You have to admit that whole mountain man look he has going on doesn't exactly scream beachy gift shop owner."

"Well, there's also the antique store," says Ryan.

"Where's that?" I never noticed one on Main Street.

"Down the road, on the way to the carnival," he answers.

"Clear down there?" I sigh. The heat of the day is starting to drain my energy.

"Come on, I'll give you a lift," he says.

"Um. No. Not on that thing," I say, pointing to the motorcycle.

He grins. "I thought you might say that." He gets up from the step and walks over to the cycle. He grabs a backpack, which he then places at my feet.

"What's this? A jet pack?"

"Rollerblades."

"Rollerblades? You just happen to be carrying two sets of rollerblades with you?"

"I was hoping you would want to go do something and I knew how you felt about the cycle. I figured you and Mrs. Martin probably wear about the same size shoe so I borrowed her gear."

"Okay. But apparently you never read Chapter Nine in my mom's second book."

"Uh-oh. Lucky for you the hospital's on the way to the antique store, if we need to make a detour."

"Or I could just ride my bike."

"Yeah, but this will be more adventurous."

"All right, I'm game."

We don the gear and I make a few wobbly loops around the parking lot. Confident I won't critically injure myself, I start toward Main Street. Just as I'm getting the hang of it, Mr. Super Athlete passes me, then does a little loop around a bench and winds back toward me.

"See, you got this," he says.

"As long as we stay at this speed," I answer.

"At this speed I'll miss my next ballgame."

"Why are you so good at this?" I ask as he circles around me again.

"I've been skating a lot with Brady and Brianna in the evenings. Since they're even slower than you are I've learned a few moves to keep myself entertained."

"Very productive of you."

"Tell me, how's your little book-reading friend these days?" Ryan asks as we glide past the bookstore.

"Cyd? Luckily I've been rather successful at avoiding her."

"I don't get it. Shouldn't you be flattered that she loves your mom's books?" he asks, circling me again.

"Sure, if I were a star baseball player like you and the books were filled with tales of my amazing athletic prowess, then I'd be flattered. But the fact that Cyd thinks all my screw-ups are hilarious does not do much to boost my confidence."

"I read one of your mom's books years ago. Now that I know you I may have to check more of them out," he says.

"Don't bother. They're all the same. In fact, I'll give you the Cliffs Notes—I leap before I look and chaos ensues."

"Hmm. Sounds entertaining. Spending time with you should be fun."

"Well, as I said before, don't believe everything you read because the last book is complete fiction. Not one horrifying scene actually happened to me. Not that they couldn't have happened to me—but they didn't. But I still got all the grief."

He loops around me again, making me dizzy. "I see why you're a bit sensitive about that book. I heard a few of the more interesting excerpts. But I guess your mom was just doing her job, writing memorable fiction."

"Maybe, but I wish it didn't hit so close to home."

"Have you thought about turning your new popularity into a positive?"

"A positive?"

"Sure. Maybe more people will start attending your musicals."

"Great, that's all I need, a whole audience of snobs hoping to see me step on the hem of my costume, ripping the entire seam and exposing my backside."

He laughs. "Maybe, but then they can see your impressive can-can kicks. I would just personally recommend everyone stand a safe distance away."

As the shops of Main Street thin out, the road slopes down.

"Oh no. You said nothing about a hill."

"Come on, you can do it." He grabs my hand and before I can panic we start down the hill. I follow his lead, bend my knees and lean forward. The air whooshes past us. I watch the path whizzing beneath my feet and am vaguely aware of the hospital off on the right side of the road. The shops have disappeared and lush green grass lines the left side of the sidewalk, which is where I plan on hurtling my body if I trip.

We near the bottom of the hill. "We did it!" I yell. My body buzzes with excitement like I've got caffeine coursing through my veins. This must be the rush that an adrenaline junky feels. I totally understand the appeal.

"Don't slow down," he warns. "We've got to get up the other side now."

I was afraid of that.

We work our way up the hill. I try to smoothly push from one leg to the other like Ryan but my thigh muscles feel like they are being ripped out of my body. He easily makes it to the top while I gasp for air. The hot sun beats unmercifully down on me. Cursing Ryan and his stupid idea as I go, I begin to side step up the hill. I have to keep wiping away the moisture that trickles down my face. Hope Mrs. Martin doesn't mind rollerblades and helmet drenched in sweat.

Finally I reach the top—completely exhausted. Leg muscles I didn't know I had burn. Ryan lounges at a picnic table at the edge of a soccer field.

"You made it," he says encouragingly.

"You are going to pay for that. You could have helped me somehow," I say and plop down on the bench.

"I'll buy you a soda when we reach the store. I think we're about halfway there."

"Oh my gosh, it's so hot," I whine. "Now I know why I spend my days at the beach."

Just then the swoosh of a sprinkler system near us turns on. It's one of those rotating sprinklers that makes an arch of water as it spins. Mesmerized, I stare at the drops of refreshing water that fly through the air, shimmering in the sunlight. I envision the coolness of the water against my skin. My spine shivers at the thought of the spray showering over me. Suddenly I can't stand it anymore and peel off the wrist guards, knee pads, rollerblades, and helmet. Ryan watches me as I skip toward the sprinkler. Pure delight fills me as I twirl through the frigid water, my aches suddenly a distant memory.

"You are insane," Ryan says as he takes off all his gear as well. Soon we're playing in the sprinklers like little kids. We try jumping over the arch of water and sliding under it. We attempt to outrun the spray but our bare feet slip on the wet grass. When one set of sprinklers stops we try to figure out which section of grass will be the next one to become our personal water park and race over to it. We chase each other around the park, laughing hysterically, only vaguely aware of the people walking by, watching our madness.

Finally we collapse, completely exhausted and drenched in the wet grass, my hair pasted against my face.

Ryan turns his head toward me and smiles. "I don't think we can go interview Mr. Harper like this," he says, pulling at his wet, grass-stained shirt.

"Probably not," I agree. "It's all your fault, you know." I prop up on an elbow and wring out my shirt. Glad I wore my swimsuit under my clothes; wet T-shirts can be much too revealing, as written about by my mother.

"My fault?" he asks incredulously.

"Yes, if you hadn't gone all personal trainer on me, I wouldn't have gotten overheated." I lie back to stare at the sky. Puffy white clouds float across the bright blue background. "Doesn't that cloud look an awful lot like a swirly ice cream cone?"

He laughs. "You sound like Brittany. Hey, there's a sailboat," he says, pointing toward one of the largest clouds.

"You mean that giant slice of pizza?"

"Are you hungry or something?"

"Famished."

"It is probably past lunch time," he agrees.

"I guess we should head back to town, I've got an appointment. But please, I beg of you, no more rollerblading."

We gather up the gear then walk back toward the marina via the beach.

"So, what would you be doing all summer if you weren't here in Paradise? Hanging with all your baseball buddies at the lake?" I ask him, the ocean rushing over our feet.

"No. If I weren't here I'd be at camp," he replies.

"For the whole summer?"

"Yep."

"Oh." A picture of his family life starts to form. He doesn't come from cool circus folks at all—his parents are the type that send their kids off for the whole summer so they won't have to deal with them. No wonder they aren't coming to visit him.

"What's your pressing appointment? More interviews? I could join you," Ryan says as he picks up a flat seashell and throws it side-armed into the ocean. It skims along the surface.

"No. I'm meeting Niko."

"You know, I bet you could survive a day without seeing him."

"I lasted a whole week without seeing him when Lily and I were on our road trip."

"Wow. A whole week." Sarcasm drips from his words. "So, what're you and Rico Suave doing this afternoon?"

"Actually, *Niko* has been teaching me to scuba dive."

"Really?" he asks, surprised. "You thirty feet below the surface. How's that going?"

"Pretty good."

"Nothing your mom could write about?"

"Well, I did actually get stung by a jellyfish because I forgot to turn off my flashlight when we ascended from our night dive. They apparently are very attracted to lights. Gosh, now that I think about it my mom actually wrote about a jellyfish sting in her latest book. That's weird, life imitating art."

"She knows you well."

"Great. At least no one had to pee on me. Turns out, vinegar is the acid of preference."

"Good to know."

When we get back to the marina Niko is outside Poseidon's waiting on us. He rises from the bench he's gracing as we approach.

"Thanks for keeping my girl company," he says to Ryan. I blush, liking the possessiveness of his words. It's nice to have someone feel that way about me.

"Your girl?" Ryan scowls. "I think Josie is her own person."

"Mr. Mullins said you two stopped to see him this morning," Niko says, ignoring Ryan's rudeness.

"Yes, we were going to talk with the antique store owner but never made it that far," I say.

"I know Mr. and Mrs. Harper. I will drive you over later and you can then speak with them."

"No, thank you," Ryan snaps. "Josie and I can go on our own."

I glare at Ryan, amazed how quickly he transforms from Jekyll to Hyde every time Niko is around. It's these moments that make me think Ryan's not the nice guy he pretends to be. I mean, Niko's the kindest person I've ever met. If you can't get along with him something's not right.

"That would be sweet, Niko, we could use the help," I answer.

"But, Josie, we haven't ruled out *all* our suspects yet," says Ryan. At least he has the decency not to come right out with his insane theory that Niko's the thief. But his unfounded suspicions are really starting to tick me off.

"We have no suspects." I shove all the gear I'm carrying at him. "Tell Mrs. Martin thanks for letting me borrow her rollerblades. It was fun."

"Yeah. It was," Ryan dryly answers.

Niko puts his arm around my shoulder and leads me toward the dock.

Josie,

What's the word, theater nerd? Chrissy is driving me crazy. She's constantly around. She wants to be like BFFs. Today we went for mani's and pedi's. I really don't want a twenty-something-year-old buddy. Even her employee discount at the mall is losing its appeal. I wish my dad would grow up. How pathetic.

I was thinking of heading back home early but my mom has decided to go on a backpacking trip to Europe. Backpack? Europe? I didn't even know she had a passport. How will she ever survive without her down pillow and daily latte? Why can't my parents act like parents?

Okay, I've put this off long enough. I really hate, despise, detest being the bearer of bad news but as a friend I must. Please sit down. Are you sitting down? I'm serious.

Okay, here goes. I was scanning messages when I got home from the mall and what popped up but a picture of you. And Ryan. With his arm around you. Cute picture I might add. But the comments were not so cute. Lots of crude stuff using plenty of baseball metaphors. Our classmates are not as clever as they think they are.

Anyway, Missy had reposted it—not sure how she got it but since I know you haven't been online I can only assume Ryan posted it. Maybe you were right about him after all. I debated about telling you but thought you'd better know what's said about you. I'm really sorry.

Your Friend Forever,

Liz

Chapter 11

The thought of all my classmates further trashing my reputation makes me sick. But strangely I'm more upset that Ryan betrayed me. He knew I wanted to stay out of the Lake Forest spotlight this summer. Even though I was still a little unsure of him, I stupidly thought we were becoming friends.

Without seeing it, I know exactly when the photo was taken. It's the only photo I have ever taken with Ryan: the one Mr. Martin shot of us at the Fourth of July baseball game with his children. Ryan's arm was around me and the kids surrounded us but it sounds like the kids were cropped out. What a sell-out.

A quick glance at the clock tells me where I can locate my true confidant. On the beach, down by the lighthouse, I find my trusted advisor taking his daily walk.

"Well, if it isn't my bestie, I thought you would be at the carnival," says Mr. Thompson when he sees me. Today is the annual Coral Island Residents Day at the carnival. Granted, not the catchiest name, but a day to enjoy the rides without the tourists.

"Niko's picking me up soon. But there's something I'd like your advice on."

"Of course, my dear, let's talk while we walk back home."

"What do you do when someone you thought was your friend betrays you?"

We stroll along in silence for a moment.

"Do you know much about the Cold War?" he asks.

"Not really, something about Russia?" I answer, already trying to decipher the correlation.

"Precisely. Russia and the United States had technically been allies during World War II but the two superpowers never fully trusted each other. As the years went on their suspicions escalated. Personally, I was getting tired of life on a ship and wanted to be with my beautiful wife and raise a family properly. So when I had an opportunity to switch to a position in Naval Intelligence at a base in Germany, I grabbed it.

"It was fascinating work, intercepting Soviet communications and implementing covert operations. But over time my new world of double agents and espionage took its toll. Being part of the surveillance missions made it nearly impossible to trust anyone. Were our personnel really trusted allies or moles working for the enemy? Were Soviet defectors truly leaving the evils of Russia and wanting to provide intel to us or were they double agents leaking false information?

"Interrogations of trained military men yielded no clarifications but only more layers of confusion. There was no way to decipher the full story when your superiors never shared the big picture. After years of the tight camaraderie of the ships, it drained me to be in a place where I was suspicious of colleagues, neighbors, and friends. Over time I realized the only way to make it through was to focus on what was important: my faith and my family. I would have to rely on my commanding officers and hope they could interpret all the conflicting information to keep us safe."

"Hmm, okay," I say, puzzling out the riddle that his stories always are.

"In other words, sometimes in life we are surrounded by confusion. The only things we really know are our own hearts and intentions. Others, even those we think we know, might betray us and test our faith. You cannot control the Judases in your life, you can only follow your faith and be the person God wants you to be. The big Admiral in the sky will always watch over his crew."

I think about his words—who God wants me to be. Well, that is the question of the summer, isn't it? The one I've been trying to figure out.

"Thanks, you always know just what to say to make me feel better. You know, I've never met anyone who has lived as fascinating a life as you have," I say.

"If you think I have good stories you should really come with me to the VA hospital next time I volunteer and hear some of the adventures told there."

"You know what, I'd like that."

When I get back to Lily's, she and Niko are sitting on the back porch.

"Hi, sorry to keep you waiting. Shall we get going?" I ask.

"Have fun," Lily says as we start to leave. "I'll see you over there. Tom is on his way to pick me up."

"Okay," I say and wave good-bye.

She never has given me any strict dating rules, but she has kept an eye on Niko and me. I've seen her check on us when we are down on the beach during our scuba diving sessions. But what Lily doesn't know is she needn't bother with the chaperone thing because Niko has never tried anything. I now know a lot about regulators and buoyancy control, but is a kiss really too much to ask for? Instead, I've had to settle for handholding and pecks on the cheek and forehead. I always wanted to date a gentleman but enough already.

"I guess you are ready to go," he laughs as I skip toward his truck, determined not to let Ryan ruin my day.

"I love amusement parks. Something about them makes me smile."

"Well, you make me to smile," he answers as he helps me into the cab of the truck.

"How was your tour today?" I ask as he climbs in behind the wheel. It's Friday afternoon and before I got the mail and my beautiful summer day was twisted into ugliness, I had seen him take a group out on the boat.

"Well, today the tour was interesting. It was a large group who stays in Myrtle Beach for a family . . . reunite?"

"Reunion?"

"Yes. But they all were fighting about everything, even those plastic coins and jewels that the kids will dive for. I finally must separate them into two groups. I do not know how they will make it through the rest of the vacation."

"You should have just started singing, they would have all fallen under your spell then."

"I think that works for you only," he answers as we drive across the island.

The carnival almost seems like its own living entity. The joyous laughter—the oxygen it craves, the competing screams of delight and terror—its pulsing blood, the tantalizing aromas—its very soul.

At least that's how deep-thinking Niko described it. Personally, I was reminded of my brother's favorite video game with constant motion, sparkling pastel colors, bright balloons, and bubbly music.

Like a living pinball machine, I pull Niko from one ride to the next, just like when I was a kid and dragged my dad to all the rides at the Mall of America. Finally, Niko pleads for a break and offers to wait in the long line for fresh-squeezed lemonade and a funnel cake. Lily and Tom Mullins wave at me from a picnic table near the merry-go-round, shaded from the afternoon sun by the canopy of a flowering tree.

"Are you having fun?" Lily asks when I join them.

"Of course. Although I think I might be wearing Niko out."

"Maybe I should have invited you today instead of your aunt since she won't go on any of the rides," teases Mr. Mullins.

Aunt Lily laughs. "*Maybe* I'll go on the Ferris wheel, but no spinning rides for me."

"Well, she has a point," I say. "Getting sick and puking on your date would not be cool. Although it would give my mom something interesting to write about."

"Josie!" I turn to see Brianna Martin scurry toward me. Behind her strides Benedict Ryan, Brady riding high on his shoulders.

Okay, God, please give me strength to deal with him. "Hi there," I say, and give Brianna a hug. "Are you having a good time?"

"The best!"

"Where's Brittany?"

"Riding the kiddie rides with Mom and Dad."

"Would you like to join us?" asks Ryan. "Brianna knows all the best rides."

"I'm sure she does," I say, struggling not to be rude in front of the kids even though I wish I could tell him off for betraying my trust. "Thanks, but I'm here with Niko."

Ryan's smile disintegrates.

"There you go, Tom," Lily says. "I'm sure Brianna would go on the rides with you."

"Oh, expert-of-carnival-rides, what do you recommend for someone who doesn't like to spin?" Mr. Mullins asks Brianna.

"The bumper cars would be good. Or the train ride," Brianna states matter-of-factly.

"Excellent suggestions," Mr. Mullins says as Lily laughs.

"How have you been, Ryan?" Lily asks the traitor in our midst.

"Good. I recently got back from another series of away games. But we'll be home for a while now."

"We hate when he's gone," whines Brady.

"Thanks again, Mr. Mullins, for talking to us about the break-in the other day," Ryan says as he lowers Brady off his shoulders.

"I hope the thief is caught soon. Everyone is on edge just waiting for him to strike again," says Aunt Lily.

"You know, I've been thinking, there must be something that ties all the thefts together," says Ryan.

"Like the fact that they all had expensive items?" I say, trying to sound condescending.

"Sure, but how did the thief know that?" Ryan asks.

"What're you getting at?" asks Lily.

"I was thinking maybe it's an inside job, someone known to them," Ryan answers.

"What do you mean?" asks Mr. Mullins.

"Well, the thief doesn't waste any time. He knows exactly what he wants and goes directly to the items of value, like he knows the homes and businesses."

"Who would know them all?" I ask skeptically.

"Maybe someone who does work for them, like a decorator or a repairman, possibly cleaners."

"That would give them access to the homes and establish their trust," Lily agrees.

"When do you want to get together and make a list of possibilities?" Ryan asks me.

"I'm too busy to work with you." I ignore the look Aunt Lily shoots me for being rude.

"Too busy to talk with everyone who's been targeted and find out who has been in their homes and businesses?" Ryan asks. I resist the urge to tell him off and slap that cute face of his. My restraint is truly one of my greatest acting accomplishments ever.

Suddenly it dawns on me who would be on that list of people who have been in all the shops and homes—Aunt Lily. He better not be implying that she had something to do with the break-ins.

"Ryan, can me and Brady go see the crazy mirrors?" Brianna asks, her big blue eyes pleading with him.

"Sure, but stay right there where I can see you."

"We'll go with them," Lily offers. She and Tom follow the kids as they skip over to the distorted mirrors to check out their reflections.

"Thanks," Ryan calls after them, then he sits down across from me. "I'll stay here and keep Josie company."

I stand up, ready to deliver a blistering speech about his less than noble character then make a dramatic stage left exit, when I see Cyd skipping in our direction. Her eyeglasses are the same bright pink as the cotton candy she holds. Her father faithfully follows along loaded down with prizes and balloons. Stuck between a rock and a hard place, I plop back down.

"Why are you so good with kids?" I ask, forced to play nice.

"Lots of practice with my little sister," he answers with a shrug.

"I didn't know you had a sister."

"There's a lot you don't know about me," he says seriously.

"Oh, like you know so much about me?" I snap.

"I know you keep choosing the wrong type of guy."

"*What?*"

"You keep going for the smooth talker."

I glare at him. There is no way he can compare Niko with Cameron. "Stop trying to ruin my summer. Niko is a great guy, nothing like that pinhead Cameron who dumped me at the first sign of trouble."

"You always deserved better than Cameron. But Mr. Rebound's not right for you either."

"Really? Why not?"

"I still think there's something not right with your big summer romance."

"Like what?"

"I don't know, he just doesn't know you."

"And you do? You've known me for what, like three seconds? Just 'cause we're from the same town doesn't mean you know me."

"I know you better than you think. And one thing I know for sure is that you're not yourself around him," he answers, then gets up and strides over to the kids, oblivious to the two teenage girls who totally check him out as he walks past.

I watch him as he joins the kids. The three of them giggle as they make goofy faces in the mirrors. He's wrong. He doesn't know anything about me. Just because of the dumb books or because of the group I hang with at school he thinks he knows me. But I'm not the same Josie I was at the beginning of the summer. I barely know myself, so there's no way he knows me.

Niko brings our food over and invites Mr. Mullins and Lily to join us. The four of us dig into the warm funnel cake, pulling apart the warm strands of dough. Puffs of powdered sugar cover us in white. Our laughter only causes more powdered sugar to snow down on us. After promising her it doesn't spin, Mr. Mullins finally convinces Lily to try the rollercoaster.

Niko and I are about to tackle a few more rides when Mr. Spencer walks by wearing a Hawaiian shirt and tan shorts revealing thin, bony legs. Niko invites his landlord to join us.

"Oh, only for a minute to catch my breath. I think I'm getting too old for this."

"That is not true, your energy is larger than most people I know," Niko answers.

"Have you been on any of the rides?" I ask him.

"A few, I like the Ferris wheel, but I'll leave the rest of them to you young people. It's fun to be here though. I haven't come for years. Usually I have no one to watch the store."

"Who's holding down the fort for you?" I ask.

"Valentine. Marco and his girl insisted I come with them today. Val offered to take care of the shop for a few hours."

"We are most happy to help you out. You deserve the fun, too," Niko says.

"You boys treat me too well."

Marco and Tina, her pink hair tucked behind her ear, stroll up and join us. They look really happy together—too bad they will have to go their separate ways at the end of the summer.

"Hey there," says Tina.

"Hi," I answer. "I hear you guys have been slowing Mr. Spencer down."

"Yep, he's hard to keep up with," Tina teases.

Mr. Spencer throws back his head in contagious laughter, his whole body shaking.

Marco pats him on the shoulder. "Are you almost ready to go? Or do you need to ride the rollercoaster?"

Mr. Spencer holds his hands up in protest. "No, no. No more torture for me."

"Well, we better get back so we can get to the restaurant for our shift."

We say good-bye and the three of them head toward the exit. Tina wraps her arm around Mr. Spencer's, the older gentleman glowing under the attention they shower on him.

"You guys are really nice to him."

"He is a wonderful man. Our family is far away, financially is the way we can take care of them. It feels good to do good deeds for someone else."

"Next time you fill in for him I'd like to help."

"Good. I will like to teach you to make a perfect malt."

"Sounds great," I answer. He may not be so eager to teach me if he knew of the blender disasters of my past. My mom was cleaning the kitchen ceiling and cupboards for weeks after one particular mishap.

We walk down the rows of game booths and Niko stops at one. He plunks down his money on the counter. The attendant hands him three balls to try and knock down three pyramids of glass milk bottles. Niko throws three impressively accurate pitches and easily knocks down all three towers. He chooses a little white teddy bear with a pink bow on its head and hands it to me. I squeeze it tight, then give Niko a hug. I've always thought it was extremely romantic when guys won prizes for their girls. I can't believe I'm one of the lucky ones now.

We continue to walk around the fairgrounds, holding hands as we enjoy the music and the entertainers. As we watch a clown doing tricks with small white poodles, Niko's phone starts to ring.

"Excuse me a minute, Jozay, it is Byron Mullins," he says when he glances at it.

"Oh, okay." I smile. I know he's Niko's boss but that guy has the worst timing. He always seems to be interrupting us.

The crowd disperses as the clown finishes his act and moves on. I stroll over to watch an artist draw caricatures of some kids, fascinated how he exaggerates certain features, transforming them into a cartoon. Oddly I feel just like that drawing—a caricature of myself, a distortion of who I really am. I wonder what the real me looks like.

"Where's Rico Suave?"

I turn to see Ryan behind me.

"Stop calling him that. Not that it's any of your business, but he had to take a phone call. Something came up at work."

"He sure gets called away by work a lot."

I have no idea what he's insinuating but I'm not going to let him get away with it.

"He has a lot of family obligations and has to work hard. Not everyone can play baseball all summer."

"Or work on their tans," he counters, totally ruining my holier-than-thou attitude.

The best I can do is glare at him again.

"Did he win that for you?" he asks with a glance down at my bear.

"Yes, as a matter of fact he did," I proudly answer, and hug the soft little bear close to my heart.

"Sweet." He grins his McNaughty grin.

I feel like slapping that arrogant look off his face when Brianna Martin waddles up behind Ryan. She struggles to walk as she lugs the largest stuffed animal I've ever seen. The giant brown teddy bear is seriously almost as big as she is.

"Look what Ryan won for me!" she squeals in delight.

I look from her to Ryan.

He shrugs and grins.

Oh, he's infuriating.

I want to throw something at him as he helps Brianna carry her enormous prize. After all, all's fair in love and war, but realizing he only has a six-year-old girl to win prizes for gives me some satisfaction. He may be Mr. Hotshot Baseball Star but he doesn't seem to have much luck with the ladies. Of course, that's not a huge surprise if he always backstabs them like he did to me.

"Ready to try more rides, *mi amor*?" Niko sweetly says as he comes up behind me.

"Of course. Everything okay at work?"

"Nothing that cannot wait for tomorrow. Mr. Mullins, Junior, can be . . ." He searches for a word.

"High-strung? Demanding?" I suggest.

"Serious."

"I've noticed."

"I saw you talk to your friend Ryan."

"He's not exactly my friend."

"You did look like you would strangle him. Is he bothering you?" he asks, his eyebrows creased in concern.

"No, not really."

"Jozay, you have never told me much about your home. Maybe there is something you wish to share about it and Ryan?"

No—definitely not. I never want Niko to know about the problems at home.

"He just likes to annoy me," I say.

"Or keep his eye on you. I think he wants to watch over you as you are from the same hometown."

"My aunt's watchful eye is annoying enough."

"You cannot blame her to make sure I have honorable intentions," he teases. And my anger at Ryan instantly disappears as I watch Niko's dimples form.

The hours fly by while we ride everything at the carnival. And as the sun sets, we share a pizza, then finish the evening with a ride on the Ferris wheel. We circle to the top of the giant wheel and marvel at the sparkling lights of town on the one side of us and the peaceful darkness of the ocean on the other. The ride halts when we are at the very top, to let some riders off. Our basket sways gently. I turn toward Niko and he smiles at me. Then he slowly leans in toward me. His fingers stroke my jaw, his soft lips find mine, my heart leaps. This time it actually is the perfect setting for our first kiss, high above the world. As the ride starts again he puts his arm around me. I snuggle into his chest hugging my bear, and blissfully live in the moment.

Liz,

I guess you're still at your dad's. I hope you get this. It's been raining like crazy here for the last few days. I hope there won't be a hurricane. Sorry your summer's not the one of your dreams. But sometimes difficulties make us realize what we really want in life. Maybe you can concentrate on figuring out who you want to be this year.

Thanks for letting me know about Ryan and the picture he posted. But you know what? I'm sick of worrying about what people at home think about me. I've been spending a lot of time on the beach reevaluating life. In fact, I've been trying to figure out how to make both our lives different this coming year. I don't want to become that cautious meek person again. Somehow we need to find a way to embrace experiences instead of running from them.

The summer's been going too fast. Besides meditating at the beach I've been busy helping Lily with her restoration projects, hanging out with her neighbor—an elderly gentleman who has somehow become my BFF over the summer—and of course spending lots of time with Niko. We often hang out at the beach or the ice cream shop he lives above and help his landlord. He actually taught me to scuba dive, and I'm now a certified diver. Niko's not like any other guy I ever met. He's so caring and thoughtful and has a lot of depth, unlike the ridiculous high school guys we know. I know it's just a summer romance, but he's really made me realize there are nice guys out there.

Miss you.

Josie

Chapter 12

Romans 8:31 *If God is for us, who can be against us?*

Oh. I like this one, despite the odd house with siding made of old license plates that accompanies it. I am totally going to remember this verse. It's like a little ray of sunshine penetrating the otherwise dark and gloomy day of relentless rain that has engulfed the island. A tropical storm has hit and we are inundated with sheets of rain and whipping wind.

Sick of being cooped up, Lily and I brave the deluge and sprint over to the Thompsons' cottage. Water seems to come from every direction. Despite the rain jackets, our clothes are soaked and stick to our bodies, which reminds me of the time in third grade when I fell into the fountain at the museum during a field trip. But unlike that day, where I had to wear the dripping clothes all day, Aunt Lily thought ahead and we brought dry clothes along.

The Thompsons' small home serves as a living memorial to the fascinating life they've led. I wander around the crowded living room, careful to avoid tripping on the stacks of military history books that range from the American Revolution to the war on terror. While Lily and Mrs. Thompson whip up some lemon cookies, Mr. Thompson proudly gives me a tour. He shares details about all the souvenirs and medals.

A seashell reveals that he lived in Hawaii when it was attacked by the Japanese. Apparently his father worked as a janitor at the naval base in Pearl Harbor. But on the day of the attack he was away, on the north side of the island, for a mini vacation with his family. Mr. Thompson was just a young boy and despite the fact that few African-American men were in the Navy then, that day he vowed he would grow up to serve his country on those Naval boats he so admired.

A snow globe brings a story of being in the Baltic Sea off the coast of Russia, standing on the deck of his ship and being overwhelmed by the brilliant flowing colors of the aurora borealis.

And a small pendant is a reminder of a young recruit who met a beautiful young lady at a dance one spring evening and vowed to marry her, which he did.

After the tour we settle down at their kitchen table with tea and cookies as rain pelts the windows.

"You are an endless supply of fascinating stories," I tell Mr. Thompson. I never tire of hearing his tales.

"I keep telling you to come with me to the VA hospital. The guys there could entertain you for months."

"I'm in. Let me know the next time you go."

"After he retired from the military I wanted him to teach history since that's his passion. He loves when he has a captive audience for his stories," Mrs. Thompson says.

"No one cares about all that anymore," Mr. Thompson grumbles.

"I would have enjoyed history class if you had been my teacher," I say.

"I keep telling him he needs to record all these memories of his," Mrs. Thompson agrees. "I would hate for them to disappear."

"Who needs to write them down? I remember them just fine," he states stubbornly. As if to emphasize his point, a loud crash of thunder rattles the windows.

"Josie, have you and your friend done any more investigating into the thefts?" asks Mrs. Thompson.

"Not really. We kind of ran out of leads. And to tell you the truth, I really don't want to spend any more time with Ryan than is necessary."

"I don't know why you don't like Ryan," says Aunt Lily. "He seems very nice."

Sure, nice to your face, but watch the knife he plunges into your back when you least expect it. "I just want to avoid people who remind me of the drama at home," I answer politely.

"Speaking of, how long are you going to ignore poor Cyd Hollis's phone calls?"

"I was hoping to avoid her for the rest of the summer," I reply.

Lily laughs. "Kitten, most people would sell their soul to have an 'in' with the powerful Clive Hollis."

"Well, I'm not most people."

"Don't burn your bridges, you never know who might be an important ally someday," says Mr. Thompson. "During World War I, the Russians and Germans were in a fierce battle in the Russian wilderness. Neither could get the upper hand, though, because both sides were being viciously attacked by starving wolves. The bitter enemies called a truce and actually worked together to kill the predators."

"See what I mean? You make history intriguing," I tell him.

The lights in the cozy kitchen begin to flicker sporadically, a visual Morse code, flashing an unknown message.

"How often is the weather like this?" I ask.

"Luckily not very often," answers Lily.

"And we haven't had a hurricane in years," adds Mrs. Thompson.

"I bet you faced lots of storms when you were in the Navy," I say to Mr. Thompson.

"You know it. Have I ever told you about the time we were in the South Pacific during a tsunami?"

We settle back to listen to another one of his intense real-life tales. The afternoon flies by as we talk, play games, and devour the delicious cookies Mrs. Thompson and Aunt Lily baked.

As the darkness descends on the gloomy day, we gather up our stuff and prepare to face the elements again for the trip home. Mrs. Thompson hands me a container of cookies but before we can make the wet dash back to the cottage, I grab Aunt Lily's arm and begin to hum.

"Oh no, Kitten," she says, shaking her head.

"Oh yes," I answer.

Mrs. Thompson laughs. "I think you must. I'd join you but I don't want to risk pneumonia."

Lily looks at me, then with a conspiratorial smile we channel our inner Gene Kellys. We make our way back to the cottage belting "Singing in the Rain" as we splash through puddles and twirl in the curtains of water.

After hot showers and dry clothes Lily turns on the stereo with the volume extra loud to drown out the thunder during our dinner prep time. Being a perfect day for soup, we make a pot of creamy clam chowder while we sing and dance to Jimmy Buffett.

"Oh, Josie, 'Margaritaville' will forevermore make me think of you," says Lily after dinner.

"I know. I just love it here, even when it storms," I answer as I peer out the dark window.

"It is a pretty great place to live."

"You have the best life ever. I hope I grow up to live life to the fullest like you and not get trapped in small-town America."

"It is a good life here, but your life back at home is pretty amazing."

"No, I can't picture myself being like my mom, stuck in Minnesota. I think I'll leave like you did."

She looks at me, then curls up on her marshmallowy couch, tucking her feet underneath her. Kahlua snuggles next to her.

"Did you know that your mom wanted to live in New York?"

"You're kidding," I say and sink down in beside them. My mom. In New York? Hard to picture.

"When we were in high school she and I used to talk about our dreams for the future. I was going to live on the beach and paint. She would move to New York City and become a mystery writer."

"See, that's what I mean—you actually fulfilled your dreams. She compromised on hers."

"You know, sometimes I think she made the wiser decision."

"Are you crazy? You have the perfect life. No worries, no one to bring down your dreams. You can do whatever you want."

"The funny thing about dreams, they're one-dimensional. Don't get me wrong, I love my life, but there are times I'm envious of hers."

"How?" I can't even imagine it.

"She's made compromises, but now she has it all. A wonderful husband, amazing kids," she says with a wink, "and the career she always wanted. I would say that's just about perfect."

"But instead of writing cool mysteries in New York she's stuck in Minnesota writing about adolescence."

"She's writing about what she knows and loves—her kids. That's pretty incredible inspiration if you ask me."

"My mishaps are her inspiration?"

"No, watching you grow into a beautiful, strong, talented young woman is her inspiration."

***

The next morning Lily and I stroll along the beach to check out the damage. The usually pristine sand is scattered with branches and debris. We try to clean up the beach directly behind the house. Kahlua does her part by finding a small stick and carrying it in her mouth as we work. The wind and rain have thankfully stopped but the sky remains overcast. Puffy gray clouds litter the sky like old stuffing pulled from a pillow.

The persistent ringing of the phone welcomes us back to the house.

"Josie, it's Niko," Lily says with a glance at the caller ID.

I pick up the phone. "Hello?"

"Jozay, I hope you did not have trouble through the rain," his concerned, sultry voice says.

"No trouble, we're all safe and sound. How's everything in town?"

"Some trees have fallen to cause damage. That is why I have called. Here at Mr. Spencer's a large branch crashed into the glass window."

"Oh no. Is everyone okay?"

"Yes, but the shop has a mess. Glass, leaves, and water cover everywhere. We now are helping him to clean. I thought you maybe would like to join us."

"Of course. I'll be over soon."

"Wonderful," he says.

Of course I want to help sweet Mr. Spencer, but a chance to spend the day with Niko is hard to resist. Aunt Lily offers to drive me over; she doesn't want me to ride my bike in case it starts to rain again.

Like a real-life video game, she maneuvers her little car through town around fallen branches and overturned trash cans. She parks behind a pile of trash and walks in with me. An enormous tree branch is lodged in the store, the plate glass window shattered. Niko and his cousins stand in a huddle assessing the disaster and their plan of attack.

"Oh, Larry, what a mess," Lily says as we step around the glass and water puddles. When she places a plate of Mrs. Thompson's cookies on one of the tables, she's swarmed by the guys. "You didn't need to go to such trouble to have a party," she jokes.

He tosses his head back with his hearty laughter. "You've seen through my strategy, Lily."

"Well, it looks like you're in good hands," she says. They chat a few more minutes, then she heads back home.

I help Niko mop up the muddy mess, telling him about the damage on the beach. Val and Marco finally get to the huge tree branch blocking the counter and haul it out to the front sidewalk. After much discussion they decide it's no longer hazardous, so let an anxious Mr. Spencer go behind the counter. Their overprotectiveness of him is touching.

"You guys are too good to me," he says, appraising the damage. "How would I ever be able to clean all this up on my own?"

When the branch slammed through the front window and onto the counter it smashed most of the candy jars that usually line the workspace. I could only imagine the soggy, sticky mess that greeted him as he made his way back. But we weren't prepared for his sharp, quick cry. It stops us all in our tracks.

"What is it? Are you injured?" Marco rushes over to him.

"No, I'm all right. But my money. It's gone." His voice trembles.

"The cash register is not there?" asks Niko.

"No, it's here. But my safe is gone."

I stand helplessly as the guys all charge the counter. Mr. Spencer wobbles out to sit on one of the stools. He seems to have aged ten years in mere seconds.

"How much did you lose?" asks Juan.

"Everything. My life savings. I know I was foolish but I don't trust banks," he says as his hands shake. "How could this happen?"

The five Consuelos cousins exchange worried looks.

"We should call the police," I say.

"Yes, I suppose we should," says Mr. Spencer, his face ashen. "But the phone lines are down."

Niko pulls out his cell phone and starts to dial.

"Did you guys hear anything last night?" I ask Carlos.

"No, we weren't here. We were all at Mr. Spencer's home," he answers.

"The electricity always goes out here in town so I insisted they stay with me during the storm," Mr. Spencer explains.

While we wait for the police to arrive, Mr. Spencer and I sit in stunned silence. I hold his hand, trying to give him some comfort. How could the little crime spree have escalated into such devastation?

The Consuelos cousins pace around, looking like they are about to rip someone's head off at this violation of their beloved landlord. Thankfully our wait is short. The officers were already making their way down the street, stopping at all the businesses. They explain that someone took advantage of the storm and looted most of the stores in town. With the electricity out, many of the alarms and surveillance cameras that were in place weren't working, making it ridiculously easy for the thief.

The officers take Mr. Spencer's statement but don't offer much hope. After the police leave for the next store, Marco drives a still-shaking Mr. Spencer back to his home. A visibly angry Niko announces he'll drive me home.

"I can't believe it. I hope he's okay, he looked so devastated," I say as I climb into his truck. I've got to get serious about this investigation. Too many good people are getting hurt.

"He is a very special man. This, he does not deserve," he says through a clenched jaw.

We approach the last stop sign in town when Niko's phone buzzes. He glances down at the number then turns to me, his eyes hard.

"Jozay, I cannot drive you the rest of the way to home."

I stare at him blankly.

"It is work. There is an emergency from the storm."

"Oh. *Really?*" He's going to leave me on my own? "Um ... okay. I'll just walk home." All that way with a storm threatening. I don't want to come off sounding needy so I reach for the door handle.

"I am sorry. I must see you later," he says, then reaches over and gives my hand a quick squeeze.

"It's okay. I understand," I lie as I climb out of his truck.

I watch him turn and drive away toward the marina, then sigh at the looming hill ahead of me. I picture the long trek I still will have after I reach the top. Maybe I should walk back to town but with the phone lines down and all the confusion from the thefts it's probably better just to bite the bullet and head home. As I trudge along the barren road I cautiously glance up at the dark sky. Maybe it's my imagination but I swear the light is fading like dimming stage lights.

When I reach the top of the hill the sky seems to be the same color as the dark rocks that form the precipice to my right. Instinctively, I pull my sweatshirt tighter around me, then glance past the cliffs down to the beach. The churning water menacingly crashes onto the sand and rocks. A big fat drop of water splashes on my forehead and rolls down my face. Fantastic.

With the rain beginning to sprinkle down on me, I pick up the pace. The rumble of thunder mixes with the whine of an engine. I edge closer to the side of the road when a motorcycle pulls up alongside me. Ryan flips up the visor of his helmet, revealing his annoying grin. He looks perfectly dry in his helmet and leather jacket.

"Get caught in the rain?" he asks.

"No, Captain Obvious, I just wanted to try out my new waterproof mascara."

"Want a ride? I have a spare helmet," he says with a nod to the back of his bike.

"On that? With you? I don't think so."

"Suit yourself," he says and turns his head to check for traffic before he pulls back on to the road.

The dark clouds suddenly open up; buckets of rain pour down on me.

"Wait! Wait. Okay, fine."

He unstraps the helmet and hands it to me. I pull it on then climb on the motorcycle behind him. To avoid falling off, I cling to his waist as he pulls away.

The storm worsens and the onslaught of rain makes it nearly impossible to see anything. I squeeze tighter to Ryan. We only go a short distance before he pulls off the road and into the lighthouse parking lot. Probably a good decision because driving a motorcycle in zero visibility doesn't seem like the brightest move.

He parks at the base of the lighthouse, grabs my hand, and pulls me toward the shelter. He yanks open the door and we rush inside the dark, cold lighthouse. Stiff from being wet and cold, my fingers fumble as I try to take off the helmet. Ryan peels off his wet jacket. I stand there in a puddle shivering, completely soaked to the bone — for the second day in a row.

"I've never been in here," he says, looking around while I snap on the lights. The metal walls of the lighthouse make the usually friendly space frigid and unwelcoming.

"Really? The view from upstairs is amazing, not that you can see anything at the moment."

"Let's go check it out. Maybe we can see when the storm breaks."

We climb the spiral stairs toward the observation area. His long, athletic legs easily climb the tower. Once again I lag behind, but at least the effort takes my mind off my wet, clingy clothes, a layer of skin I wish I could shed. Rain violently pelts the windows, obscuring any view.

"Sorry we didn't make it to your aunt's. I was worried a car wouldn't see us on the road," he says, watching me tremble when I make it to the top.

"I know. Actually, I was glad you stopped," I answer, trying to control my chattering teeth.

"Why were you walking alone anyway?"

"Niko couldn't give me a ride home, something came up."

"Rico Suave bailed on you in your time of need," he says with a snort. Just when I thought he was being nice.

"An important work situation arose."

"Oh, and that extra five minutes it would have taken to drive you home was that critical?"

"I offered to walk," I lie, angrier than usual because he has a point.

"He knew you were walking. When it started to rain he should have come looking for you."

"Can't you mind your own business?" I say and turn my back on him.

I hear him take a deep breath.

"I'm sorry, but someone has to look out for you," he says in a calm voice.

I spin back to face him. "I can do that on my own, thank you. I didn't ask for your help and I don't want it."

"I'm just trying to make you understand that he's not the amazing guy you think he is."

I fight the tears that threaten my fragile composure. I'm drenched and freezing, upset with Niko for not driving me home, and furious with Ryan for pointing it all out.

"I saw him drop you off at the stop sign," he continues.

I glare at him. "What, were you spying on me?"

"No, I had gone into town to get something for Mrs. Martin. But when I saw him make you get out of the truck when it was obviously about to storm again, I knew I had been right about him. He's been leading you on and playing some kind of game."

"If you were that concerned about me and my safety then why didn't you pick me up then instead of making me walk all the way up the hill?"

"I followed him."

"You *what*!?"

"I followed him to see what was so important that he would leave you vulnerable like that. And he drives to the dock and talks to his boss, like that couldn't have waited a few more minutes."

"Then what did you do?" I ask incredulously.

"I got in his face and told him that I've been watching and was on to him. I told him he should watch his back because I knew exactly what he was up to. Then I left to find you."

"Why are you doing this?" I snap, the brunt of my anger directed toward him.

"What? Protecting you?" he asks, his green eyes full of emotion.

"Protecting me from what? A great guy? A fun summer? A life away from the jerks back home?"

"Why do you still care what they think?" he asks passionately.

"It's easy for you not to care, you're naturally part of the popular crowd since you're athletic and good-looking. Is it really that much to ask to want to be invited to the cool parties?"

"But you are nothing like them and never will be," he answers.

"Gee, thanks."

"No." He throws his hands up in frustration. "I mean, those people you're talking about aren't cool. They're judgmental, mean, and all the same. Josie, you're unique. You have this enthusiasm that touches people. You try to hide it but it shines through, and I can't get enough of it."

His words bounce around the room as I stare at him. What is he talking about? He's cute and popular, why would he notice me?

Finally he starts talking, words flowing from him like a dam that suddenly broke open.

"The first time I really noticed you was during *Thoroughly Modern Millie*. A friend forced me to go and I was bored to death until you came on stage. You were just one of the dorky tap-dancing secretaries in the scene. But you seriously lit up the stage. Your smile drew everyone in and when you had that little tap solo you captured everyone's attention. After that, I'd see you in the halls at school, trying to blend in and be like everyone else, but you couldn't. You have this way of just doing things despite the consequences. Your free spirit is intriguing and I knew I had to get to know you."

I keep staring, not comprehending his words. I mean, I know what he's talking about but my "free spirit," as he calls it, is not intriguing—it's my worst trait. It's what causes all those Josie moments that fill my mom's books.

"Don't look so shocked," he continues earnestly. "You must know how you affect people. You were surprised I saw any of your theater productions. Well, I've gone to all of them since then. Please don't look at me like I'm a stalker."

"If you felt that way why didn't you ever talk to me at school?"

"I wanted to approach you and ask you out a million times, but I never knew what to say. And you always had a ton of people around you. Then you started dating Cameron. But the unimaginable happened—I came all the way to South Carolina and here you were. I couldn't believe it. I told you that first night at the restaurant it was fate. Finally, my chance to be with you." His voice cracks with emotion.

Before I can react he takes one quick step toward me. With his strong hands on either side of my face, he leans in and kisses me.

Stunned, I hesitate as his lips touch mine, then pull away.

"No," I say quietly, trying to catch my breath.

This isn't right. He can't like me, he betrayed me.

"Josie," he says, and takes another step toward me.

"No, Ryan. Please leave."

"Don't do this."

"Please leave," I repeat.

His shoulders sag. "I didn't mean to make you mad. Come on, I'll take you home."

"No."

"I don't want you walking in the rain."

"No, I said leave. The rain has almost stopped. I'll walk the rest of the way, it's only three houses."

"Josie, I'm sorry. But I meant everything I said." He gives me one last look before slowly retreating down the spiral stairs.

He looks completely defeated and I almost apologize, but I need time to think through everything. Nothing makes sense.

It's darker than it should be at this hour because of the ominous clouds, but the downpour is just about over so once again I can see out the windows of the lighthouse. I peer down from the high tower and watch as Ryan climbs on his motorcycle. He looks up at me once, then pulls away toward Seaview Boulevard.

Could he really like me? He was totally convincing but it can't be true. Everyone knows tier one people date other tier one people. Him being interested in me just doesn't fit into the world as I know it. And if he truly cared for me why would he post that photo and cause all the drama to restart?

My fingers touch my lips as I remember the warmth of his hands on my face and the urgency of his kiss.

His motorcycle winds through the entryway, then turns left onto the road. He is almost to the top of the hill on his way to town when a truck comes barreling up behind him. In disbelief I watch the speeding vehicle clip the back of his motorcycle. Ryan struggles to keep the bike on the road when the truck rams into the back tire again. The second hit knocks the motorcycle over. The bike skids across the wet pavement toward the rocky precipice. I watch in horror as Ryan and the motorcycle hurtle off the cliff.

Chapter 13

"NO!" My scream reverberates through the hollow metallic structure of the lighthouse.

Despite my trembling muscles, I race down the spiral stairs. My wet shoes slip out from under me, and my back and head slam into the steep metal steps. Pain surges through my body.

Ignoring my aches I run as fast as possible across the parking lot and playground. 911. I need to call 911. Instinctively my hand slips into my back pocket for my phone. I'm an idiot. Why did I give up my phone for the summer?

Pivoting, I sprint toward the road to flag down a car. A minivan comes into view. The driver's startled expression changes to concern when he sees my face. He cautiously pulls over and lowers his window. I try to explain what happened but my words don't seem to make any sense. He touches my arm and tells me not to worry, then dials the police.

My head throbs and every breath brings a sharp pain in my side, but I run back toward the cliff. My muscles burn from the exertion. Tears stream down my cheeks as I try to make my way across the sharp porous rocks in search of Ryan.

Oh, dear Jesus, please help him to be alive. At the bottom of the cliff on the beach, a black mass pollutes the gray sand. The motorcycle. But no sign of Ryan.

"Ryan! Ryan!"

My ankle twists on the uneven rocks. I stumble and scrape up my hand. There is no answer to my calls, only an eerie calm and the dim sound of a siren. Realizing I'm useless on my own, I force myself back to the park to flag down the ambulance.

The paramedics and a police car pull into the parking lot; their urgent lights bring hope. Choking on the words, I quickly tell them what happened. Despite my pleas, the policeman refuses to let me go with the paramedics as they begin to search the cliffs. Instead, he hands me a blanket to wrap myself in and has me sit in the back of his patrol car. He asks if there is someone he should call. Since I don't know the Martins' number I give him Aunt Lily's.

Despite the blanket, my tremors continue. My wet clothes are plastered to my body but I'm sure the uncontrollable shaking isn't from being wet. I've never been this terrified.

After the officer makes several phone calls he sits beside me in the back of his cruiser to ask me some questions. In more detail I describe everything I saw. He takes notes, then leaves me alone with the horrible vision of Ryan plummeting off the cliff replaying in my mind.

After what feels like an eternity I see movement from the shoulder of the cliff. The darkness rapidly descends but I see the paramedics carefully hoist a stretcher up over the rocks, a body strapped onto it. Ryan. *Oh, please God, let him be alive.*

As soon as they reach level ground they lay him down and begin their frantic work. They begin to attach things to him but their urgent shouts are disconcerting. I tell myself these must be good signs. You don't work on a dead body.

Their precisely choreographed chaos makes my head spin. To avoid being sick I lean my head on the back of the seat of the patrol car. As he's loaded on the ambulance, Aunt Lily arrives. She slides into the backseat and pulls me into her arms. The dam breaks and I burst into tears.

"Come on, Kitten, let's get you home."

"No, I have to go with him. He has no one."

"Let's get you dry and warm, then we'll go to the hospital. Mrs. Martin is already on her way there."

I reluctantly climb into her car and watch the ambulance pull away. The red and blue strobe lights disappear over the hill.

I'm sorry, Ryan. I'm sorry for everything.

***

We wait. I stare at the doors to the OR, willing them to open, for someone to come out and tell us some news. But no one comes.

The minutes stretch into hours, the ticking of the clock a time bomb of bad news waiting to explode. Despite dry clothes my muscle tremors continue. Mrs. Martin and Aunt Lily talk quietly but I don't hear their words. I just keep praying and making bargains with God. Things I will do if only He will spare Ryan.

I've been staring at those doors for so long that when they finally swing open and a man in blue scrubs walks toward us, I can't be certain it's real. Maybe he's a mirage, a desperate hallucination. When he opens his mouth I hear nothing, only the throbbing blood in my brain. He looks at me, concern radiating from him. No. Not bad news. No! Wake me from this nightmare. But all I see is black.

***

"Josie . . . Josie . . ."

My eyes flutter open to see strangers hovering over me. I scan the faces until I focus on a familiar face, Aunt Lily.

"Did Ryan . . ." I choke on my words.

"No, Ryan is okay at the moment. He's stable and in the ICU. Josie, you fainted."

"Get her something to eat, okay?" says the man in the blue scrubs.

With the crisis over, the medical personnel scatter. Great. Just like me. Ryan's fighting for his life and I grab the attention.

Mrs. Martin hands me a hot chocolate and we settle back in our chairs. We've been here so long they seem part of us now—the vinyl and metal extensions of our bodies.

Aunt Lily scrutinizes me after I take a few sips of the cocoa. "Are you ready to hear this?"

I nod, trying to keep the tears inside my head.

"He's pretty battered. Broken ribs, punctured lung, and his left leg is broken. But there is no head or spinal trauma. Overall he was lucky. But he's not completely out of the woods; they will monitor him closely for internal bleeding."

I nod and feel the betrayal of tears rolling down my cheeks. Stop it. You must stay strong. "Would it be better if he were on the mainland?" I manage to ask.

"Don't worry, Josie," Mrs. Martin says. "We have some world-class doctors here on the island. Several who wanted a less stressful lifestyle have moved here recently. The trauma team is top notch."

"Now," Lily says, turning her concerned eyes on me. "Mrs. Martin has convinced the ICU to let you go in since Ryan has no family here and you know him the best. Can you be strong for him?"

"Yes."

My wobbly legs somehow get me to the bathroom where I splash cold water on my face. When I look in the mirror, though, the face of a ghost stares back at me. How can someone look that terrified?

We walk to the ICU, the stark fluorescent lights exposing all my fears. The beeps of machines dissolve any strength I have left. But I tell myself I have to do this for Ryan. A nurse leads Mrs. Martin and me down the cold, sterile hallway. She pulls back a curtain and walks into a room.

I stare in disbelief. Tan, handsome, and normally full of life, Ryan looks unnaturally frail lying in the bed under the harsh glaring lights. He's hooked up to machines and tubes that buzz and drip in an unnerving rhythm. His eyes are shut but he doesn't look like he's asleep. I know this image will haunt me for a long time. The vision of nightmares.

Mrs. Martin, whose mothering instincts kick in, goes straight to him. She touches his forehead and starts to talk to him. I can only stare at him, unable to move, willing myself not to faint again. Josie, you must do this. You owe this to him.

The nurse leans close to me. "It's okay, hon, you can touch him. Hold his hand, let him know you're here."

I shuffle to the bed and Mrs. Martin tells him I'm here. With no idea where to touch him—every inch of his skin bruised, tubes snaking into his flesh—I glance at the nurse. Her nod encourages me to slip my hand under his and gently hold it.

"Ryan, I'm here. I'm sorry."

Eventually Mrs. Martin says she must leave but that she'll be back tomorrow. The nurse pulls a chair next to the bed for me. When she notices my quaking body, she hands me a blanket. I pull the fraying, bitterly antiseptic-scented blanket around me, but the gnawing cold that grips my insides refuses to budge.

I realize my life this summer has finally been what I always dreamed of—full of romance, adventure, and excitement. But seeing his strong body now so fragile as it lies on that starched hospital bed, fluids dripping in and out through invasive tubes, I know the price to pay for such a life is just too high.

***

After a sleepless night, I wander zombie-like into the kitchen. I was exhausted when I got home from the hospital but the hot shower I thought would make me feel better was powerless to thaw the numbness of my soul. Every time I closed my eyes the image of Ryan's unconscious body, his chest rising and falling in rhythm to the machines, burned in my mind, making sleep impossible.

Aunt Lily fixes me something to eat and gently questions me. I tell her everything I told the police, reliving the horrific scene, although I purposely leave out what happened in the lighthouse. I can't bring myself to think about the kiss.

"Are his parents on their way?" I ask.

"Not yet. They're out of the country on a cruise, which means their cell phones are turned off. The Martins have contacted the cruise line and were assured they will locate the McNaultys."

After I try to force a little food down to appease Aunt Lily, she drops me off at the hospital. When the elevator doors open to the ICU, uncontrollable wails from behind one of the thin curtains greet me. I imagine a family gathered around a bed, sobbing, overcome with grief. Not wanting to be part of their misery, I hurry down the hall.

I peer into Ryan's room at his perfectly still body, tubes still attached everywhere. Why did I fight with him? Why didn't I have him drive me home? Why did I push him away?

"Hard to see him like that, isn't it?"

I turn to see Mrs. Martin sitting in a chair, her eyes red and puffy.

"I know. I just can't believe it."

"Did you know that he was supposed to be a camp counselor this summer?" she asks.

A camp counselor? When he said he would have been at camp instead of here for the summer I thought he meant he'd be attending some luxury sports camp or something. "No, I didn't know that."

"I guess he worked at a camp for underprivileged kids last summer and loved it. He wanted to go back but got this opportunity to play baseball. If only he had gone to the camp, he would be safe and sound now. We were supposed to watch over him and keep him safe. I don't know how I'll be able to look at his parents."

"He has loved staying with you. This isn't your fault."

"We lent him the motorcycle. What were we thinking? It was much too dangerous."

"He was a careful driver," I assure her. "But someone ran him off the road."

"Did the car skid on the wet roads?"

"No. It looked deliberate. In fact, the truck hit him twice. No, I'm sure it was on purpose."

176

"But who would do such a thing?"

"I don't know."

"Well, if you gave the police a description of the vehicle, they can hopefully find the person responsible."

"It wasn't much of a description. I was pretty far away and didn't see any more details."

"Praise God you witnessed it, though. I can't bear to think about how long he would have been there on the cliff if you hadn't seen the accident." She wipes away a tear. "Well, now that you're here, I'll go home for a while. I'll be back this afternoon."

She hugs me, then leaves. I stare at Ryan, the shame and guilt for how I treated him right before he was hit building inside me. I sit down on the chair next to his bed and hold his hand again. His usually handsome face is now bruised and scraped. A gash below his eye is evidence of the broken visor of his helmet. My eyes travel down to his lips and my insides do a little jump as I remember his kiss. The intensity when he reached for me and held my head in his hands was amazing. I was so surprised and stunned by what he said that I pushed him away, still not believing him. Why did I have to send him away? Why didn't I just give him more time to explain or ask some questions?

I was furious at him for posting that picture, but I didn't want anything bad to happen. What if he doesn't get better and I'm never able to talk to him again? What if I can never ask for forgiveness? *Oh God, is there some way to help him?*

There is. Somehow, I've got to find out who did this to him.

Chapter 14

I don't know how long I've been at his bedside, lulled into oblivion by the beeps of the monitors, willing his body to heal. But the tap on my shoulder by the nurse makes me jump. She informs me my visiting time is over.

As I emerge from the cocoon of the hospital, the cloudless blue sky and bright sunlight are in stark contrast to the turmoil I feel inside. Even though it's a beautiful day the remnants of the storm are still evident by the trash and debris swept into piles along the sidewalk. I walk the few blocks to the marina, hoping to see Niko. I could really use a friendly face about now. Maybe he can help me figure out what to do. All I want is to have someone else carry the burden for a while.

Niko's and Marco's trucks sit side by side in the parking lot. Relieved they are here, I walk down the pier toward the *Jewel of the Sea*. The Consuelos cousins are all on the boat cleaning the deck after the storm. Carlos sees me first and waves. He meets me at the back ladder and offers his hand to help me climb aboard.

"Jozay!"

The others circle around to say hi.

"Hey, *bonita*," Niko says as he leans in and kisses my cheek. "I hope you came to rescue me from this cleaning."

"Maybe she came to make sure you're not slacking off," jokes Juan.

"Well, you are always welcome, especially if you brought more of those cookies," adds Val.

Niko looks closer at my face, which gives away my mood. "What is wrong?"

"Something horrible happened last night. My friend Ryan was involved in an accident and is in the hospital. He was in surgery for hours and we still don't know if he'll be okay."

I fall into Niko's arms and the others murmur words of sympathy.

"What happened?" asks Marco.

"He was on his motorcycle and someone forced him off the road. He skidded over the cliffs near the lighthouse. They found his body about halfway down." A shiver runs down my spine at the memory.

"A vehicle pushed him off the road?"

"Yeah, a big black truck, like the size of yours," I answer. "Somehow I've got to help the police track down whoever hit him."

Marco flinches. Val and Niko exchange a glance. Carlos looks away. Juan closes his eyes. The sudden silence is palpable.

I don't need my mad detective skills to realize something's wrong. I look at Niko for some assurance but he looks past me. I follow his gaze toward their black trucks in the parking lot.

Marco begins to speak in Spanish and Niko shoots him a hard look.

"Niko, what's going on?" I ask, taking a step back.

"Nothing," he replies, his forehead creased.

"Do you know something about Ryan's accident?" I probe.

"No. Of course not," he answers unconvincingly. The hair on the back of my neck rises.

His cousins start a barrage of rapid-fire Spanish directed at him. Their demeanor instantly changes from friendly to hostile.

"What's going on?"

"Nothing," he says again as he glances at his cousins.

Instinctively I move toward the ladder, but he grabs my arm.

"Jozay, wait."

"Let me go," I say and try to pull away from him. A useless attempt, like a seal who tries to flee the jaws of a shark.

"I cannot do that," he says, his hand a vise tightening on my arm. Who are these people I thought I knew?

"Did one of you force Ryan off the road? He could have died." I turn to scream for help when Niko forcefully spins me toward him.

"Jozay, listen to me. This is not as it seems. Please, let me talk."

Before I can answer, the engine of the boat suddenly roars to life. Juan untethers the boat and Marco steers it out of the marina toward the open water. Suddenly terrified, I realize I need to get away. But Niko's death grip on my arm makes it highly unlikely.

My mind reels as the boat speeds away from land. Where are they taking me? What are they going to do to me? *God, please protect me.*

"Jozay, if you have at all cared for me you must listen," Niko pleads in my ear.

"Well, since you're kidnapping me I don't see how I have another choice," I snap.

I try to think of a way out of this but even if I could get away, jump overboard, and attempt the long swim back to shore, there's no way I could outswim Niko. Helpless, I stare at him. Could I really have been that wrong about him?

Eventually the boat stops and Marco joins the rest of us as the *Jewel of the Sea* bobs in the ocean, far off the coast.

"Jozay, do not be frightened. We only need to talk to you," Niko finally says. His grip loosens and I yank my arm away.

"You dragged me all the way out here to 'talk'?"

"I am sorry. We panicked. Please, life can be more complicated than you know."

No kidding, like when your boyfriend and his relatives turn out to be child abductors. "What I know is that my friend is lying in a hospital fighting for his life and you know something about it," I counter in an attempt to hide my fear.

Niko turns and looks at his cousins, communicating without words.

"What is it?" I demand.

Niko sighs. "Do you remember yesterday, I had a call of an urgent work matter?"

"Yes, how could I forget when you made me walk home in the monsoon."

He ignores my sarcasm. "We had been sent to the mainland to take care of something when the accident happened."

"I don't believe you."

"Jozay, it is true."

"Then what are you hiding? You wouldn't just drag me out here for nothing."

He sighs. "Marco this morning noticed damage on the front bumper of his truck. We did not know what happened. Yesterday, after I said good-bye to you, Mr. Mullins had us to take the ferry off the island. We were to drive his SUV so all of us could fit. Our trucks stayed parked at the marina. We got back late from our assignment and went straight to Mr. Spencer's home so to check on him. This morning is when the damage of the truck was found."

"You expect me to believe someone mysteriously took your truck, ran Ryan off the road, then re-parked it at the marina?" I ask Marco.

He doesn't answer, his usually friendly face menacing.

"I tell you it was not us," Niko answers.

"You're protecting someone. I know you're leaving something out. Tell me the truth."

"That is the story. Please have trust in me and do not ask any more," Niko demands.

I'm surprised by the strength that fills me, but I refuse to be intimidated by the five men facing me. "Not good enough. I'm telling the police to check out your trucks. They can figure it out."

Niko looks at his cousins. "Jozay, you cannot do that."

"You can't protect them."

His gaze travels between me and his cousins, then he walks over to one of the crates on the boat and pries it open.

His cousins erupt in Spanish again.

Inside sits a mound of watches and other pieces of jewelry. I stare at the merchandise, not comprehending. Then the lightbulb turns on. Finally it all makes sense.

"You guys are the ones who have been stealing everything in town. Did Ryan somehow figure it out? Is that why you ran him off the road? He told me not to trust you. I should have listened to him."

"Jozay, no. We did not hurt him. The stolen items are not from us. We only have been transporting them to hide."

"Why?"

"If we do not obey we will lose our jobs."

"Who's making you do this?"

"Mr. Mullins."

"That doesn't make sense. He's been burglarized as well."

"This is his scam. We knew nothing of this when he hired us, but he needed help. He knew that we are the support of our family back in the Dominican and could not afford to turn him in. All summer we did as we were told and hid the larger stolen items in the cave on the beach and the jewelry here. He was to keep the items hidden until he could get everything off the island to sell them. He will also collect the money of his insurance."

Could Lily's charming suitor really be the villain? "Why would he keep everything and risk someone finding them? Why not just move them off the island right away?"

"He became paranoid. The police have the harbor master and ferry operator to report any unusual patterns or behavior. Mr. Mullins could not make any new trips to raise suspicion. He was to wait until the end of summer to move all the items at once when the *Jewel* would be scheduled to go down the coast for maintenance."

Val continues the story. "But he's so greedy he took advantage of the storm and looted the whole town. Yesterday when we realized that he had basically destroyed Mr. Spencer, we couldn't sit back anymore and had it out with him. We told him he had to return everything or we would go to the police. But he threatened us. Said he'd plant some of the stolen items and frame us for all the thefts."

Niko gently takes my hand. "The guys are not citizens and would be in terrible trouble. Listen, you may not understand but our family is dependent on us. Our grandmother, cousins, elderly aunts and uncles—we are all they have. If the guys lose the cruise ship jobs or we go to jail our family will be to suffer."

"But what does any of this have to do with Ryan?" I ask.

"I am not all sure but yesterday after you left my truck, Ryan followed me and confronted me in front of Byron. He was saying he knew what I was up to. Mr. Mullins maybe was afraid Ryan knew the scheme."

"You think one of them ran Ryan off the road?"

"Probably Byron, he does the dirty work," Carlos answers.

"Is everything they stole either here on the boat or in the cave?"

"No. We do not know what they stole from the storm or where they keep it. But we think there is now too much for the cave because we were ordered to go down the coast and with cash purchase a storage unit. That is what we were doing at the time of the accident."

I look from one cousin to the next and realize they're telling the truth. Their anger has been replaced by fear and hopelessness. And worse yet, they are all looking at me for help.

"I'm sorry, but unfortunately, it's too late," I tell them. "It's only a matter of time 'til they track down the truck. I gave the police a description last night."

Chapter 15

After an uncomfortably tense ride back to the marina (what is there to say when your actions will most likely destroy your boyfriend's family?), Niko drives me home. Nothing was decided, nothing sorted out, nothing solved, only more confusion.

I quickly check with Aunt Lily, who's painting in her studio, but with no news from the hospital I head to the beach, where I sink down in the sand. My conflicting feelings make my head spin like when I pirouette across the floor without spotting my turns.

I'm terrified that Ryan won't recover. I'm guilt-ridden that I didn't work closer with him on the investigation and instead tried to avoid him. I'm outraged at Byron Mullins for hitting Ryan. I'm shocked that Tom Mullins could be involved in all this. I'm scared that the two of them could get away with it all. I'm angry with myself for steering the police straight toward Marco, ruining his life and forever affecting the Consuelos family. I'm sad about how all this will affect my relationship with Niko.

And for the life of me, I can't get Ryan's kiss out of my mind. I've never been kissed with such passion before. Neither Cameron nor Niko ever made me feel that desired.

"Hey, kiddo, mind if I join you?" says Mr. Thompson from behind me.

I shake my head and he somehow lowers his big frame down in the sand to sit next to me.

"Lily told me about your friend's accident," he says in that gruff voice of his.

"It was horrible. My mind keeps replaying the scene."

"Trauma does that. Let me know if you want to talk about it."

"Actually, I'm really confused. I have two friends in trouble but I don't know how to help them, or even how I feel about either of them. No matter which one I help I'll hurt the other. How can there be no good answer?" I confess to this grandfatherly figure I've come to care so much about.

We sit quietly for a few minutes watching the waves roll onto the beach.

"Did you know out there," he points toward the water, "just sixty miles off the coast of New Jersey, at the bottom of the ocean rests a World War II German submarine?"

"I didn't know that the Germans were ever that close," I say, not really in the mood for a history lesson today.

"Yep. While the citizens here on the East Coast were minding their own business, thinking the war was happening far from home, they were in more danger than they thought. Of course they worried about being attacked but no one knew the enemy was actually that close."

"Oh," I say, wishing he'd get to the point.

"Deep sea divers discovered the U-boat in the early nineties."

"Wow, that's interesting," I murmur.

"It just goes to show you that things are not always what they appear to be."

I turn to him. "What're you saying?"

"Sometimes, the real story rests below the surface. If you don't know the answer, it's because you don't have all the facts."

"So, like those divers who found the sub, I need to dive down and explore in order to discover the truth?" I answer, trying to think like him.

"Sounds like a good way to be sure which course of action to take."

"You're the wisest person I've ever met," I say, leaning my head on his shoulder.

"Will you tell that to Mrs. Thompson for me?" he asks.

"Sure."

"Josie?"

"Yes?"

"I think I'm stuck down here, can you help me get up?"

***

When I get back to Aunt Lily's I pick up the postcard of a building that looks like a giant television that waits for me on the table.

James 5:13 *Are any among you suffering? They should pray.*

Wow. It's amazing how God always seems to be speaking to me through her cards.

The ringing of the phone breaks the stifling silence.

"Hello?"

"Oh, Josie, it's Mrs. Martin. Ryan woke up a little while ago. All my Hail Marys must have worked," she gushes.

"That's wonderful," I say, relief washing over me.

"Still no word from his parents but I was able to contact his uncle in Colorado who's a doctor. It's a relief to have a family member in charge now."

"Thanks for the update. I'll have my aunt drive me over."

As I wait for Aunt Lily to get ready I contemplate the two polar opposites that are Niko and Ryan.

On the one hand there is Ryan, a privileged, wealthy, all-American boy whose parents sent their kid away for the summer so they could go on their luxury vacation.

On the other hand there is Niko, caring and sensitive, whose underprivileged family means the world to him. He works night and day for everything he's got and would risk it all to protect those he loves.

Ironically, Niko's family works for next to nothing providing entertainment on the type of exotic trip that Ryan's parents are on right now.

I wish I could somehow help both of them. I want the person responsible for Ryan's accident punished. But now thanks to me the police are searching for a black truck that will lead them straight to innocent Marco. There is no possible way the authorities will even listen to his story. Who would believe that a successful businessman is behind the accident when everything points to Marco, someone who is poor, desperate, and not even a citizen? He's an easy target.

Maybe Mr. Thompson's right, if I dig a little deeper and talk to both of them maybe I'll get some clarity. But first I should probably follow my mom's advice and pray.

***

By the time I reach the hospital it's evening. The setting sun beautifully colors the sky in shades of pink. When I enter Ryan's room I'm surprised how thrilled I am to see him. He still looks terrible, red cuts and purple bruises coloring his face. But he's awake and he's attached to fewer tubes. He rolls his head toward me, too weak to lift it from the pillow. The corner of his mouth turns up in greeting but his eyes are dull and heavy.

"I'm so happy to see you," I say as I sit next to him.

"Really? I would have admitted myself to the hospital sooner if I knew that was how to get your attention," he says, his voice raspy.

I smile. He must be feeling better if he's flirting.

"Seriously, I can't tell you how worried I was about you. Watching you skid across the road and disappear over the cliff was horrible." A shiver passes through me at the memory.

"It wasn't so great living it either."

"Any idea when you can leave this charming place?"

"Not a fan of hospitals?"

"Definitely not, they're sad and depressing. Don't you think?"

"Hmm, they don't really bother me. I guess I've spent a lot of time in them over the years."

"Accident prone?"

"Something like that."

He looks extremely tired and weak. I notice the huge teddy bear that he won for Brianna at the carnival on the chair by the window, a bouquet of balloons tied to its paw.

"Brianna gave up her bear?"

"She sent it to watch over me. Brady picked out the balloons and Brittany drew me a picture. They're upset they can't visit. But I'd probably freak them out in my current state."

"You have looked better."

He starts to laugh then grimaces in pain.

"Oh, I'm sorry. See, I should stay away from you. I cause you nothing but trouble."

"I hope you don't mean that. Besides, thanks to you they caught the guy."

"What?" I feel the blood drain from my face.

"Yeah, some detective was here earlier to get a statement and told me they found the truck that was involved and arrested some guy."

Oh no. "Did they give you a name?" I ask cautiously.

"No."

"Do you remember anything?"

"You mean besides the smackdown from you at the lighthouse?"

"I'm sorry for that." I feel myself blush. "I really thought you were lying."

"Why would I do that?"

"Seriously, why would you like me? You're a jock, you shouldn't be interested in a theater geek."

A slight grin forms on his battered face. "You're delusional. I really don't care what everyone at that stupid school thinks. I've never been one to follow the crowd."

"Then why did you post that photo of us online when you knew I didn't want them to know about my summer?" I ask.

"I didn't post any photo," he says.

"Ryan, come on, someone had to, it didn't post itself. Who else could have done it?"

"Mrs. Martin has been posting things all summer so my mom and grandma could see what I've been up to."

I suddenly feel sick as it all comes together in my mind. Ryan's mom probably commented on it or copied it to her photos. She must be friends with lots of the other moms back home. It would just take one of them to "like" it, then whichever teenagers they are friends with would see it. And it wouldn't take much to crop it and repost it.

"Oh gosh, I'm sorry, Ryan. I thought you did it."

"Why do you care what those people think of you anyway?"

"I don't know. It all seems ridiculously petty at the moment."

"Someday you'll learn to trust me," he murmurs as his eyes droop.

"I should let you rest. I just wanted to stop in and make sure you were okay."

"Will you come back tomorrow?" he asks.

"Of course. I'll see you then."

Before I head down to the lobby to find Aunt Lily, I stop in the little hospital chapel. I settle into one of the pews and thank God for protecting Ryan. The stained glass windows and simple wooden cross help me gather my thoughts.

Ryan's right, all the stupid stuff back at home is unimportant. Who cares what a bunch of insignificant people think? There are a lot worse things in life than my bruised ego.

Life is extremely fragile.

There are people lying in this hospital right now, fighting for their lives.

There are people who live in countries so corrupt that they must flee in order to save themselves.

There are people who are indebted to others and must work feverishly to send money back home to support family members who live in poverty.

There are people who can't stand up for themselves for fear of being deported and losing their livelihood.

There are people innocently sitting in jail, possibly for the rest of their lives.

Yes, there are a lot worse things in life than my trashed reputation.

Josie,

If this is indeed the real Josie. If you are an imposter—what did you do with my best friend? Where are the histrionics that I have grown to love? Where is the worry about what others will think? Could you really have changed so much in such a short time? Is that what a warm ocean breeze does to a person? I wouldn't know, stuck here in the hot muggy Windy City.

Since I have no one else to talk to, I've shared your letters with Chrissy. She thinks you sound wise beyond your years. Then she gave me some advice to share with you. Ready for this gem? Any problem you face can be solved with your unique talents. Deep—I know. I'm not sure how sarcasm and eight years of ballet will solve any of my problems but hey, at least she has a motto to live by, unlike my just-survive-one-day-at-a-time philosophy.

Seriously, it sounds like you've come to terms with the stuff back home. I still can't believe Ryan turned out to be such a tool. But you're right, who cares what any of them think, although they are hard to ignore. And if we never get invited to the cool parties (although just once would be nice), we'll continue to make our own great memories.

But remember, if you do find yourself facing another crisis that seems insurmountable, your vast knowledge of musical theater may just help you out.

Peace out,

Liz

Chapter 16

After a restless night of sleep, or more accurately a sleepless night of attempted rest, I ride my bike into town to Spencer's Ice Cream Parlor. Huge plastic tarps cover the gaping hole where the storefront window should be—a bandage over the open wound of Mr. Spencer's life. I gather up my courage and enter.

Niko, Val, Juan, and Carlos are sitting in a booth. Their shoulders sag with defeat. The jovial mood that usually fills this place has vanished. Sadness and despair fill the void. Niko walks over to me and kisses me on the cheek while the others stare. I was expecting anger, since my report to the police led to Marco's arrest, but I honestly still don't think I did anything wrong. How was I to know how it would all turn out?

"Where's Mr. Spencer?" I ask.

"He is to rest for a few days," answers Niko as he pulls up a chair for me, then sits back down in the booth next to Carlos. "We worry for him. The theft has been hard on him."

"And now he's worried about Marco," says Val, a little too vehemently if you ask me.

"We are all worried about him, thanks to you," adds Carlos. Geez, I really walked into the lion's den.

"That is not fair," replies Niko. "Jozay did not know Marco would be involved. She had to tell what she saw to the police." I'm grateful for his defense.

"I heard Marco was arrested. I really am sorry. What are the charges?"

"Hit and run. Mr. Mullins has hired him a lawyer who is to go with a careless driving angle. But he is not a citizen; it will be complicated. It is unknown if he can be out on bail."

"Mr. Mullins hired a lawyer for him?" I ask, surprised.

"Probably so we will be quiet. We could never afford one but now we go deeper in debt to him."

"You can't let him get away with this."

"What are we going to do?" hisses Val. "No one will believe us. If we say anything, he will implicate us in the thefts, then we will all go to jail."

"There has got to be a way to get proof. I could help you."

"He is too smart for a trap. He will never tell the truth," says Niko.

"And he controls everyone who gets in his way," adds Carlos.

"How?" I ask.

"Blackmail their families, plow them off the road, demand Niko to date them," mumbles Juan.

He quickly looks up at me, then at Niko, then slumps farther down on the leather bench.

"*What*?" I ask.

Niko looks down at his hands.

My head starts to reel. "Is that true? Mr. Mullins *told* you to date me?"

"Can we talk alone?" Niko asks.

"You ass ... tronomical jerk," I say before I storm out.

Niko follows me out to the sidewalk.

"Jozay, please listen to me," he says, grabbing my arm.

I whip around and stare him down with any icy glare.

"You were spending too much time on the beach and made it hard to move items to the cave. Then Mr. Mullins heard you were to investigate the thefts. He was nervous. He demanded I keep you occupied."

"So, this whole romance was some *assignment*?"

"No. I did enjoy spending the time with you. I had more fun this summer than I have ever before had. And that was because of you."

"But you didn't like me."

He sighs and runs his hand through his thick, dark hair.

"No, not that way. As you dug more into the burglaries, Mr. Mullins kept me to go further with the relationship with you. I did not want to hurt you. I think you are like a little sister. I'm sorry."

A sister?!

I'm completely mortified, tears on the verge of breaking my anger. Not wanting him to see me upset, I yank my arm away and climb on my bike. I wish I had a car I could jump into and peel away in, showing my disgust with the squeal of my tires. Pedaling away on a bicycle with a basket and bell just doesn't have the same effect.

The floodgates open and tears stream down my face as I ride aimlessly away to berate myself. I really believed he liked me. How could I have been that stupid? No wonder it took him forever to make a move. I thought he was being chivalrous when really he was gathering the courage to kiss his "sister." Sister! How humiliating. Where's my mom at a time like this? She would find the whole situation perfect for her next book.

I pedal harder, trying to race away from the pain.

What is wrong with me? Am I that desperate, to be totally fooled by some cute guy who gives me an ounce of attention? I thought I was coming to this island to fix my problems but I've only substituted one pathetic existence for another. I escaped from home where I was so determined to fit in that I lost myself in the process. But I was no better here.

As I ride it dawns on me that the real problem isn't the kids back home or Niko or Mr. Mullins. The problem is me. Things don't work out well when I pretend to be something I'm not. I'm not the quiet meek wallflower I tried to be back in Lake Forest and I'm not the beach chick with the perfect life. Mr. Thompson has been right all along. I need to be true to myself. The problem is, how do you do that?

Please, God, help me to discover myself again. I know you made me just the way you wanted me to be—please give me confidence in that knowledge. And help me not to worry about what others think. Please guide me through these struggles to become the person you want me to be. Thanks. Amen.

My tour de failure has taken me down by the carnival, then back toward town. Eventually I end up at the hospital, somehow drawn there by a guiding force.

I peek in Ryan's room and am glad to see he's awake. He's propped up on his pillow, watching a baseball game in silence. He rolls his head toward me when I enter.

"Hey," he says.

"You look much better," I say and sit down next to him.

"You're not a very good liar."

"I'm serious, you've improved from looking like roadkill to death warmed over."

"You sure know how to make a guy feel good."

"Anytime."

"You, on the other hand, don't look so great. What's up?"

"Ryan, there's something I have to tell you."

"Sounds serious. Are you going to proclaim your undying love for me?"

I roll my eyes. "The person they arrested for your accident is Marco, Niko's cousin."

He looks at me for a long moment. "Are you telling me that your boyfriend tried to have me taken out?"

"No. Marco didn't do it." And I go on to explain what the Consuelos guys told me about the thefts in town, being blackmailed by Mr. Mullins, and their belief that Byron was the one who ran Ryan off the road.

He listens carefully, no emotion showing on his face at all.

"You believe them?" he finally asks.

"Yes. You should have seen them. They're terrified."

"Then I guess we inadvertently solved the mystery of the thefts."

"I guess so. I'm sorry I didn't work with you more on the investigation. If I had maybe we would have uncovered the truth sooner and you wouldn't be lying here now."

"I never really cared about solving the crime spree. I just wanted an excuse to spend time with you."

I try to smile.

"Josie, if what you say is true, then we've got to tell the police. We can't let an innocent person take the fall."

"I know, but it's complicated."

"How?"

"Well, Niko and his cousins are sure the police won't believe them and Mr. Mullins has more than enough evidence to pin the thefts on them. To complicate matters, I'm not sure what the relationship is between Aunt Lily and Tom Mullins."

He searches my face. "Is there something else you're not telling me?" Dang, he's perceptive.

The last thing I want to do is bare my soul to Ryan, but seeing him lying there completely vulnerable, I realize we've been through a lot together the last day or two. I risk the "I told you so" and go ahead and tell him about Mr. Mullins forcing Niko to date me.

"I guess my plan to be the girl with the hot summer romance is out of the question now," I attempt to joke.

"You don't need to be anyone other than yourself. You're amazing the way you are," he says.

I blush.

"I'm serious," he continues. "I think I've seen the real you from observing you back at home and from the time we've spent together here. You're like no one else I know, and I like that."

"But don't you ever feel like you have to act a certain way to fit in?"

"I guess when I feel that way I just focus on my youth group leader's advice about being yourself."

"Your youth group leader?" I wish I could take back the incredulous tone with which I responded.

"Yeah, Matt. He's the one who hooked me up with the Martins. They all went to college together."

"Hmm. I never thought of you as the youth group type."

"I told you there was a lot you didn't know about me."

"I'm beginning to believe that. So, what's his great advice?"

"Well, there's two parts. First, you need to spend as much time as possible with the people who make you feel comfortable—the ones you can safely share your dreams, secrets, and problems with. For instance, I could never share my feelings with the guys on the baseball team back home. They would totally judge me and never let me live it down. But my youth group would be completely supportive, so when I'm around them I'm being myself."

"Makes sense. I guess I'm lucky to have Liz. What's the second part?"

"Help others. When you help those less fortunate, you really start to see what's important and you don't have the time or need to pretend to be something else."

"That's exactly what Mr. Thompson told me. And that's why I was looking into the thefts," I say.

"Halfheartedly," he adds with a grin.

"You speak the truth. Well, I like this youth group leader of yours. I may have to come check it out for myself when we get home."

"Great. You'd like everyone."

"Too bad more people couldn't hear that advice. High school can be such a vicious cesspool."

"Yeah," he agrees, "but it won't last forever. Matt likes to remind us that lots of high school kids are trying to fit in and be something they're not so it's really hard to find good friends and yourself in that environment. But he says to hang in there because college is different—the people are more real and the social stigmas disappear."

"I hope that's true."

He smiles at me. "Listen, Josie, I'm sorry Niko hurt you."

"Thanks. You don't seem overly surprised though."

"I told you something didn't seem right with him."

"Because a guy like that wouldn't be interested in me?"

"Of course not, any guy would be lucky to be with you. No, it was the way he looked at you. It was a respectful look, not an I-can't-get-this-girl-out-of-my-mind look."

"Really?"

"Yep, I know that look well. I've perfected it," he says seriously.

I feel myself blush again.

"Josie, I told you it was fate that we were both here this summer. This wasn't exactly how I would have planned it but at least you finally got to know me."

This whole summer has been one convoluted mess. There's one guy who likes me and I don't believe it. And another one who I think likes me but really doesn't.

"Are you always this calm and confident?" I ask.

"It's called believing that things will turn out the way they are supposed to. Listen," he continues, "we were all duped by Mullins. He blackmailed the Consuelos family, forced them to do things they normally wouldn't have done. He fooled you and Lily. He stole from half the town and his madman nephew nearly killed me. He needs to be stopped."

"I know, but what do we do?"

"First, you should ask your aunt what's up between her and Mullins and see how close they are. Then somehow you need him or Byron to confess."

"And how exactly am I going to do that?"

"I don't know, you're the one who's supposed to be Nancy Drew," he says, sinking farther into his pillow.

"Mr. Thompson will be extremely disappointed in me. But seriously, any ideas?"

"Well, when you were in the musical *Thoroughly Modern Millie*, the main characters got the confession while hiding in a laundry cart."

I stare at him. "I still can't believe you've seen my shows."

"Why?"

"It's just hard to wrap my mind around that fact," I answer. "Maybe we could lure Byron to one of the mansions by telling him someone has a rare jewel on display. I could hide behind the grand piano. When he breaks in, I'll wait patiently until his hand is on the precious gem. Then I'll turn a spotlight on him to blind him. When he tries to run away I'll trip him since he won't be able to see well yet. He'll slide across the floor and I can take the piano bench and hit him on the head, knocking him out until the police arrive."

He looks at me. "I give up, what musical's that from?" he asks.

"Why do you think it's from a musical?"

"Because I know how your mind works."

"Well, it's not, I just made it up."

"You made all that up?" he asks.

"What? It could work."

He shakes his head and grins. "Maybe, if all the convoluted pieces of that plan fall together perfectly, you could catch Byron, who is probably the thief. But Tom Mullins might go free since he'd most likely let his own relative take the fall."

"Just like Ms. Hannigan tried to do in *Annie*," I agree.

"See, I knew it would somehow come back to a musical," he says triumphantly.

"Then let's hear your bright idea."

"Well, how would your mom write you out of the situation?" he asks.

"Hmm, let's see. She'd probably have me follow Mr. Mullins. I think he'll take the stolen goods on his boat and since I don't have a boat to drive I would need another way to track him."

"Mr. Hollis's helicopter?"

"No. Don't be silly, I don't know how to fly a helicopter. She'd most likely have me swim to the mainland while he loads the boat. Maybe I'd come across a random horse and gallop along the beach following him as he heads down the coast. Unfortunately, when I get off the horse to nab him my foot gets caught in the stirrup and I end up flat on my back with my leg suspended in air."

He chuckles then winces. "Don't make me laugh."

"Sorry."

"Did that really happen to you?"

"Hey, equestrian riding is trickier than it looks."

"All right, well, that plan's a bust." He thinks for a moment, then says, "You know, in *Rudolph the Red-Nosed Reindeer*, the abominable snow monster is lured to his demise by that cute little deer with the bow."

I can't help but giggle. "I think the nurse better decrease your pain meds; they might be affecting your brain."

"There's a thought—maybe we can load him up on narcotics."

"Truth serum."

"An invisibility cloak would be useful."

And so goes the afternoon, brainstorming until the nurse once again kicks me out.

Chapter 17

"I think I have an idea."

Niko sighs. "Jozay, I know you do feel bad for Marco but do not get involved, please," he says as he loads the *Jewel* with scuba tanks for a dive trip.

I have stopped by the marina to tell him my plan. His surprise to see me is obvious. After our painfully embarrassing breakup scene yesterday, I'm sure he thought he was done with me for good.

"I'm already involved and there is no way I'm going to let Marco be blamed for something he didn't do."

"What do you have in mind?" he asks, easily lifting the heavy oxygen tanks onto the deck of the boat.

"Somehow we've got to trap one of the Mullinses into confessing."

"That is not possible."

"We've got to at least try."

"But remember we were his accomplices. This I think ends badly for us no matter what. We cannot double-cross him."

"You can't let him keep blackmailing you, he'll never let you go. I know you don't want to be scared of him forever."

"But our families, they depend on us. If we go to jail or lose our jobs what will become of them? You have no understanding."

"He won't protect you. You will always be in danger of him pinning all of this on you. Has he moved the stolen merchandise to the storage unit yet?"

Niko stops working and sits down on one of the benches, probably resigned to the fact that despite his objections I won't let this drop.

"No, he grows more paranoid and will not draw attention to himself in case anyone is watching. But he told us in the next day or two to be ready to clear out the cave items to transport everything down the coast."

"It seems that we need to make a move before he takes everything away. You won't have any leverage once it's gone and have no access to any of it," I say.

"Maybe. But I think neither of them will ever tell us the whole plan. They are too smart."

"Which one do you think would be more likely to talk?"

"Byron. He is what you call a loose gun."

"Cannon?"

"Yes, loose cannon."

"We need to get him away from his uncle and lure the truth out of him."

"How?" he asks skeptically.

"Greed. That's what motivates them. I have an idea but I'm going to need your help as well."

"I guess it may be worth a try."

"Absolutely, you can't give up without a fight."

"Jozay, I did not know you were so strong. Can I ask why would you help us after I have hurt you?"

"I don't know, I feel like I've made a mess out of everything and need to fix it."

"Can you say what is the plan?" he asks.

"I'm still working on it but right now the wolves are circling and I need to go chat with Germany."

***

Cyd bursts into Spencer's shop, waves enthusiastically, and scurries over to my table. Her orange glasses match her bright orange T-shirt and socks. With Mr. Spencer still away, Val mans the counter. I ignore the suspicious look he sends my way.

"Josie!" she gushes. "I'm glad you called. I've been wanting to talk to you for weeks. I was afraid you were avoiding me."

"I'm sorry about that, Cyd. Where's your dad?" I'm surprised he actually let her out of his sight.

"He's across the street. He understood we needed some private girl time."

"I'm glad you could come. Hey, I've been wondering about your name. Is Cyd short for something?"

"No. My full name is Cyd Charisse Hollis."

"Cyd Charisse, like the famous dancer?" I ask.

"You know her!" Her excitement echoes off the walls, causing another glare from Val.

"Sure, she's in one of my favorite musicals, *Singing in the Rain*. That's a really cool name. I'm just named after my dad, Joe."

She shrugs. "My mom was hoping I'd be a graceful dancer like my namesake but it didn't really happen."

I smile as I remember her less than graceful twirls. "Well, Cyd," I say, ready to bite the bullet. "I need your help with something."

"Sure, anything!"

"First, there's something I need to confess."

"What?" She leans closer, excited to be my confidant.

"I lied to you. My mom is Tabitha Baker."

Her eyes widen before her face crinkles in confusion. "But why'd you lie?"

"I'm sorry. After *Saving Sadie* came out, the kids back at my high school were really cruel and teased me relentlessly because of all those embarrassing stories in the book. The worst part was that this time the book wasn't even about me. Anyway, the pranks and taunts became so bad, I had to leave. That's why I'm here this summer, to get away. I really didn't want anyone here to know about the book for fear the humiliation would happen again."

"I'm sorry they were mean. I know how that feels. But," she argues, "it's wonderful that your mom writes about you."

"No, not really. But the reason I'm telling you this is because I need your help. In exchange, I will answer all your questions about my mom. I will also have her send you signed copies of her books." I realize Cyd probably would have helped me anyway, but she deserves the truth.

"Wow!"

Val tenses at the loud screech as he wipes down the counter.

"What would you like to know?" I ask.

"Hmm. Tell me about your mom."

I debate telling her about the kooky postcard I received this morning of a tree with hundreds of hats dangling from its branches. While thinking of the card my mind wanders to the verse that accompanied it: 1 Peter 4:10 *Serve one another with whatever gift each of you has received.* It was oddly close to Chrissy's words of wisdom. I just wished I had some real gifts that could actually help Niko and Ryan. Wonder where one goes to find some useful ones. Too bad Paulie doesn't sell any of these types of gifts at his store. In the meantime I'm stuck with the plan at hand.

"Like, what do you and your mom do together?" Cyd asks when I continue to stare blankly off into space.

"Oh. Well, normal mother-daughter stuff, I suppose. We watch old movies together. We like to get our nails done. Oh, and we bake."

"She sounds wonderful," she gushes.

"Well, I'm sure you and your mom have special things you do together. I know you were recently in New York with her. That must have been fun."

"No. She's always frustrated with me for being clumsy and not glamorous like she is. But I don't see her very often. She lives in Paris with her new husband and doesn't really care to see me much."

Shocked, I don't know what to say. Here I thought this rich little girl had the ideal pampered life. I guess money can't buy everything.

Cyd continues, "After she left us, my dad brought home one of your mom's books. I loved it. She always has characters like me, that don't do the perfect thing and are always in crazy predicaments. But it always turns out great in the end for these girls. When I heard that Ms. Baker wrote about her daughter, I was super excited. I knew there was someone out there just like me. And this girl made people laugh and feel good about themselves. See, I knew that even if my mom didn't think I was great, other people could."

Tears well up in my eyes. I had no idea my stupid foibles could help anyone.

Cyd smiles excitedly. "So, what can I help you with?"

***

Feeling energized after finalizing the details of the plan, I head to the hospital, armed with flowers and chocolate. Even if our plan doesn't work at least we're going down fighting. The front desk tells me Ryan's new room number. He has improved enough to leave the ICU and has been moved to a step-down unit.

I enter his new room but he's not there. Along the wall, hanging above a small couch, is a huge get-well banner signed by his baseball team. I place the gifts on the side table before I venture to the nurses' station.

"Excuse me, do you know where Ryan McNaulty is? Was he taken somewhere for tests or something?"

The elderly nurse smiles at me. "No, he conned the candy striper into taking him to the pediatric wing."

I follow the signs up two floors and down a long corridor. The primary colors of the walls are in such stark contrast to the rest of the drab white hospital. It's like Dorothy leaving Kansas and entering Oz.

Near the nurses' station is a large lounge where an animated movie plays on a large TV. Several children watch the show while others play with toys. Ryan, in his wheelchair, is at a table with four little kids playing a board game. His broken leg sticks straight out and an IV pole stands next to him. Two of the children at the table are bald. I assume they are cancer patients, their tiny little size heartbreaking. How can life be that unfair?

I stand there and watch, amazed at how easily he interacts with them. They laugh and joke with him, obviously thriving under his attention. I've seen him with the Martin family so I knew he was great with kids, but this is something else. These kids are sick. I've spent a lot of years babysitting and I know I would feel uncomfortable coming down here and playing with them. It's great to see this caring side of him.

Ryan finally sees me and waves me over. He introduces me to the kids and explains he just lost an intense game of Candy Land. After they convince me to join them I choose the little blue person and start down the path of the game I used to beg my mom to play, over and over.

Before we reach the Candy Castle, the nurses come to gather everyone for lunch. Ryan promises the disappointed kids that he'll come back later.

"Well, do you feel up to being my private nurse? I can't make it back up to my room by myself."

"Um, sure, I guess. What do I have to do?"

"Don't worry, I won't make you change my catheter." He laughs, probably at my mortified face.

I push his wheelchair while he pulls the IV pole along.

"You really must have spent a lot of time at hospitals," I say as I carefully avoid banging his outstretched leg into the elevator. "I didn't realize baseball was such an extreme sport."

"Actually it wasn't me in the hospital, I was just visiting with my mom. She's a physical therapist and used to take me with her to interact with her patients."

"Oh." This new information does not click at all with the image of Ryan and his family I have had all summer long. That doesn't sound like the uncaring mother on her luxury vacation that I had pictured in my mind.

"Mrs. Martin said your parents are on a cruise."

"Yeah, I finally spoke with them and told them I'm fine and not to cut the trip short."

"Are they somewhere exotic?"

He laughs. "I wouldn't call cruising with cartoon characters and princesses exotic. They took my sister on her dream cruise," he explains.

"Without you?" I ask, trying to figure out the situation.

"They took me on one when I was her age. They wanted to postpone 'til after my season when I could go but I told them I'd pass. A whole week of character dinners sounds like torture."

"I can understand that."

"Hey, there's a balcony down the hall from my room. I would love some fresh air, do you mind taking me there?"

"Sure."

Once we make it through the doorway, I try to situate him in a spot with a beautiful view of the ocean.

"When you get home this leg of yours will be tough to maneuver around those parties," I say as I inch him around a table.

"What parties?"

"You know, the ones that all you popular kids get invited to," I tease.

"I told you, I don't hang out with that group."

"But you're a jock, you must get invited. You don't go to any?"

"When I made varsity last year I went with the team once but I quickly realized it wasn't my scene."

"Why not?"

"That crowd is not cool. There are a few that are rude, mean, and involved in stuff they shouldn't be. The rest just follow along, afraid if they say anything in opposition they'll be outcasts, too."

"Oh." Somehow Liz and I always thought hanging out with the "in" crowd and being invited to their parties would be cool and fun.

He grins. "Sorry. If you were hoping to use me to get in with the party crowd, you're out of luck."

"No." Surprisingly, none of that seems important at all anymore. "I hate that our school's like that. I wish we could change the atmosphere there," I add.

"I bet if anyone could do it, it would be you," he says, smiling at me.

"I think your confidence in me is misplaced."

"I have faith you could accomplish anything you set your mind to."

"Hmm. I'm not so sure about that."

"You know, you should come with me to my youth group sometime and meet some genuinely nice people," he says.

"I'd really like that. My church doesn't have much of a youth group."

"Ours is great, we do a lot together. In fact, I was supposed to go with a bunch of them this summer and work at a camp."

"Right. Mrs. Martin mentioned you were going to be a counselor."

"Yeah, we did it last year and had a blast. The kids were great. But I couldn't pass up this opportunity to play baseball for the Pirates."

"Too bad. If you were at that camp, hiking and singing campfire songs, you wouldn't have nearly died."

"But I wouldn't have gotten to know you then."

"Well, I'm not sure getting to know me is worth surgery, months of rehabilitation, and ending your baseball season, but I agree it was nice to get to know you, too."

"Glad to hear it." He grins his McNaughty grin, but on his bruised and gashed face it looks more vulnerable and less mischievous.

"After I was so rudely kicked out last night by your by-the-book-nurse, I think I figured out a plan to trick Mr. Mullins."

"Oh, this should be good." He leans back to listen, obviously expecting another crazy idea. But as I lay out my actual plan his face loses its easygoing expression and hardens in concern.

"Josie, that's stupid. You can't put yourself in danger like that."

"You agreed we can't let an innocent person be sent away. And I have to make sure the person who did this to you pays. Besides, the Bible says, '*If God is with us then who can be against us*,'" I say, proud I remembered the verse.

"God of course protects us but that doesn't mean you should put yourself in a dangerous situation. Bad things can happen to good people. Josie, you can't do this on your own. If Byron Mullins is evil enough to run me off the road who knows what he's capable of."

"I'll be safe. Besides, Niko will be there to protect me."

His face darkens further.

"What's the matter?"

"I should be the one to protect you."

Chapter 18

"Lily, my dear, thank you for inviting me to dinner," Mr. Mullins says after he kisses her cheek. He enters the cottage, armed with a huge bouquet of roses—charming and polished as usual. I watch them closely but still can't tell how she feels about him. They seem compatible yet it doesn't look like they're about to start singing about their undying love when they look into each other's eyes. But what do I know about matters of the heart; I fell for cute dimples and an alluring Spanish accent.

"I wish I could take credit, but this little dinner party was Josie's idea," Lily answers.

"Well, it was a superb suggestion, Josie," he adds as he takes the glass of wine I offer him.

I shrug. "It seemed like a fun idea."

"Jozay's ideas are good always." Niko comes up behind me, his arm around my waist, continuing the farce that we are a happy couple.

"Josie," says Mr. Mullins, "Lily told me it was your friend Ryan that was involved in Marco's accident. I hope he's doing better."

Good time to flex my acting muscles. "Thanks for your concern. He's going to make a full recovery."

"I felt horrible that Ryan was injured and felt I should explain why I hired a lawyer for Marco." He makes a great villain—evil lurking underneath his smooth, polished demeanor.

I force a smile. "Niko told me how Marco lost control of the truck on the wet roads and panicked when he hit Ryan, since he's not a citizen. He said you felt sorry for him and wanted to help because he's been a faithful employee."

"Yes. I honestly believe it was an accident. I know you told Lily you thought it was deliberate but I don't agree. How extraordinary that you witnessed the whole thing," he says, taking a sip of wine.

I should have known Lily would have told him everything. "Well, I was pretty shaken up after watching him plunge over the cliff. But after thinking about it for a few days, I also realized Marco would never try to hurt Ryan."

"Good." He smiles. "Hopefully this whole situation will work out."

"Yes, hopefully."

"Tom, these flowers are beautiful," Aunt Lily says. "Can you help me get a vase for them?"

"Of course," he says and follows her and her sixties-style dress into the kitchen.

When the doorbell rings, I take a deep breath. *Please, God, help this plan to work.*

Even though I know who will be on the other side of the door, it takes me a moment to recognize the man in front of me. Mr. Hollis has completely transformed. Gone is the ridiculous toupee, the baseball cap, and the polyester jogging suit. Tonight he looks like the Hollywood producer he is, wearing an expensive sport coat, dress pants, and crisp button-down shirt.

"Josie!" Cyd squeals and rushes in to hug me. She looks festive in a Hawaiian sundress. Her glasses of course match the blue of the ocean on the fabric.

"I'm glad you could make it." I had been worried she wouldn't be able to convince her slightly reclusive dad to come.

"Mr. Hollis, you look so . . . so . . . great," I add.

"I made him ditch his disguise for the evening," Cyd says proudly.

"Disguise?"

"He likes to blend in when he's on vacation."

"I find that if I wear designer clothes it's hard to go unnoticed. But if I dress in my jogging suits people treat me like a normal person, even if they know who I am," he explains.

"Oh, well, you look really handsome tonight."

"Mr. Hollis," Tom Mullins says, coming out of the kitchen with outstretched hand. "I didn't realize you would be joining us this evening. What a wonderful surprise."

"I usually don't come to many dinner parties but Cyd insisted. How's the restaurant business these days?"

"Wonderful," he answers, pumping Mr. Hollis's arm. "Have I told you about my new dinner cruise venture? I'm expanding my business and looking for some investors to join me."

"Shall we go out on the porch? Our other guests are there," Lily says, unintentionally—I think—but nevertheless rescuing Mr. Hollis from a sales pitch.

We all join Mr. and Mrs. Thompson out on the porch. Cyd and Kahlua immediately bond over a game of fetch. The two of them are a match made in heaven, both blessed with an abundance of energy. Niko hands Mr. Hollis a glass of wine and introductions are made. Typical small talk accompanies the appetizers that Lily serves.

Mr. Hollis seems uncomfortable and watches Cyd intently. But his second glass of wine starts to relax him. After some gentle coaxing he begins to boast about Lily's restoration work. Which leads to a long discussion about his private art collection. He's in his element describing his favorite pieces to the rapt audience. I can see Mr. Mullins' greedy mind churning behind his cool demeanor. It must be driving him crazy, Mr. Hollis's collection tantalizingly close but his alarm system impenetrable.

After Niko and I help Lily bring dinner out to the porch, we all settle around the table, the glistening ocean the perfect backdrop to our scene.

"I think a toast is in order," says Mr. Mullins.

"Josie, since this was your idea, would you do the honors?" asks Aunt Lily. Everyone raises their glasses and looks at me.

"Sure," I answer with no idea what to say. Toasting is new to me. But I turn to what I do know, and try to remember the wise words of Tevye from *Fiddler on the Roof*. "To each of us and our great fortunes. Much happiness. Good health and long life. L'chaim!"

The smiles turn quizzical before Mr. Thompson sounds a hearty, "Mazel tov!"

The others join in. "Cheers!"

"Everything looks very delicious," Niko politely says to Aunt Lily.

"Thank you, Niko. I keep forgetting to ask how Larry is holding up."

"Mr. Spencer will be fine. He continues his rest. The break-in and Marco's accident are still hard on him."

"I was shocked that all the businesses in town were robbed during the storm," says Mr. Hollis.

"A travesty," agrees Mr. Mullins.

"Are you still investigating the thefts, Josie?" asks Mrs. Thompson.

"No. Without Ryan to help I think I'll leave it to the professionals," I answer.

"That sounds like a smart idea," says Aunt Lily. "Things have really escalated and it could be dangerous."

"Dear, you should tell everyone your new scheme," says Mrs. Thompson, deftly changing the subject.

"Team?" hollers Mr. Thompson, pretending not to hear. "What team?"

"No, the crazy idea you were telling me about this afternoon."

"Oh no, now what?" teases Lily.

"It's not crazy. I've been doing a lot of research."

"Let me guess, something about World War II?" I ask.

"Well, that's what got me thinking. Josie, remember how I told you about the German sub that some divers found off the coast of New Jersey?"

"Of course," I reply.

"The way they first realized that the U-boat was there was because of seagulls." He states it matter-of-factly, like we should all know what he's talking about.

"I'm not following," says Lily.

"Divers often locate shipwrecks that way."

"That's right, I've read that," says Mr. Hollis. "Plankton grows on the decaying shipwreck, which causes fish to swarm the area to feast on the plankton."

"Yes," says a gleeful Mr. Thompson, thrilled someone understands him. "And then the seagulls congregate since there is an abundance of fish."

"And this is relevant because . . ." Mr. Mullins prompts.

"As some of you know, I've always been interested in pirate folklore, especially the tales that surround Shipwreck Cove."

"There were pirates here?!" exclaims Cyd.

"Yes, that's one of the reasons I chose to build on this island," explains her father.

"Well," continues Mr. Thompson, "it has always been assumed that the little pirate vessel sank after hitting the cliffs."

"Because that's where the wreck is," says Mr. Mullins.

"I want to see the wreck!" Cyd jumps in.

"Niko takes snorkeling tours to the site," I tell her.

"Really?! Please, Daddy, can we go?"

"Sure, honey, we'll do that this week," says Mr. Hollis, appeasing his daughter. "Mr. Thompson, please continue."

"What if the boat actually crashed into rocks farther out and then the current brought the doomed vessel in closer to shore?"

"That's a possibility," says Niko. "There are very many rocks off the coast."

"I see where you're going with this. That would mean the treasure could be farther off the coast," ponders Mr. Hollis. "Since everyone assumed it had been brought to shore they never looked farther out. Just think, it could still be there."

"Treasure!" Cyd screeches.

"On my daily walks, I've noticed a consistent gathering of seagulls a half mile or so out from the cliffs," states Mr. Thompson. "I never thought anything of it until I read the book about the discovery of the German sub."

"I have noticed the birds as well," agrees Niko.

"But wouldn't the treasure be too far down to dive for?" Mr. Mullins asks. "The ocean floor drops off sharply."

"Actually," says Niko, "there are sand bars and mounds of coral around there. We must show caution and navigate around the shallower areas when we bring the tourists into the cove."

"Fascinating," Mr. Hollis says, leaning back in his chair.

"Well, that is quite an interesting theory," adds Tom Mullins.

"I have a buddy who loves to dive and has agreed to humor me and come next week to help me check it out," says Mr. Thompson.

"You really could be on to something," Mr. Hollis agrees.

"Please, please, *please*, Daddy. Can we search for pirate treasure?" pleads Cyd.

"You know, I have a crew that just finished filming down in Florida. What if I have them come and check it out? I bet I could get them here in a couple of days," says Mr. Hollis, almost as enthusiastically as his daughter.

"While they're here, they should check out the cave on the beach. That's where people thought the treasure could be hidden," I add helpfully.

"A cave on the beach!" Cyd gasps. "This place is way cooler than I thought."

"Great idea," says Mr. Hollis. "I'll have them film everything. This could be the project I've been dreaming of."

"Don't you need some permits or something?" Mr. Mullins asks, his index finger tapping the table.

"Not for this research phase, it's all public land."

"Hmm, wouldn't that be something if you found the pirate treasure," says Aunt Lily.

"See, dear, they don't think my ponderings are outrageous," Mr. Thompson says as he nudges his wife.

We move on to other topics during dessert. But, by the way he squirms and doesn't engage in the conversation, I can tell Mr. Hollis can no longer concentrate, excited about the possibilities of the project. And Mr. Mullins contributes less to the conversation than before.

Overall I'd say it was an enjoyable evening. If you can call it enjoyable when all evening I had to resist the urge to stab Mr. Mullins with the steak knife and pull away from Niko every time he touched me. (I'm still a bit perturbed by the whole "sister" comment.) However, the key lime pie was delicious.

The Thompsons are the last to head home.

"How'd I do, kiddo?" Mr. Thompson whispers in my ear as I hug him goodnight.

"You deserve a standing ovation." All my accomplices played their parts perfectly. None of them knew the whole story, except for Niko. I couldn't risk someone not believing me about the thefts and spilling the beans to Mr. Mullins.

"I've been wondering," I say as I help Lily clean up and load the dishwasher, "is there anything going on between you and Mr. Mullins?"

"Oh, is that what this evening was about? Matchmaking?"

Yeah, like I'd match you up with an insurance-scamming, blackmailing crook. "It kinda seems like you two are more than friends," I say.

"You are observant. It's a complicated relationship. He's been pursuing me. At first I was quite interested. I mean, he's a handsome, intelligent, successful man. But to tell you the truth something hasn't felt right. There's something under the surface that I don't quite feel comfortable with. I don't know, it's hard to explain."

"No, that makes complete sense. Wait for the man of your dreams." When the phone rings, I grab it and shut myself in my room. "Hello?"

"It is me," says Niko. "I hope you do not plan on sleep tonight. Mr. Mullins took your bait. He has ordered me to take Byron tonight and clear out the cave."

"Excellent. We'll capture the move on video."

"Not only that but his greed is so great, he wants to search for your imaginary treasure. I am to take him in the morning to the seagull area for a preliminary dive to check for the treasure."

"Good, while you keep him occupied off shore, I'll follow Byron. If we keep watching them, sooner or later one will accidently show us where the items they stole during the storm are kept. Eventually they'll have to move everything and we'll catch them red-handed. Thanks for letting me know. I'll see you in a little while."

"Jozay, thank you very much for helping my family. You are very special."

I hang up, then dial Ryan. Somehow my quick call to update him on the situation turns into a two-hour conversation. We discover we both love miniature golf, old Hitchcock movies, and spumoni ice cream. We commiserate over the pros and cons of having younger siblings. We share our favorite holiday memories. And we debate who is the greatest superhero. We would have talked longer except the nurse makes him get off the phone so she can check his vitals. Geez, they are such sticklers at that place.

Chapter 19

Some may call me sheltered, but I have actually never snuck out of a house before. I guess I never had the need. But using a door at Aunt Lily's in the middle of the night is out of the question. Kahlua, with her bionic hearing, goes crazy whenever she hears one of the doors open, sure she's about to go on a walk.

Sneaking out doesn't seem like it would be that difficult, especially from a one-story beach house. But the multistep process is trickier than I thought. First, you have to open the window, which during the day seems a relatively quiet operation, but at one-thirty in the morning the gentle squeak amplifies to ridiculous loudness. After the window is open wide enough to fit your body through, you must crawl out without hitting your head or scraping yourself on the metal track of the window sill. Then you must gently drop to the ground, careful to miss the prickly bush, which I was not entirely successful at.

Surprisingly, the gorgeous beach, inviting during the day and romantic at twilight, is absolutely frightening in the middle of the night—every twig a possible rabid animal waiting to attack, the usually lovely beach grasses now hiding places for whatever evil lurks in the night. And thank the good Lord that when I reach the cave the deformed shadow that staggers toward me is not some monster but actually Niko.

"I was afraid you maybe fell asleep and I would have to wake you by not disturbing Kahlua and Lily," he whispers.

"There was no way I could sleep. I'm so nervous. You know, somehow this plan sounded better in the daylight."

"It will work. It has to." He takes my hand and expertly leads me through the all-encompassing blackness of the passageway in the rocks. Tonight I'm less worried about disease-carrying bats than running into a madman and his evil uncle. Once inside the cave he drops my hand then travels the circumference to turn on the battery-operated lanterns.

I guess I was expecting piles of merchandise covered in tarps or something but there is still nothing in the cave except for the pirate chests. "So where is everything? In the chests?"

"No, those actually do hold the supplies of the tours."

I wander the space examining the crevices in the rocks but see no other hidden area. He smiles, takes off his shoes, and proceeds to climb the far wall of the cave. When he nears the top it becomes obvious there is a ledge at the top that is not apparent from down below.

Niko reaches into the darkness and tosses down a bundle. A rope ladder unfurls down the natural rock wall. He motions for me to come forward and I climb the ladder to the high ledge. Only more blackness greets me. Niko hands me his diving survival ring, a set of tools on a metal ring that clips onto his BCD scuba vest. It holds anything he may need in case of an underwater emergency— a flashlight, compass, small knife, and metal ball to bang on your tank to get everyone's attention. I turn on the flashlight and the near-invisible space lights up. It reminds me of the bed above the cab of my grandparents' camper, a long compact ledge. Not exactly Solomon's gold but it's full of boxes and carefully wrapped items.

"This is amazing. It's completely invisible from down below," I say, fascinated.

"I know. A perfect hiding spot. Even with all the visitors I bring through, no one can be suspect of anything being kept here."

"I wonder who discovered this."

"I do not know. It would make a good place to hide the pirate treasure, no? This is where you can videotape our conversation. He cannot see you from the shadows." He hands me a small duffel, which holds the underwater video camera he uses on his dives. "I must go to meet Byron at the marina. We are to bring the *Jewel of the Sea* over for loading. You will be all right?"

"I'm fine."

"Keep the flashlight, the darkness of this cave is great." He turns to climb down.

"Niko, this will work," I say in encouragement to his worried face, but also to convince myself.

"I hope so."

I pull the rope ladder up and can't help but shudder when Niko turns off the lanterns. He was right about the complete darkness. I can't even see my hand in front of my face. It's beyond overwhelming, more like insane asylum scary. I quickly turn on the flashlight.

Dear God, thanks for helping everything go smoothly so far. I would greatly appreciate it if you could make this part of the plan work as well. Thanks. Amen.

To pass the time, and keep myself from totally freaking about the weird shadows, I peak into the boxes and under the bubble wrap. The amount of items the Mullinses have stolen surprises me. I try to videotape the loot but am pretty sure there is not enough light for it to turn out. After a thorough investigation I move on to reciting the Bible verse Ryan shared with me—*Do not fear for I am with you.* I keep repeating it until a sense of calm washes over me. Continuing with my good faith effort to rely on God, I move on to recalling the Bible verses my mom sent me this summer. When I make it through my new repertoire I shift to my comfort zone and silently sing show tunes, but I stick with songs from *Joseph and the Amazing Technicolor Dreamcoat*, figuring that's pretty close to biblical recitation.

As I try to remember the words to "Benjamin Calypso," a Bible verse I didn't realize I even knew pops into my head. *Trust in the Lord with all your heart and do not rely on your own understanding.* Suddenly it all comes together in my mind. The words of wisdom from Mr. Thompson, the priest's soul-searching advice, the comfort and understanding of Aunt Lily, and my mom's inspirational postcards, they all make sense. Each of them has been trying to tell me in their own way but now sitting here in the dark cave unsure what the future holds, I know they are right. I can never stop bad things from happening but I can trust in God to get me through them. That's all I need—faith.

So, that's how God speaks to us—through our thoughts. Coolest. Thing. Ever.

Dear God. You are truly amazing. Thanks for speaking to me and helping me know I'm on the right track. You really are my lighthouse, guiding me through the storms. I give this whole situation to you. Please protect us tonight and help us to uncover the truth. Amen.

By the time I hear Niko's voice I am full of hope. I switch off the flashlight, once again plunged into darkness.

"Let me lead the way for you."

"Don't be an idiot, turn on a flashlight," Byron snaps.

"I did not bring one. I will go to turn on the lanterns," answers Niko. Soon a faint glow fills the cave.

Niko climbs the wall to once again retrieve the rope ladder. The panicked look in his eyes worries me. Suddenly I'm not sure he can pull this off. After all, he's not a trained thespian. Can he be convincing? To offer reassurance, I reach out and squeeze his hand. He nods, tosses down the ladder, then jumps down. I position myself against the rocks and start to record. The moment I see Byron I know we've got a problem. He's wearing a baseball cap pulled low over his forehead, shadowing his face. I don't think he will be recognizable on the video.

"What's wrong with you, Niko? Get back up there and hand down the stuff," Byron demands.

"No, not yet," answers Niko.

Byron stops pacing and looks at him.

"I want some answers first," declares Niko.

"What are you talking about?"

"I am tired of doing what you order. Before I help I want to know the truth. What happened with that boy and Marco's truck?"

Byron laughs. "Get back up there and hand down the items or I'll climb up myself."

Uh-oh.

"I have lied to good people and hid every stolen item. You can tell me the truth at least."

Byron scrutinizes him. "What're you after?"

"Just the truth. I do not care about your money. You have something far more valuable, my cousin's future—his life."

"Sorry, Niko, all roads lead back to the Consuelos boys, including fingerprints on all the stolen items. I don't think you want to add theft to Marco's list of charges, do you?"

"I know you were who ran that boy off the road."

"Prove it," he challenges.

Oh no. Come on, Niko, at least call him by his name.

"You could help Marco. You could make someone to come forward and verify Marco's claim that he was with us. Somewhere must be surveillance cameras to prove it. You could tell a story about a teenager who took Marco's truck for some fun."

"Niko, you're really not in a position to bargain," he says, amused.

"I can refuse to help you now. You cannot move everything by sunrise alone. You could take some of it but the rest would be in my hands."

"Then I call the police anonymously and they find the items here with your prints all over them."

"Until Marco is free, I will not tell you the coordinates for the treasure location," he says, using his last bargaining chip. He may be gorgeous but a negotiator he is not.

"Who cares, we could hire someone else to dive for it."

"Yes, but by the time someone new is hired the film crew of Mr. Hollis will be here. Or I may dive down to search for treasure myself."

"At the moment I don't care about possible pirate treasure. Get up there and start handing down the stuff or I call the police and tell them where Marco hid the items he stole during the storm."

"He did not steal anything."

"That will be hard to prove when they find evidence in your apartment."

"There is not anything in our apartment."

"There can be very quickly. You and your cousins went into business with me and you are not pulling out of this deal now."

Silence.

It didn't work. Poor Niko looks completely defeated when he climbs back up to start handing down all the stolen merchandise. He knows he blew it. I've got to think of a way to salvage the plan.

With shaking hands he lowers down one item at a time. Soon the hidden shelf is empty and all the items are piled on the sand in the cave. Niko and Byron take their first load out. Hours seem to tick by as they take load after load to the raft then transport them to the *Jewel* waiting offshore.

While they are gone I play back the video. There's not enough here to go to the police. With his disguise you can't tell it's Byron and with no evidence or confession there is no smoking gun. All it proves is that the Consuelos guys were working with an accomplice. If we turn this over and try to convince them it was Byron it may hurt Marco even worse because the video shows Niko with all the stolen merchandise. It could sound like they are trying to frame Mr. Mullins, who is an upstanding citizen of the community. I need more. We either need a confession or some video showing Byron's face; at least that would give us some credibility. I'm going to have to follow them when they leave with the last of the items and try and get something on tape.

Soon I hear Byron's voice.

"No, Niko. I got this last load, you keep an eye out."

I watch as he grabs the final remaining heavy box of items then disappears through the rock passage. Carefully I climb down the rope ladder, feeling like a super spy. I sneak across the cave and silently make my way out. I inch forward out of the rocks, trying to locate Byron and Niko on the still dark beach, when my arm is violently yanked from behind.

"Well, well, well, if it isn't Niko's little toy," snarls Byron. I try to squirm away but his grip tightens, cutting off the circulation in my arm. He spins me toward him. "I knew something was up. Come on, time to join him." With his free hand he grabs my bag that holds the camera, but I cling to it.

For some weird reason, Liz's goofy words of advice ring through my head: *my special talents will help with the problems I face.* And just like that a vision of when I was on the swing and did my Hot Box Girl's high kick from *Guys and Dolls*, and nailed Ryan in the family jewels, comes to me.

I picture my dance and focus all my energy into my kick. With as much force as I can muster, I knee him in the intended target. Byron Mullins' eyes bug out and he bends over in pain. Then with a straight-legged can-can kick, I nail him in the chin. His head snaps back and his grip loosens. I yank the bag from his hand and swing it hard into his head. He drops to the sand like dead weight. Wow. I can't believe that worked. Thanks, Liz.

He's probably not down for long. I scan the beach for Niko. The small raft clings to the beach and I can make out the dark great mass of the *Jewel of the Sea* bobbing in the ocean. But there is no sign of Niko.

Where is he? Byron said it was time for me to join him. Hopefully that meant out on the boat and not dead on the bottom of the ocean.

With a great deal of self-coaxing I force myself to reach into Byron's jeans pocket, trying to find his phone or the key to the raft. Eww, eww. Gross.

Nothing. His pockets are empty. Now what? He's onto us now so we have to get his confession or it's over.

Byron groans and starts to stir.

I stare out at the inky darkness of the ocean toward the bobbing *Jewel*, picturing all the known and unknown creatures that lurk beneath the surface: sharks, eels, stingrays, giant killer squids.

A plan starts to formulate.

Byron shifts onto his knees and shakes his head. He stares at me, hatred in his eyes.

I sprint toward the ocean. Locating the knife on the survival ring, I quickly stab the blade into the raft, momentarily relieved by the sound of escaping air. I drape the camera bag across my body, then with a sign of the cross plunge into the ocean. As I swim in the darkness toward the *Jewel* I pray that I can outswim Byron. He doesn't look like he's in the best shape but for all I know he could be a champion triathlete. The distance from the boat to the shore seems a lot farther tonight than when Niko and I swam it that first day we went snorkeling. Of course swimming in wet clothing and carrying the camera bag contribute to the slow going. When I turn on my back to relieve the sharp pain in my side I see Byron standing above the raft. He curses, pulls off his shoes, shirt, and jeans, then splashes into the ocean with just his boxers on. I'll give him credit, he thought through this whole swimming-with-clothes-on thing a little better than I.

At last I reach the boat. Before I climb the ladder I check behind me. Byron has swum about a third of the way to the boat. With a huge breath of air I dive down to clip Niko's dive tools onto the metal handle that Niko uses for towing the raft, and make sure to turn the flashlight on. I scramble up the ladder then pull it up behind me, making it nearly impossible for Byron to board the boat. Except of course if he climbs the anchor line, which I have no idea how to raise.

"Niko!" I scream and dodge around all the items from the cave now cluttering the deck.

A pounding down in the cabin leads me to a thick wooden door. Wondering how Niko let Byron trick him, I undo the two deadbolts. The door flies open and we run back up to the deck.

"I'm so glad to see you, Jozay," says Niko.

"I was afraid he killed you," I breathlessly say to him.

"Where is he?"

"Come on, we need pull up the anchor," I order. He raises it as Byron reaches the boat.

"Let me on board!" Byron screams as he treads water alongside the *Jewel*.

We stare down at him. The dive light illuminates his scrawny white legs as he treads water. He paws at the side of the boat trying to hang on to something but only finds the smooth siding.

"What happened?" Niko asks me.

"He figured it out and was waiting for me when I left the cave. We don't have enough evidence on the tape. We have to make him confess."

"I screwed it up," he says, running his hand through his hair.

"Oh well, on to plan B."

"There is a plan B?"

"Sort of. Now that he found us out we've got to get the rest of the information out of him now."

"How?"

"Do you have a searchlight on board to shine in the water?"

He looks confused, then quickly understands. "Jellyfish?"

"Jellyfish." I nod.

He shines the bright beam of his spotlight on Byron.

"What're you doing?" He squints at the blinding beam. "Niko, your family is ruined," screams Byron. "Ow!" He slaps at his arm, then his chest. "What is that?"

"Jellyfish," I say as I pull out the camera, praying it still works after Byron's hard head smashed into it. "They're always worse after storms."

"They are drawn by the light," Niko adds.

Byron starts a manic dance, his pale white legs flailing in the water as he is swarmed by jellyfish, whose mushroomy bubble-heads rhythmically bob around him. The scene oddly resembles spaghetti noodles bouncing in a pot of boiling water.

"I'm not sure you can make it back to shore," I tell him.

"This spotlight will follow you the whole way," Niko says.

Byron's face shape-shifts in agony as the pink tentacles continue to lash at him.

"I think too many stings can be dangerous," I say.

"People have died," Niko tells him. "We will help you if you give us answers."

"Yes, Byron Mullins, tell us why you and your uncle, Tom Mullins, have been robbing everyone on the island."

"I don't know what you're talking about," he screams. His head sinks slightly underwater, exhausted from the struggle and pain.

"Okay. We'll leave you just like you left Ryan after you ran him off the road. Niko, start up the engine." I seriously hope Byron doesn't call my bluff because I don't know if I could really leave him out here alone.

"We did give a chance to him," Niko says, then he turns toward the boat's controls.

"Wait! Please help."

"Talk," I say. "And remember this is your chance to come out ahead. I'm sure your uncle will be more than happy to pin all this on you."

"Fine," he gasps. "I'm not dying for this. He's overextended on all his credit from buying this dumb boat. And stupid enough to already have signed the purchase agreement for a dinner cruiser. With insurance fraud and the black market he thought he found an easy way to raise capital 'til the new business lines started to succeed."

"Where are the items you stole during the storm?" I ask.

"In the storm shelter at Tom's house."

He reaches his hand toward us, genuine fear in his eyes. His head bobs under the water again. "Please . . ."

"First tell us about Ryan's accident," I say.

"The kid was nosing around too much. We needed him to stay away so I ran him off the road."

I sigh in relief. *Thank you, Jesus!*

Niko lowers the ladder and reaches an arm to Byron. He pulls Byron onboard and Byron collapses on the deck. I grimace at the swollen red streaks that cover his body, scourged by jellyfish tentacles.

"Jozay, there is still vinegar downstairs for the stings."

"I was going to offer to pee on him," I state.

Byron tries to snarl at me but his lip is grotesquely swollen and doesn't move.

"Hey, just trying to help. I hear it's an effective remedy."

Niko zip-ties Byron's arms behind his back. "Okay, I will radio help."

Thank you, God, for this incredible summer, for helping me find myself, for bringing amazing people into my life, and for showing me that the stuff at home doesn't matter.

You are the best. Amen.

***

The next twenty-four hours are intense.

We spend forever at the police station. A freezing interrogation room full of skeptical officers carrying loaded weapons is not exactly the most fun place to be in the middle of the night. You wouldn't believe how hard it is to convince people that a pillar of the community can be the thief in their midst. Even with Byron's taped confession they were reluctant to believe us. But eventually they got a search warrant for the restaurant and Mr. Mullins' home.

Later, a detective told us that all the items that had been reported stolen just days before during the storm had indeed been in Mr. Mullins' storm shelter. He also explained to us the hit-and-run charges would be dropped against Marco but that he, Niko, and their cousins were accomplices, even if it was under duress. He recommended they get a good lawyer.

Aunt Lily is shocked about Mr. Mullins and the whole situation. I'm sure she feels betrayed by him. She tells me she's disappointed that I took such a dangerous risk and didn't confide in her. But I can tell she's proud of me for being so tough and helping someone besides myself.

My parents are stunned when we call and tell them the story. At first my dad is furious that I was involved in an illegal situation. I'm sure he's going to order me to come home, but when I enlist his help in finding a good lawyer for Marco and all the Consuelos boys, he feels useful and calms down.

My mom bombards me with a million questions, but instead of being annoyed at her overprotectiveness, I realize that I miss her. I suddenly miss our chats when she'd put everything on hold and make me an after-school snack. I miss our chick flick nights when we'd curl up with bowls of cereal. I miss how she decorates for every season, making the house a home. Time really does heal all wounds, I guess.

Mr. Thompson can't stop bragging how he knew all along that he and I would solve the mystery. Mr. Spencer is thrilled that Marco will be cleared and that his retirement won't be in jeopardy.

I, however, am not allowed to set foot out of the house until I'm old and gray, so I can't get to the hospital to see Ryan. But we talk on the phone, a lot. We continue to get to know each other and discuss ideas about making some changes around the school, like creating a safe haven in the lunchroom where everyone can hang out no matter what group they belong in. Mostly he's relieved that the plan worked, but he makes me swear not to save the day ever again without him. I agree and promise to stop by when things calm down and the adults stop hovering.

Chapter 20

Finally, after some coaxing and begging, Aunt Lily agrees to let me go to the hospital. I can't believe how anxious I am to see Ryan. My heart still leaps in my throat whenever I remember the kiss we shared in the lighthouse. I'm annoyed at all the time I wasted misjudging him. He's not at all what I thought he was. Since the accident, I've really gotten to know him. He's funny, great with kids, has strong values, loves his family, and I can't get him out of my mind.

Mr. Thompson was absolutely right. Helping others does make you forget your own troubles and helps you realize what's important. Lately, I've been so focused on all the problems Ryan, Niko, and his cousins face that I completely forgot about anything that happened back at home. The only thing that mattered was justice for those hurt by the Mullinses.

And one other thing became crystal clear. I've realized I like Ryan and want to be with him. But I'm worried that he will think I'm only using him as a rebound after Niko. Somehow I've got to prove that it's him I'm crazy about. After thinking about it all night I've decided how to show him.

So, somewhat optimistically, I enter the hospital and make my way to his room. Outside his door, I take a deep breath. Come on, girl, you can do this.

I enter and he smiles at me. Deliberately, before I lose my nerve, I stride straight to his bed, place my hands on either side of his face, lean down, and kiss him. He seems stunned at first and pulls slightly back, then I feel one of his hands in my hair and the other on my shoulder. He draws me in closer as our kiss intensifies. Whoa. As the kiss lingers I sink onto the side of the bed, trying not to crush his fractured ribs.

Finally, we part. My heart beats out of control.

"Well, I'm glad to see you, too." He grins, gently stroking my cheek.

I smile back in complete and utter bliss, sure that if I died right now, I would be the happiest girl in heaven.

"Josie," he says as he glances over my shoulder, "I'd like you to meet my parents."

Oh. Holy. Crud-muffin.

I slowly turn to see his family. His parents, a tanned couple with the same light brown hair as Ryan's, sit on a small couch, both looking down at the floor, the corners of their mouths curved up in amusement. His sister is staring at us wide-eyed, her mouth hanging open.

"Oh, um, hi," I lamely mutter, sure I have just turned an unnaturally deep shade of red. I quickly push myself off the bed and stand awkwardly looking at them.

"Ryan was just telling us about you." His dad grins the McNaughty grin, identical to Ryan's.

"He said he didn't know if you liked him," adds his sister, still looking mystified.

"I guess we all know the answer to that now," states his dad, while his mom elbows him in the side.

"Please, don't be embarrassed," Mrs. McNaulty says, and tries to contain her smile.

I glance at Ryan. He winks and takes my hand.

"Wow. Um, when did you guys get here? I didn't know you were coming," I manage to say.

"Neither did Ryan. We got in about an hour ago," answers his mom. "We had always planned on surprising him with a visit after our cruise. But with help from the cruise line we were able to arrive here sooner than planned."

"We owe you our gratitude for getting immediate help to him after the accident and staying with him while he was in the ICU," adds his dad.

"It's the least I could do."

"Maybe we should let them have a moment alone," says his mom.

"Why? I like watching them," his sister complains as they pull her out of the room.

"Oh my gosh. I'm sorry. Obviously I didn't know they were here," I gush as they leave.

"Are you kidding? That was a moment I've dreamt about. But can I ask what exactly that kiss meant?"

"That I've been an idiot and furious with myself that it took this long to get to know you. And hopefully, maybe, you will give me another chance?" I hold my breath, anticipating his answer.

"You'd be seen back at home with me?"

"I'd be the luckiest girl in town."

"Even though it may tip the balance of the Lake Forest Universe?"

"I hope it does."

"What if I don't know much about musicals?"

"I'll teach you. Seriously, I'm sorry I was so dumb for such a long time."

He pats the bed and I gingerly snuggle in next to him.

"When things are meant to be, they always work out."

"I wanted to rush right over here after the sting operation but Aunt Lily wouldn't let me out of her sight."

"I was worried about you. That really was too much of a risk."

"At least it all turned out. Did the kids in the pediatric wing keep you occupied since I couldn't visit?"

"For a while, but when I couldn't concentrate on Chutes and Ladders they sent me away."

"Ah, I'll bring some juggling balls over later. Maybe you can redeem yourself. It was probably great to see your parents. When are they planning on springing you out of this popsicle stand?"

"Soon. That's what they're working on, arranging a medical transport. My dad's a pilot and using his connections."

Instantly my life becomes gray, my joy dissolving faster than the Wicked Witch in a rainstorm.

"Oh, I didn't think about you leaving this soon. I'm going to miss you."

"I'm going to miss you, too," he says as he runs his fingers across my temple and through my hair. "You could come back home with me."

"Believe me, I'm tempted. You have no idea how much I'd like to push you around. In your wheelchair, I mean. But there's something I have to take care of here before I leave. But no doing anything exciting back at home without me."

"I don't think I'll be doing anything exciting for a long time, except maybe this."

I look up at him and am assured by the warmth of his lips.

Ryan,

How are things in Lake Forest? I hope you're recuperating well. It sounded like your sister was going to keep you quite busy with all the animated movies she wanted to watch with you. You should be well versed in princesses when I return.

Life's not the same here without you. But I've been so busy it's actually been hard to find time for the beach! Believe it or not I've been spending a lot of time at the hospital. Suddenly that dreaded building has a special place in my heart. Aunt Lily, Cyd, and I have been going over to the pediatric wing to do some art projects with the kids. They just think Cyd is the greatest and they always ask about you.

Don't be jealous but I've been spending a lot of time with another man, an older guy. JK—I've been recording the stories and words of wisdom of Mr. Thompson and his veteran buddies. They seem so happy to have someone interested in their incredible adventures. My mom's publisher said she'd like to look at it when I'm done compiling.

I've also been putting the final touches on the proposal we talked about for the principal. I really hope he okays our ideas. Wouldn't it be amazing to have our school a place where everyone feels comfortable?

Oh, the attorney my dad's office sent to help Marco and the guys was able to work out a deal. Their testimony will help the prosecution's case, so the Consuelos men are in the clear. The Mullins men on the other hand will hopefully be on their way to jail.

I'm heading home next week but first Lily is throwing a bon voyage party for me.

I can't wait to see you. I miss you!!

Josie

Epilogue

My dad picks me up from the airport and on the long ride home we talk about Marco's legal situation. He keeps throwing legalese into the conversation like I've now acquired a passion for law. I don't want to burst his bubble but nothing sounds more dull and boring.

When we finally drive down the tree-lined street and pull up to our red brick house, my stomach knots up a bit. Suddenly I'm nervous to see my mom. A lot has happened between us; how do we move forward? Is it going to be awkward forever?

Please, God, give me the right words.

As soon as I enter the mudroom from the garage, it happens. The scent of chocolate chip cookies washes over me and memories flood my mind.

There I am climbing up on the kitchen stool lugging along my favorite stuffed animal, Corky, my hair in lopsided ponytails. Mom lets me crack the eggs and patiently retrieves the shells that fall into the bowl. She helps me hold the hand mixer and when I turn it on too high we giggle at the puff of flour that engulfs us.

The sweet smell transports me to all the times she had gooey cookies waiting for Riley and me as an after-school snack. We'd dip them into glasses of milk and reveal the adventures of our day.

The heavenly chocolaty aroma fills me with the comfort she knew I needed when I got the devastating news that I didn't get the role of Sandy in our eighth grade production of *Grease*.

"Josie!" My mom rushes over to gather me in her arms. "I missed you so much."

I bury my head in her shoulder and breathe in her scent as tears fill my eyes. "I missed you, too." Dorothy was right—there's no place like home.

"Hey!" yells Riley. "What about me?"

I pull back from my mom and wipe away my tears. "Hey, Scarecrow, I think I might have missed you most of all."

"Really?" His eyes grow wide.

"Yeah, totally. There was no one to bug me every few minutes," I say and tousle his hair.

"Did you bring me anything?"

The souvenirs I brought for everyone are a big hit. Riley's thrilled with the kite I bought him. I give Dad some books about World War II that Mr. Thompson said were must reads. And I give my mom a paperweight that I found at Paulie's gift shop that reads, *Dreams are like stars . . . you may never reach them, but if you follow them they will lead you to your destiny.*

She contemplates the meaning, then smiles. "That's really profound. When did you become so wise?"

"I realized that our dreams don't always come true the way we expect them to but usually God has something better planned for our lives."

She and Dad exchange a look.

Riley begs Dad to help him with the kite. As they begin assembling it, Mom loads a tray with lemonade and the warm, gooey cookies then leads me into the living room. On the coffee table sits the most enormous, colorful bouquet of flowers I've ever seen. The burst of gorgeous flowers brightens the room.

"Wow, these are incredible." I scan my brain to see if I've forgotten their anniversary or something.

"Yes," she says, setting down the tray. "They're for you. From someone named Ryan."

I glance at her, then curl up on the couch, unable to control my smile.

She hands me a cookie, takes one for herself, and sits on the far end of the couch.

"Josie, I'm so sorry. I'm sorry that my writing has caused you such grief this summer. I'm sorry I ever wrote that book. I'm sorry I wasn't more sympathetic when you were being teased. But most of all I'm sorry I said you were self-centered and should get over it."

"No, Mom, you were right. Hearing those words was the push I needed. I know it was hard on you for me to be away but it gave me some perspective. If I hadn't gone I wouldn't have met so many amazing people. Like Niko and his cousins, who are completely dedicated to their family. They worked selflessly to send money back to the Dominican Republic to give their families a better life. I learned about immigrants and refugees and the struggles they face. I spent time at the hospital and played with little kids who were battling cancer. I met an elderly military vet who told me stories about the many friends he lost fighting for this country. He also helped me see how helping others can put your own life into perspective. The priest at Lily's church showed me how to pray and listen to God's advice. And most importantly, with the help of your postcards, I learned to give my problems over to God. Getting away from my sheltered Lake Forest High world was exactly what I needed."

She stares at me with the strangest look on her face. "Wow. You constantly amaze me. I'm glad you had such an insightful summer, but I really should have been more aware of your feelings. I didn't realize how much it bothered you that I wrote about you."

"Well, I do give you plenty of material to write about, being completely uncoordinated and accident prone," I tease.

"Is that how you see yourself?"

"Duh."

"I've never seen you like that. Ever since you were a little girl you were excited about life and always ready to plunge right in. That's why these interesting moments happen to you. Your adventurous spirit causes you to seize new experiences. I've always admired this trait of yours. In fact, that's why I write about you—I wish I was more like you."

Stunned, I stare at her. Tears fill both our eyes and we hug again.

"Although I haven't seen that girl in a while," she adds when she pulls away.

"I think I rediscovered her this summer," I reply.

"Well, don't worry, I think you'll be happy to know my next book will be about an adolescent boy."

"NO!" screams Riley from the other room.

I smile. "That's okay, Mom. You do a great job writing from a girl's perspective. You know, I met your biggest fan this summer and she made me realize that my screw-ups can actually inspire people. They show that no one is perfect and we should all embrace who we are. Besides, I think I have the perfect story for you, full of action, mystery, and romance."

"Does this story have something to do with a boy named Ryan?"

"It's the story of the most romantic summer adventure ever."

Acknowledgments

There are a few people I must thank for helping get this novel published.

First and foremost, God, for leading me down this writing pathway. All my success is because of Him.

My husband for his unwavering support in every venture I try.

The Mental family for giving me so many moments of joy and inspiration.

My Friday night cohorts, Kelly and Kristie - the first people I told of my aspirations to write a book, who encouraged me through the years over margaritas and merlot.

Anna-Maria Crum, my writing mentor, without her expert guidance I never could have published any of my stories.

eLectio Publishing for giving me the opportunity to publish this book and working with me to make this project a reality.

To all my theater friends, for the many great memories that helped spark my characters.

And to all the readers, thank you for taking the time to read this book – I hope you enjoy it!

Reader's Guide / Questions

- Josie's school is very cliquey. Have you had experiences like that? Does getting away from problems help or is it better to stay and work through them?

- Her mom's postcards and bible verses give Josie the encouragement she needs. Are there certain bible verses that have spoken to you?

- The priest on Coral Island talks about being a friend to Jesus. Do you have a two-way relationship with Him? Have you heard him "speak" to you?

- A recurring theme is helping people less fortunate. Do you think this is a good way to find yourself? Is there a way you can help others less fortunate?

- Josie's mishaps help Cyd feel like she's not alone in the world. Have other's experiences helped you? Do you think anything you do could help others?

- Do you think Ryan and Josie are able to change the culture back at their school?

- Josie gives her mom a gift with this message on it *"Dreams are like stars…you may never reach them, but if you follow them they will lead you to your destiny."* What does this mean to you?

- Who was your favorite character and why?

CPSIA information can be obtained
at www.ICGtesting.com
Printed in the USA
BVHW030701280821
615512BV00005B/96